C000171614

Dwellers of the Deep pounding action that t. Saga is known for, with battles so ﹍﹍, immersive, you will find yourself reaching for your sword. Expansive in scope, Dwellers transforms the Saga into truly epic fantasy, and drops the reader into the Byzantine web of political intrigue that swirls about the Kingdom of Lomion.

In Glenn G. Thater's world of Midgaard, some kill for love or honor; others die for blood and souls. In Dwellers of the Deep, the fourth volume of the saga unfolds across a vast ocean of bleak expanses and forbidden islands that harbor secrets best unspoken, ancient magics best left buried, voracious monsters of the gelid depths, and a god of the outer spheres whose wrath will shake the very foundations of Midgaard.

Within these pages, heroes and villains abound. But are the heroes those that quest with Theta to keep shuttered the portal betwixt the worlds, or those that sail with Korrgonn for god and glory, to restore Azathoth's reign? Only you can decide. But in the end, Ob will tell you, evil is as evil does, and in Midgaard, only one thing thing is certain--nothing is as it seems.

1

BOOKS BY GLENN G. THATER

<u>THE HARBINGER OF DOOM SAGA</u>
GATEWAY TO NIFLEHEIM
THE FALLEN ANGLE
KNIGHT ETERNAL
DWELLERS OF THE DEEP
BLOOD, FIRE, AND THORN
GODS OF THE SWORD
THE SHAMBLING DEAD
MASTER OF THE DEAD
SHADOW OF DOOM
WIZARD'S TOLL
VOLUME 11+ (FORTHCOMING)

HARBINGER OF DOOM
(COMBINES *GATEWAY TO NIFLEHEIM* AND *THE FALLEN ANGLE* INTO A SINGLE VOLUME)

THE HERO AND THE FIEND
(A NOVELETTE SET IN THE HARBINGER OF DOOM UNIVERSE)

THE GATEWAY
(A NOVELLA LENGTH VERSION OF *GATEWAY TO NIFLEHEIM*)

THE DEMON KING OF BERGHER
(A SHORT STORY SET IN THE HARBINGER OF DOOM UNIVERSE)

To be notified about my new book releases and any special offers or discounts regarding my books, please join my mailing list here: http://eepurl.com/vwubH

GLENN G. THATER

DWELLERS OF THE DEEP

A TALE FROM THE HARBINGER OF DOOM SAGA

ISBN-13: 978-0692598382
ISBN-10: 0692598383

December 2015 Amazon Print Edition
Published by Lomion Press

PREFACE

Although much of the story presented in *Knight Eternal* (Volume three of the Harbinger of Doom Saga) was only recently discovered and translated, the climactic duel between Claradon Eotrus and the Wild Pict, Kaledon of the Gray Waste, has long been known to scholars via Leonardo DaVinci's rather dry translation in *Of Prehistory*, his weighty and long out-of-print tome of ancient stories, myths, and legends. Down through the centuries the final line of *Knight Eternal*, "*Then Claradon Eotrus fell*," haunted scholars, for the immediate events of the battle's aftermath were never known, save for brief references in later tales.

I am pleased to report that recent translations of several newly discovered ancient manuscripts have brought to light another point of view of that fateful battle and the exciting events that followed. Drawing heavily on those translations, this fourth volume of the Harbinger of Doom Saga reveals the fate of the young Eotrus and details the continued saga of his band's epic pursuit of Gallis Korrgonn, son of Azathoth.

Dwellers of the Deep transforms the Saga into truly epic fantasy, action-packed, yet cerebral, reflective, and philosophical, as go most Thetian tales. *Dweller's* source material consists of four distinct documents each born of a different civilization. The chapters centering on Theta's group were translated from the Fifth and Sixth Scrolls of Cumbria, which despite the similarity of their names hail from different eras, though both were discovered in the same region of northwestern England. The Fifth Scroll is some twelve hundred years old and likely the product of a Northumbrian scholar, while the Sixth's Celtic origins extend back more than two thousand years to the Brigantes tribe of pre-Roman times.

The chapters centering on Korrgonn's group are more familiar to Thetian scholars as several sources that contain variations of those tales have survived the centuries, the most complete found in the writings of Ptolemy.

Dweller's chapters that center on the happenings in Lomion were unknown to modern scholars until the recent translation of the "first chamber" Grenoble Tablets, which predate the oldest Cumbrian scrolls by some twenty-five hundred years. Numerous other Grenoble Tablets are in translation and promise to add significantly to the breadth and depth of Thetian lore. Written in various regions and languages and over so wide a timespan yet telling portions of the same tale, these sources demonstrate the enduring and widespread popularity of the Thetian stories. One must conclude that in ancient days these tales were as widely told and as much beloved as any stories known today.

Besides continuing the pulse-pounding action that the Thetian Saga is known for, *Dwellers of the Deep* drops us into the intricate web of political intrigue that swirls about the Kingdom of Lomion. The alert reader will note curious parallels to modern political ideology and the timeless concerns that nations and peoples struggle with today. The truths and philosophies explored in the saga offer lessons seemingly lost on nation after nation, since they fail to learn from and inevitably repeat the errors chronicled in the historical record.

An interviewer recently almost stumped me when she asked how I would characterize the Thetian world of Midgaard in a single word or sentence. Fantastical? Wondrous? Mythical? Epic? Imaginative? Though it is all of those, and more, my answer was one that I'm proud of because it crystallizes the Angle Theta saga for me. "In Midgaard," I said, "nothing is at it seems."

Glenn G. Thater
New York, USA

1

Weighty deeds weighed heavy on the grand weave of magic that populated the ether, inducing sorcerous waves that erupted in all directions — waves that carried information of import, sometimes esoteric, but often seemingly mundane. From time to time, these chaotic impulses of ethereal knowledge could be detected, captured, and interpreted by honest Seers of uncommon skill and by certain eldritch devices. Grandmaster Pipkorn, archmage of Lomion, possessed two such devices — the fabled Rings of the Magi, two of the original twenty forged by Grandmaster Talidousen in ancient times, rare and venerable hangers-on from days long lost yet more enlightened. One Pipkorn bore on his right ring finger, the other, recently gifted to Par Tanch Trinagal, House Wizard for the Eotrus.

Talidousen rings, as they were sometimes called, did not give up their knowledge freely. They yielded only to those that held a measure of mastery over them. Such masters always paid a weighty price for the privilege, and no one, save Talidousen himself, ever held greater mastery over the rings than did Pipkorn, for he had plumbed their depths for longer years than even he remembered. And so the magical weave communed with Pipkorn, shared secrets seldom spoken, whispered of forces that disturbed and influenced it, and hinted at those rare beings that plucked the weave's fabric and unlocked its mysteries, whether they dwelled in the Tower of the Arcane, or a far-off land across the sea, or some forsaken, subterranean depth never visited by man. This afforded Pipkorn knowledge that others could never possess, though the ring was ever fickle, stingy, and vague in its offerings, as if it had a mind and purpose of its own. Nonetheless, with its knowledge came power, great power.

Pipkorn started when he felt the familiar tingle in his right ring finger that heralded some event of import; a reliable signal to perk up and pay heed or else risk regret. At such times, his Talidousen Ring would vibrate ever so slightly while at other more urgent times, it would oscillate so violently it emitted an audible buzzing and vibrated his arm to the elbow. When that happened, his finger, sometimes his entire hand, burned as if thrust into flame.

Thankfully, the latest vibrations were mild and caused but little discomfort. Too much danger was already afoot; Pipkorn had no interest in any of it boiling to a crisis just now, though he knew such was coming.

He polished the green gemstone with his fingers as he approached the ponderous marble font tucked in the alcove adjacent to his sleeping chamber. The font was the heaviest of the treasures he spirited from the Tower of the Arcane on the day of betrayal and secreted in this hidey-hole of exile — an ancient, foreboding stone structure that lacked the comforts and amenities of the Tower, but was functional, secure, and had thus far served him well.

Pipkorn was glad he had saved the font,

despite the arduous efforts involved in secreting it and himself in this dark corner of the Southeast district of Lomion City, for the font had oft proved a useful tool over the years, and, strangely, he'd even grown rather fond of it. Years ago, after he had tired of polishing the silver font that then graced his laboratory, he commissioned a master stonemason out of Tarrows Hold, a rather tall dwarf with flaming red hair, arms as hard as tree trunks and near as thick, to carve the marble font for him to precise, though unnecessarily stringent specifications. An interesting character was the dwarf, a stonemason, soldier, brawler, adventurer, and artist, all rolled into one, though Pipkorn had no recollection of his name. The dwarf had done his work well, though he'd taken a full year in the effort. The font was cut in the shape of a large bowl; its interior carved along a precise curve, smooth and polished. How exactly he'd accomplished it remained a mystery. An ornate wood lid sat in a groove at the font's rim and safeguarded its contents.

Pipkorn didn't actually need the font. He could put the ring's gem up to his eye and see through it clear and crisp, though its view was narrow of field and lacked depth. The font provided an easier, more comfortable method for tapping the weave, and offered a much wider and more expansive view. Pipkorn had long ago resolved to employ a font whenever feasible and took to carrying a portable one on his travels, though none provided the clarity of the marble. In olden days, he filled it with clear water, until he discovered oil worked the better. He experimented with numerous oily concoctions, homemade, local, and exotic, both plain and scented of spirit and spice. For whatever reason, the pungent stuff worked best. His chosen brew was a clear, thick olive oil flavored of garlic and thyme, imported from Crondin, long considered the best on the continent. The oil made the image a bit clearer, the colors a bit deeper, brighter, and more lifelike, but it was sound that it most enhanced. It made voices as clear and loud as if one stood amidst the speakers. With the gem alone, they often sounded muffled and distant.

Though Pipkorn had worn the ring daily for years, no marks marred his finger when he pried it off, which was no easy task. The ring was snug, but by no means tight, yet it resisted removal until Pipkorn pulled, twisted, and turned it just so. Owing to some enchantment Pipkorn could not lift, a different combination of movements was required each time to get the ring off. This caused Pipkorn endless frustration because he had never deciphered the secret to predicting the next combination, and he had long ago given up trying. Finally, he got it off, but wondered what other secrets of old Talidousen's ring still eluded him. He placed it gently into the font's oil, near the center.

The ring floated, gemstone up, its glossy surface barely covered with the thinnest film of oil. Then the ring began to turn, to spin clockwise of its own accord, faster and faster until it hummed. The concentric ripples it created in the oil broke gently against the basin's walls. Of a sudden, the oil's surface grew indistinct. It blurred, then became opaque. When it suddenly clarified, Pipkorn gazed through a magical window to another place. Images appeared across the oil's surface and sound issued from it. The ring had created a mystical connection to its twin borne on the finger of Par Tanch Trinagal. That connection secured, Pipkorn saw through Tanch's eyes, heard with his ears, and to a limited extent, even knew his thoughts — all laid bare for Pipkorn's perusal.

The air in the secret Temple of Hecate hung heavy and close and smelled of sweat and smoke. Who would have guessed that a grand hall of soaring ceiling, mahogany panels, and marbled floor that seated thousands hid below a dilapidated warehouse in the bowels of Southeast, the foulest district in the fair city of Lomion. Who would have guessed that untold thousands of Lomerians secretly worshipped the Chaos Lords of Nifleheim, praying to them as gods, and that those cultists had the resources to build such a place and the discipline to keep it secret. And keep it secret they must, for worship of the Chaos Lords had long been outlawed throughout the Kingdom of Lomion, owing to their adherents' rumored penchant for human sacrifice and other foul practices.

Despite the ban, for years there had been rumors of chaos temples hidden somewhere in Lomion City. Most folks considered them tall tales, but Par Tanch knew better, for the wizards of the Tower of the Arcane whispered about them, and what tower wizards whispered of always held some truth. Such was the way of things.

Tanch envisioned the chaos temples as grimy

hovels or dank dungeons manned by a handful of wretched lunatics, gibbering away, huddled in the dark, biting the heads from chickens. He never dreamed that the temple could be as this.

Beneath the massive, domed ceiling the faithful aligned shoulder to shoulder in innumerable rows; a sea of concealing cowls and blood-red robes. Thousands crowded the hall to hear Father Ginalli's booming sermon in worship of Azathoth, the one true god — long now absent from Midgaard, the world of man, long now residing in the outré realm of Nifleheim, only to return when man proved worthy, or so went one tale.

Ginalli, Azathoth's high priest, stood at the lectern and read boldly from a thick, leather-bound tome of sacred scripture. Par Tanch didn't pay attention to the words; he didn't much care. He was never one for religion; if the black rites of those mad cultists could even be called religion. His back ached; his neck was stiff. He was tired and drained. He longed for the quiet comfort of his chambers at Dor Eotrus. That's where he belonged, not in a den of madmen, and certainly not on some fool's quest. He was no adventurer, no soldier, no war wizard. He was a simple man of simple needs and little ambition. He never wanted to be House Wizard for the Eotrus. It was a weighty mantle and a step in the spotlight that he had neither the nerves nor the stomach for. If Par Talbon and his apprentices hadn't got themselves killed, he never would have been house wizard — he would have turned down the position, if somehow, it was ever offered, and it

13

wouldn't have been. It was Talbon's fault he was in this mess. Damn him.

But after everything that happened, when Claradon asked him to take the position, how could he say no? They had been friends for years, since Claradon's days at the Caradonian Chapterhouse in Lomion City. It was Claradon's support alone that had persuaded Lord Aradon to take Tanch in after the Caradonians dismissed him. Without that opportunity, Tanch had no idea where he would have ended up — though wherever that was, it wouldn't have been as good a life as he had in Dor Eotrus. He owed a debt to Claradon and his family that he could never repay. That's why he was on this mission, to give back what little he could to the Eotrus for all they had done for him, though he was far out of his element. He yearned for their quest to come to a happy end and for things to return to normal, though he conceded they would never be normal again. They couldn't be. Not after what they had been through. Not after the terrible losses they had borne.

As the service progressed, Ginalli's voice boomed louder and deeper, though he could have jabbered about the weather for all Tanch knew, staring at his feet and willing the ordeal over. Then it happened. A group of burly cultists emerged from the wings carrying a squirming, rotund man to the altar. They tied him down.

The tip of Father Ginalli's golden staff flared bright red, almost afire, as he leveled accusations of dubious merit against the man — Mr. Miscellaneous Merchant from Who-Cares-Where.

Tanch glanced at Lord Angle Theta. While intently watching the sermon, the big foreign knight tightly gripped the misshapen ankh that hung from a cord about his neck. That strange token glowed dimly in his grasp. Tanch noticed Theta's lips moving, subtly, as if he whispered to himself, and knew at once what went on. Sorcery — secret and dark, no doubt. But to what end?

Ginalli's voice grew still louder and demanded attention, though it echoed strangely, as if it came from within Tanch's head, instead of without. Tanch lost all interest in Theta's magic or mischief, whatever it was, and felt compelled to focus his full attention on Ginalli's rant against the merchant; the priest's voice shrill, his eyes — the wild eyes of the fanatic.

Tanch's vision blurred; his hearing dimmed. He floated as if in a dream. He looked to his comrades: young Lord Claradon Eotrus, stalwart and true; Ob the gnome, his gruff Castellan; and Theta's servant, the enigmatic simpleton, Dolan Silk. Each wore vacant expressions and slowly rocked back and forth, their eyes glazed over and watery.

Behind Ginalli appeared two Lords of Chaos, the very same creatures that crept from the mystical gateway lately opened in the Vermion Forest. One was called Mortach, a giant, living skeleton; an undead horror out of hell, loathsome and malevolent. The other, Gallis Korrgonn, the abomination that possessed the remains of Gabriel Garn, beloved weapons master of House Eotrus. Even as Tanch watched, Korrgonn's eyes began to glow golden and bright, and two horns

15

erupted from his forehead. Tanch froze, his breath caught in his throat, the hairs rose on the back of his neck.

The seating area behind Korrgonn brightened, and the sinister, deformed, inhuman aspects of the Arkons of the League of Shadows came into Tanch's view. Tanch shuddered and his head swam. It was all he could do not to scream; not to flee in terror from those cursed chambers. But the throng about him failed to stir; those sights of no alarm to them at all.

Through a murky haze and debilitating waves of dizziness Tanch cringed as Mortach's long dagger plunged into the bound merchant and laid him open, throat to groin.

Even as Mortach and the priests collected the man's lifeblood in golden chalices to share with the faithful, guards dragged a long procession of bound and struggling citizens, men, women, and children, toward the sacrificial altar. Dead gods, they were mostly children; their eyes wide with fright. Tears streamed down their faces. Tanch's stomach churned; bile rose in his throat. He wanted to save them, though he knew he could not. He wanted to call up every magic he knew — each cantrip, conjuration, and incantation, every spell and sorcery, but he dared not or else invite the merchant's fate or worse. The masses of mad cultists would pull him down and tear him to shreds, and his comrades too. Even Theta could not survive here, so outnumbered. He wanted to run, but his legs betrayed him, weak and trembling. He could do naught but stare in horror as the cultists dragged the captives, one after another, to the sacrificial altar. Their piteous screams were stifled by rags the cultists stuffed in their mouths.

Even more shocking than those heinous sights was the crowd's reaction to them. No cries of alarm; no shouts of protest; no shocked gasps. Instead, nods of approval; whispers of support; even a scattered smile and cheer. The wretches thought those murders right and proper. Truly a den of madness and monsters; the stuff of fevered nightmares. No place for any goodly man was that, though Tanch dared not flee, if even he could find the strength.

On instinct, Tanch mouthed words of protection; ancient words taught him by his old master. Mystical words of power from the old tongue of the *Magus Mysterious* carried down from the Dawn Age; words lost if ever known by normal men and each nigh unpronounceable. From deep within, he felt his arcane powers stir, and with a rush of adrenaline that made him shudder, his vision cleared, his mind calmed, and his tension ebbed.

It was as if he awoke from a dream; as if a veil lifted from his eyes, and a plug of wax was plucked from his ears. With this clarity, the scene before him suddenly changed. Now it appeared altogether different. Now Tanch saw it the way it truly was.

Mortach was no monster. His true face was handsome, almost perfect to behold, with long straight hair, black as pitch. His form, tall and lean, but powerful. Beside him, Korrgonn wore no stolen face, but his own. Even more beautiful than

17

Mortach; his skin of golden tone; his eyes, a piercing blue; his body, tall and stately. Each chaos lord held an aura of majesty about them; a spark of the divine. With every breath, they exuded strength, wisdom, and power. These were more than mere mortals; they were holy messengers of the heavens, of paradise.

No blood dripped from the dagger Mortach held. The chalices were filled not of blood spilled from the captives' chests, but of red wine poured over their brows. The merchant stood now beside the altar unharmed.

The gruesome blood sacrifices and all their trappings were merely a performance, an illusion — religious ritual, symbolism, ceremony, and such, nothing more. Nothing bad, nothing sinister. Not a scene of horror, not a march of madness.

Tanch knew now what had clouded his mind. It was Theta's magic; there was no other explanation. But why? He turned toward Theta—

—But now Tanch was back on the deck of *The Black Falcon* as it sailed down the Grand Hudsar River and passed through the Dead Fens. Wind lashed his face; freezing rain pummeled the deck; it was bitter cold.

The Einheriar battled Theta on the Bridge Deck. Its form was blurred and indistinct, but from what little Tanch could tell, it was a monster. A creature that perhaps was once a man, but was now corrupted, a mockery of humanity, a twisted, misshapen offense to life itself.

And there was Theta with his ankh that glowed with unholy fire. A gleaming mountain of muscle and steel, Theta floated just above the

18

deck and glided hither and there, faster than any man could move.

Of a sudden, a strange beam of light emanated from Tanch's hand with a will of its own. He knew at once that the beam was his own spark of mana, a projection of the holy light of his immortal soul, enhanced by decades of mystic training, by his art.

The beam sped at Theta and engulfed the hellish glow of his preternatural ankh. The dark magic that powered the ankh resisted Tanch's light, but for a few moments, not long, but time enough, did Tanch's light hold mastery. It enwrapped the ankh and covered it. It suppressed its evil rays and dampened its unholy magic. It pulled back the veils of lies that it wove.

And while it did, the scene changed; the Einheriar changed; Theta changed.

The Einheriar was now no monster, no menace out of hell. He was a man, a warrior in gleaming armor, a long dagger in each hand. His brow noble; his expression determined, resolved. He and Theta taunted and threatened each other.

"I'm on god's side, deceiver," said the Einheriar. "I've sworn to destroy all evil and destroy you, I will."

"Dead gods, he is a holy warrior," mumbled Tanch. Sent down by the gods to face the unfaceable, to struggle against the unconquerable, to die for the lord and for all that's good and holy in the world. How did Tanch not see that before? How was he so easily beguiled?

Tanch tried to look at Theta, to see his true face now that the veil of clouding magic had lifted, but he was paralyzed with fear. He had to know. He gathered all his will and courage and forced himself to look—

—But then he was in the ancient temple in the Vermion Forest the night Sir Gabriel died. A mind-rending din pounded against his ears, so loud, so utterly overwhelming.

Tanch saw the rear of the temple. There lurked its altar; a stark slab of gray stone, stained brown and red from untold sacrifices. Atop the altar, an orb of madness and mystery, blacker than death, a sphere of the outer realms that pulsed with forbidden powers and terrible temptations.

Behind the altar, the rear wall of the temple, embossed with a geometric pattern of flaming, melting, golden coins, shimmered, fluxed, and strained. It strove to tear open the fabric of the dimensions. The magic of that ancient orb was birthing a gateway — a dark portal to the realm of Nifleheim, a place of madness, chaos, and death. A breach that would join the two worlds in an unholy union of light and dark that would herald the end of civilization, the end of mankind. For when that gateway opened, the beasts from beyond, the demon hordes of hell, would gain passage into Midgaard to ravage the world of man.

Men struggled toward the rear of the temple as they strained against the unnatural cacophony; the nauseating mist; the bone-chilling cold; the flailing pseudopods, the very arms and claws of hell; sacrificing all to safeguard mankind and avenge their fallen liege. Each, a named man, a hero — armed with honor, clad in courage, and girded with honest steel, helm to boot, sword, dagger, and axe.

One amongst them plodded at the van and trudged through the murk where brave men faltered. Angle Theta, a shiny mountain of sculpted steel and determination, red-faced and sweating despite the chill, struggled forward, slowly, as if he pulled some vast weight. Every inch was a battle; every foot a war, as Theta strained against some unseen force, some power beyond the sight of man that held him back.

And then, for a fraction of a second, the bizarre scene grew even stranger when the cloud of deluding sorcery lifted from Tanch's eyes, and another reality, the true reality, flashed into view. Two Valkyries, holy sword-maidens of the gods, appeared from nowhere, blinking into existence. Each sat atop a white, winged steed that hovered aloft behind Theta. Each gripped a gleaming silver rope that was corded about Theta's cloak and shoulders. They labored to hold the juggernaut back, dragging at Theta's cloak with all their supernatural might.

Then they were gone: Valkyries, horses, and ropes; vanished from sight, though Theta struggled still.

The orb of darkness pulsed wildly on the altar and empowered the doorway to Abaddon, but the relic could not release the vast energies needed to drop the veil between the worlds.

For long moments, Theta trudged forward, his aspect blurred and obscured by the unnatural haze within the temple and the pounding din that assailed Tanch's ears. When at last he reached the altar, Tanch's vision sharpened and cleared, and Theta's form changed. The Valkyries blinked back into view, and this time remained, still struggling in vain to pull Theta back. But he was Theta no longer. Now he was Thetan. Thetan, the evil; Thetan, the traitor; Thetan the fallen.

Tanch's face became a twisted mask of shock and horror. He wanted to turn away, but he could not.

What had appeared to be Theta's great steel helm now was revealed to be two great horns that protruded from his forehead. What had been his cloak was really two great, black, leathery wings, like those of a giant bat. Theta's face sharpened and morphed — that protruding, boney jaw; the sharp, long nose and flared nostrils; the deep-set eyes; the muscular physique beyond that of any mortal; the reddish tinge to his skin. This was Thetan; Theta in his true form, revealed at last for what he truly was. A monster. The Prince of Lies, the Great Dragon, the Lord of Demons. Evil incarnate. The Harbinger of Doom. He who betrayed the Lord and was cast out from the heavens in time immemorial.

As Tanch watched in horror, Theta raised a great hammer and smashed the orb of darkness. It exploded on impact, and crackling streaks of deadly lightning flashed along the Valkyries' silver ropes and engulfed them. The brave sword-maidens and their valiant steeds screamed, burst into flame, and burned instantly to ash.

The orb's eerie energy, released in one titanic blast, powered the vestigial gateway, tore it open, and thereby created a gap in the fabric of reality — an unholy bridge between the worlds. Such had been long hoped for by those who lurked on its threshold for years beyond count. Their prayers answered, the demons of nightmare vaulted through in triumph. Thetan's booming laughter shook the temple to its core.

Tanch felt himself falling; felt his world grow dim.

The mystical connection broke and Pipkorn staggered back from the marble font, his heart racing. "Dead gods," he said.

Tanch sprang up and gasped for air. His heart pounded in his chest; his head throbbed; drenched in sweat; his hair plastered to his face; his shirt soaked through. For some moments, he knew not where or when he was. Soon his head cleared; his vision, sharpened.

He was in his bunk, off the Captain's Den, on *The Black Falcon.*

He was awake. A nightmare. He thanked the gods it was all just a nightmare.

Tanch rubbed his hands to stifle the nagging itch and persistent burning that plagued him since the very moment he'd thrown that great blast of fire on the docks of Tragoss Mor. He shuddered at the thought of it and the power that had coursed through him, a power not his alone, but born of the Ring of the Magi gifted him by Pipkorn and affixed evermore to his right hand. That ring, its very aspect alien, whispered of secrets best not known. The golden band cupped a singular, faceted, green stone that was no emerald, its true lineage unknown, its unplumbed depths at once afire and murky beyond man's sight or reason. Tanch struggled to avoid thinking of the horrors that he'd seen in Tragoss Mor, of the death and suffering that he'd wrought. He had to block that from his mind, and distract himself with saner thoughts, but after that nightmare, sane thoughts were hard to find.

He pulled himself from bed, put on a clean shirt, and made his way to the Captain's Deck, still groggy and fatigued.

The guards admitted him into Claradon's stateroom without a word. There lay his young friend and liege; bloody bandages wrapped about his chest, looking much the same as he had the previous night. His face and skin were pale, deathly pale; his breathing shallow, but dear gods, he did still breathe, did still cling to life, where near any other man would've long since passed, his wounds so grievous.

The part-elven woman, Kayla, was at his side from the moment they carried him aboard. She tended to him however she could, though of what medical skills she had, if any, Tanch had no idea. The young knights Paldor and Glimador were there too, tired and forlorn. It was good that Glimador was there — he was Claradon's oldest friend, not to mention his first cousin. If Claradon slipped away, at least one family member that loved him would be at his side to mark his passing and mourn him. Ob was there too, and he was practically family, though as Tanch expected, he was passed out in a chair beside the bed, a collection of wine bottles empty at his feet.

24

Dear gods, please let Claradon live.

2

GODS OF THE SWORD

Like all the young, he thought himself immortal.
Now he knows better.
— Milton DeBoors

The wide avenue that led to Tragoss Mor's dock ward sang with swordplay and ran red with blood. A dozen Kalathen knights, a squadron of House Alder's marines, and two born killers battled Brother Claradon Eotrus, newly named Lord of Dor Eotrus, and his small band. Bartol of Alder's arrest warrant for Claradon and "*his mercenary*" lay trampled underfoot.

In a somber alley just off the avenue, Claradon dueled a legend — a sword master and bounty hunter famed and feared throughout the land for a generation. Kaledon of the Gray Waste was his name, better known to most as The Wild Pict, a born killer that stories claimed had slain a thousand men by his own hand. The Pict stood before Claradon, battered, bloody, and dazed, his chest smoking and scorched, courtesy of Claradon's magic. The Pict's sword was still in his hand and the fight had not yet left him, but he was weak and unsteady. In truth, Claradon fared little better — but now came his chance to end their lengthy battle and to defeat a legend.

Claradon advanced and thrust his sword at Kaledon's bare chest. The wounded Pict's parry was far too slow and failed to keep the blade from his flesh. It sank deep. Blood spurted from the wound and splashed Claradon's face, already bloodied and dripping sweat. The Pict roared in pain but returned Claradon's strike before the last of his strength was spent. His war blade slashed Claradon's breastplate, cleaved through at the center, and shattered. The young lord stumbled back in shock and disbelief.

The broken remnant of Kaledon's sword slipped from his fingers and clattered to the pavement. The Wild Pict clutched his chest and tried in vain to stem the flow of his lifeblood. His eyes burned with hatred and never left Claradon's face. He dropped to his knees. Moments later, eyes still open and staring, he fell face forward to the ground. He did not move again.

The Duelist of Dyvers, Milton DeBoors' eyes went wide and he knew at once that he'd underestimated Claradon Eotrus. When Chancellor Barusa of Alder hired him to kill Claradon and his foreign mercenary, he expected a challenge — not from their personal martial skills, but from the combined might of the fighting men that traveled with them. He never dreamed that the young Eotrus could stand up to the Pict, his friend and ally of long years, little less best him. Such mistakes were foreign to DeBoors and costly when rare they came. The Chancellor's coin was not worth this.

DeBoors rushed forward through the smoke, blood, and din of the melee; too late to save his comrade, but in good time to avenge him.

Claradon's sword hung loose from its guard;

his eyes were glassy, his face pale, his legs unsteady.

"Eotrus," boomed DeBoors.

The young knight turned, grievously wounded; sweat poured from his brow as he gasped for breath.

DeBoors aimed his thrust for the narrow gouge in Claradon's armor where that last strike of Kaledon's had laid it open. DeBoors' wicked blade passed unerringly through the center of the rent, and clear through Claradon, garment, flesh, and bone. Through the heart.

Claradon wore a look of shock. Like all the young, he thought himself immortal. Now he knew better.

DeBoors pulled the blade free. It made a curious, sucking sound as it slid out; a spray of blood followed it.

DeBoors raised his sword to take Claradon's head — a trophy for Chancellor Barusa, and a bit of satisfaction for him, but before he struck his blow, a mountain fell on him. The world spun into chaos and he sailed through the air. He crashed to the ground, the air crushed from his chest; something massive atop him; something alive. At first, DeBoors thought it a horse, felled in the battle and fallen on him; such was its bulk. But it was a man; one of Eotrus' mercenaries; a veritable giant.

A snarling face appeared over DeBoors, and two vise-like hands clamped about his neck. The power of that grip would've crushed another man's throat in moments, but the thick, corded muscle of DeBoors' neck held, though he could not manage a breath.

DeBoors' hands were pinned between his torso and the giant's; his sword lost from his grasp; no room to swing it anyway.

His throat screaming for air, DeBoors wrenched one meaty hand free and pummeled the giant's jaw. Unfazed, the giant clamped down tighter; his thick digits dug deep into DeBoors' throat, his hot breath washed over DeBoors' face; his sweat dripped into DeBoors' eyes.

The duelist squirmed, twisted, and stretched to align and leverage his next desperate strikes. His fist slammed unerringly into the giant's head, again and again and again.

The giant grunted, spit blood in DeBoors' face, and squeezed ever tighter. "Die," he said; that was all he said. In all his years, DeBoors had never battled a man of such strength — strength to match his own. Close to blacking out, he struggled to pull those hands of doom from his throat. After the uncountable battles he'd weathered, he would not fall to some random mercenary. That was inconceivable; the moment surreal.

DeBoors head-butted the giant, producing a sound akin to a hammer slamming a stone. The giant reeled and for a moment, his eyes went unfocused. That moment was all DeBoors needed to pull his other hand free and thrust the giant off.

Both men scrambled, rolled, and made their feet in an instant — the giant, nearly a head taller than DeBoors, who himself towered well above men called tall.

The giant was fast, far faster than any man

near his size should be. His massive fist appeared from nowhere and pummeled DeBoors' jaw, smashing his head to the side, a crushing blow.

But DeBoors remained solidly planted, his eyes clear and bright. He snapped his head back toward the giant and saw his eyes go wide with surprise. No doubt, he'd expected DeBoors to go down with a broken jaw, and all his fight spent. Instead, DeBoors returned the blow and sent the giant reeling — a hammer blow to the head that would've dropped a horse. The giant staggered back, but did not go down.

The giant charged, fire in his eyes, long dagger in hand. DeBoors grabbed his tunic as he came in, dropped to the ground, rolled back, kicked the giant's midsection, and sent his massive bulk flying. He crashed to the ground yards away.

DeBoors rolled over, snatched his sword from the ground, and leaped to his feet in a single motion. Pain seared through his arm. The giant's blade had found some hole in his bracer and pierced his forearm. He ignored it. A moment later, sword again in hand, he glanced toward the mouth of the alley in time to see an arrow streaking for his throat.

DeBoors flicked his blade to the side, perfectly timed, and deflected the arrow away; a metallic pinging sound marked its demise. Another arrow came on just as quickly, and then a third — launched by a slim archer who stood amidst the roaring battle in the avenue. DeBoors' blade knocked each shaft aside — a feat few men were fast or fortunate enough to do once, but three times in as many seconds bespoke of martial skills untold.

With a glance, he found his shield and plucked it from the ground. Looking up, he expected more arrows, but instead saw a swarm of fiery blue orbs rocketing towards him. Wizard's work.

"Zounds!" No time to dive for cover, he dodged to the side and ducked down behind his shield. The heater shield, his long companion, iron and oak, forged in dwarven fire in ages past, was blasted from his grip and exploded into sorry fragments. Another bolt slammed into his shoulder plate and blasted the steel away. Spheres of fiery death streamed just over his head and to either side as he dodged and spun with preternatural speed. Each bolt detonated nearby, on ground or masonry walls, raining dust, sparks, and shrapnel everywhere.

Then the giant was there again. Battered and bloody, he barreled toward DeBoors, his huge war hammer slicing through the air with enough power and speed to fell a tree. DeBoors sidestepped the blow and with a lightning flick and twist of his sword took the hammer from the giant's grasp.

Before DeBoors could finish him, and without an instant of hesitation, the giant pulled a sword from his belt and stood at the ready, glaring at DeBoors, nostrils flaring.

They moved together and traded blow for blow with dizzying speed and unrelenting resolve. The giant's slashes and thrusts came in with thunderous power and precision, not born of desperation or anger, but founded in skill, and

31

steeped in mastery of the blade; its wielder, a veritable harbinger of destruction and death.

DeBoors' strikes were no less powerful and even quicker; his sword a blur of movement; its ancient metal hummed a dull tone as it cleaved through the air, a somber song that promised only death.

Each man was nigh unbeatable. Neither had ever tasted defeat. Together, two gods of the sword, two giants among men; though in such contests no impasse could long stand. One always proved the greater, but for the whim of chance or the whisper of fate or the right hand of doom. Such was the way of things.

And when fate decreed it, the whirling blades at last proclaimed their master. One of DeBoors' strikes slipped under the giant's guard and slashed his breastplate; a skirling rending of metal filled the air as the tempered steel gave way.

DeBoors' spinning hammer-blow thundered down at the giant's head. But the giant was not done yet. He raised his mighty blade and caught the deathblow, though his sword shattered with the titanic impact. Bits of screaming metal flew into the giant's face and he fell back, bloodied.

As DeBoors plowed forward to finish him, an arrow slammed into his back, then another, though they bounced ineffectually from his steel-wrought armor.

DeBoors' senses, born and honed of olden days, alerted him to movement close behind. He spun in time to see a wide, curved sword slicing towards him. It took all his speed and reflex to snap his blade up and parry the blow in time to preserve his life. Even then, his sword was nearly wrenched from his grasp.

A hail of sword strikes rained down on him — faster and faster. Through the blur of motion, DeBoors glimpsed a gleaming knight in midnight-blue armor and massive shield; tall, broad, and powerful, with an aura of death hung around him like an old, beloved cloak.

Each time DeBoors maneuvered to attack rather than parry, the blows rained in faster.

A high strike came in and when DeBoors parried it, a kick struck him in the midsection — a monstrous blow that flung him backward several feet to slam into a wall. He dropped to the ground on his rump. The wind knocked out of him; his strength sapped. In all his days, no one had ever hit him that hard.

Eotrus, the giant, and now this one. Dead gods, how many champions did House Eotrus have? He'd underestimated this one. He would not do that again. DeBoors bounced up, sword at the ready, death flaring in his eyes. All his will and power bent on destroying his opponent. DeBoors' eyes locked on the knight's to take his measure and read his soul before taking his life.

With a sharp intake of breath and widened eyes, DeBoors, undefeated sword-master of Dyvers, froze, at once deflated and diminished, ego, body, and soul. His blood ran cold and all color fled his face, for before him stood Lord Thetan, and Thetan's falchion was poised at his throat. A trickle of blood ran down DeBoors' neck, courtesy of a prick from the sword's tip.

The sight of Thetan's face dredged a memory from the depths of DeBoors' mind. He stood on the bridge deck of a great sailing vessel — a vast fleet arrayed behind it. Lord Thetan stood at the prow. He wore that same blue armor and that same falchion hung at his side. Surrounded by his lieutenants, Thetan's eyes were locked on R'lyeh as they approached that dread isle for the long war's final battle. Gabriel was there, the Horn of Valhalla at his hip. Mithron the wise stood at Thetan's right hand. There too was Raphael the healer, and Azrael the alchemist. Modi and Magni were there too, along with the other great captains of the host. The great lord turned towards DeBoors. Thetan's steel-blue eyes locked on him and DeBoors shuddered.

"Lord Thetan," said DeBoors, his voice unsteady.

"No other, though they call me Theta now."

"I knew not it was you," he said, his composure regained, his voice strong once again.

"No matter, DeBoors. Stand down and call off your men. The Eotrus are under my protection."

DeBoors pushed Theta's sword away and took a step to the side, his shock fading and with it, his confidence returned. "You're Eotrus's mercenary?"

"I'm on a mission, like those of old, when we fought side by side in common cause.

DeBoors' brow furrowed. "That business ended at R'lyeh. It's long past and best forgotten." DeBoors moved to where Kaledon lay. Whistles sounded from all about, near and far. "The monks will come in force," said DeBoors. "We should sort this out another time."

DeBoors squatted, scooped Kaledon up, and hefted him over his shoulder even as Artol, ignoring the blood that streamed down his own face from his shattered sword, knelt beside Claradon and bound a cloth about his bleeding chest.

Theta made no move to stop DeBoors. "The Eotrus are under my protection," said Theta in a tone that defied opposition.

DeBoors paused and looked back at Theta before turning the corner at the end of the alley. "And I must honor my contract."

3
THE RETURN OF PRIOR FINCH

The top four feet of *The Black Falcon's* gangway was a no-man's land, empty, save for blood spatters on plank and rail. Two Thothian monks who dared enter were carried away by their comrades bloodied and battered. Their assailant, *The Falcon's* chief roughneck, a bristling, seven-foot-tall, hirsute giant called Little Tug.

Tug guarded the top of the gangway brandishing a wicked hammer; a huge tower shield rooted before him. The shield and Tug's vast bulk choked the ramp's entire width. Crowded behind him were two dozen of *The Falcon's* seamen, cutthroats and reavers all, cutlasses, axes, and dirks in hand. Beside them, several knights and soldiers of House Eotrus and a score of Lomerian soldiers, sharp, young, and clean-shaven, their arms and armor gleaming, almost new. More soldiers and crewmen lined the deck-rail, longbow, sword, and mace.

Scores of Thothian monks, bald, bronzed, and bare-chested, crowded the gangway and the pier alongside *The Falcon*. The two scrawny monks at the head of the contingent, just out of Tug's range, were pale; their faces and brows dripped with sweat; their terror, plain to all. Each gripped the gangway's rail with one hand and desperately pressed back against their fellows who threatened to surge forward and push them into Tug's unforgiving embrace. They knew well the fate of their predecessors and wanted no part of it.

Sergeant Vid of House Eotrus stood just behind Tug, though Tug's bulk blocked his view almost entirely. Vid was armored in chainmail and gripped a weathered poleaxe of hardened wood and forged steel that he would make good use of if Tug went down. As it was, there was little Vid could do save guard Tug's flank if arrows or bolts began to fly. Crowded beside Vid was a lanky young seaman called Chert. Pale and sweating in shirtsleeves and breeches, Chert brandished a wide saber that looked all too heavy in one hand, and a big shield that was even heavier in the other.

"You think we'll get into it with them?" said Chert to Tug's back.

Vid glanced at the frightened youth who stared straight ahead.

"Depends how that monk gets on with the Captain," said Tug, his voice a deep baritone, though he never took his eyes off the monks amassed before him.

"So you think we might have to fight?" said Chert, forgetting that Tug had bashed most of the life from two monks already.

"If we do, we do. If we don't, we don't. No sense worrying on it. Saw you through the last few scrapes, didn't I? This'll be none different. Just keep your shield up, your eyes open, and stay well clear of me if things get going. I need room to swing Old Fogey."

"Right," said Chert.

"That goes for you too, tin-can."

"I'm no knight," said Vid, "I'm just an old soldier."

"All the same to me," said Tug. "Just keep that pigsticker out of my back and I'll keep you clear of the business end of Old Fogey."

"Fair enough," said Vid.

The Black Falcon's sail fluttered in the light breeze that washed in from the south. The briny ocean air cooled the afternoon sun, and blessedly freshened the dock ward's foul and fishy stench. Captain Dylan Slaayde stood on the bridge deck with Bertha Smallbutt, the ship's quartermaster, arguing with a group of Thothian monks led by one Prior Finch. Sir Glimador Malvegil stood by with Sir Kelbor of Dor Eotrus. They studied both the debate and the standoff at the gangway, concern on their faces over each.

Slaayde's well-coifed appearance, black patent leathers, white shirt, and crisp jacket held him in sharp contrast to his crusty crew. He stood an extra step away to avoid the Prior's foul, oniony breath. "Prior, be reasonable," said Slaayde, his ready smile absent, his cheeks flushed. I've given you and your aides the grand tour, from stem to stern, including the hold. I've been more than cooperative and patient—"

"—For the last time, Captain, order that overstuffed barbarian of yours to stand down and give himself up," gesturing down toward Tug, "and the rest of your men to stand aside so I can have this ship properly searched."

"Properly?" said Bertha. "You've seen everything already. The whole ship — every hold, locker, and bunk. We've wasted the best part of the day with you."

"I haven't seen the bulk of your cargo. You know full well that you only opened a handful of crates. You will open the rest or—"

"—You want to see more?" said Bertha. Her voice grew shriller with each word. "Fine. We'll open another handful. We'll open a dozen."

Slaayde put his hand on Bertha's shoulder. "I'm a simple merchant, Prior," said Slaayde. "Here to engage in honest trade. Nothing more. I want no trouble with you Thothians. You can search a score or more crates if it'll keep your troops off my ship and prevent this matter from escalating."

"You will open every single box, barrel, and crate on this ship for inspection. Every one."

"Ridiculous!" said Bertha as she shook her head.

"One score, no more," said Slaayde. "You can select them yourself. Let's head back down to the hold and get this over and done."

"Do you think me a fool?" said Finch. "Do you think this is a negotiation? I know you've got contraband aboard. One way or another I'll find it and you will taste almighty Thoth's justice. If you cooperate, Thoth may show you mercy, if not . . ."

"You've no right or cause to threaten the Captain like that," said Bertha.

Finch glared at her. "Captain, in the name of the Thothian Theocracy of Tragoss Mor, I order you to direct your men to stand down. Now, Captain. And direct your cow," he said as he scowled at Bertha, "to open and empty every crate on this ship or I will take you into custody and—"

"—Who the heck do you think you are?" screeched Bertha. "You can't speak of me like that."

The Prior's arm shot out and slammed openhanded into Bertha's cheek. She fell backward, such was the force of the blow, and cracked her head into the deck-rail, which knocked her senseless. The big monk beside Finch, his bodyguard, chuckled. The third monk, a bespeckled, elderly fellow, looked up from his ledger for the first time, concern on his face.

Prior Finch loomed over Bertha. "I'm a Prior of almighty Thoth, you disgusting cow, and I'll speak to you any way I see fit." Finch raised his leg and prepared to stomp on Bertha as she laid dazed, blood dripping down her brow. "If you had—" The Prior's words ended abruptly in a gurgling sound when the tip of Slaayde's saber burst through his chest.

The Prior coughed and a glob of blood poured from his mouth. He stared in disbelief at the steel that protruded from his chest. The saber's crossguard pressed against Finch's back, its steel-forged blade having passed clear through him.

Slaayde pulled his blade free, his face grim, as blood spurted from the mortal wound. Finch staggered wide-eyed and openmouthed for a few steps, pitched over the rail, and crashed to the main deck below, his fall in full view of the troop of monks amassed on the pier.

For a moment, no one moved, and everyone that saw went silent; shock and disbelief filled their faces.

Glimador shook his head. "Fool," he spat.

"Treachery," yelled one monk on the pier. Others yelled the same.

"Attack," yelled others.

"Kill them," yelled still more. "Praise Thoth! Kill them! Kill them all!"

The monks on the gangway charged Tug. Finch's bodyguard roared and pulled his scimitar. Before he could bring it to bear, Slaayde's saber bit deep into his throat; a mortal wound that instantly sapped his strength and dropped him to his knees.

The bodyguard's sword clanked and rattled when it struck the deck. He desperately pressed his hands to his throat to stem the gush of blood, but it spurted from between his fingers and sprayed over Slaayde's boots and pantaloons. Fear etched the man's face. His eyes darted from Slaayde, to Glimador, to Kelbor, and back again — a pleading look; a silent cry for help, for mercy.

Slaayde stared down at him for a moment, then thrust his blade into the man's chest. The sharpened steel sliced through muscle and sternum and plunged deep into his beating heart. Slaayde pulled the blade clear and the monk collapsed face first to the deck.

The elderly monk dropped his ledger and backed away, but stumbled on a coiled rope and fell to his backside. He stared at the dark pool of blood that expanded around his fallen comrade. His eyes searched for some escape or solace. His gaze lingered on the ship's ladder that led down to the main deck. Slaayde would be on him before he even made his feet; he would never reach the ladder. He was doomed. He looked up at Slaayde but betrayed no emotion, no fear. He simply adjusted his spectacles and sat there waiting, stoically resolved to his fate.

Slaayde stalked toward him, the same grim expression on his face as when he killed the other two.

Glimador grabbed Slaayde's sword arm and stepped before him. "You fool. There must be a hundred of them over there. How's Claradon supposed to get aboard now? And how will we get away?"

Slaayde's eyes were hard; his voice harsh. "We'll fight our way out. My crew's seen worse." Slaayde glanced at Bertha. She stirred, only now coming around.

"We're not leaving without Claradon and the others."

Two crossbow bolts flew past and narrowly missed Slaayde's shoulder.

"They'd better show up fast, because we can't stay here. Stand aside. I've business to finish," said Slaayde, gesturing toward the old monk.

"He's no threat. You will not butcher him."

Slaayde stood eye to eye with the young nobleman, their faces inches apart. Slaayde's face and eyes were emotionless, resolved, dead. The dead eyes of a stone-cold killer. The gaze of a man who didn't care; all pretense to the jolly rogue long gone. He started to push past Glimador, but the young knight clamped down on his arm, all his muscle brought to bear to hold the captain back.

Kelbor moved behind Slaayde. "Stand down, Slaayde," he said, menace in his voice.

A flash of anger covered Slaayde's face, and he paused for but a moment, considering, and then took a breath, glanced again toward Bertha who stared back at him. Tears streamed down her face. He relaxed and ceased straining against Glimador. Gesturing toward the old monk, he said, "Fine. I'll leave him be. Let go of me."

Glimador nodded and released the Captain. Slaayde rushed to the ladder to join his men in battle.

More crossbow bolts flew by. One embedded in the housing for the ship's wheel.

"What do we do now?" said Kelbor.

"We hope that Seran found them and that they get here soon."

"And if they don't?"

"Watch the monk and see to the woman; I'm going downdeck. Keep your head down."

Little Tug wreaked havoc on the gangway. He cursed and taunted the monks that crumbled and shattered before his monstrous hammer. He trod on the broken bodies, their blood, brains, and guts stained the ramp as he pummeled his way down to the pier. Several corpses bobbed in the reddening water beneath the gangway, Tug's blows having launched them over the rail.

The smell of blood and men's innards hung heavy in the air as it always did over a battlefield, breeze or not. The horrid sounds and sickening sights and scents of battle were new to the young Lomerian soldiers aligned behind Tug. Several retched. They formed a column one man wide behind Sergeant Vid, all silent and shiny silver, shields and swords, their faces pale and stoic, their eyes betrayed their fear. Beside them, Slaayde's gritty reavers, old friends to blood and gore, formed a second column, their eyes wild and weapons notched, their voices raised loud and wild, urging Tug on. They chanted his name in unison, in tone and tenor that made the monks' blood run cold.

Sergeant Vid and seaman Chert crouched behind Tug; their shields protected his and their flanks from crossbow bolts fired in panic by the monks arrayed along the pier. Most shafts flew wild, but some few slammed into or shattered against their shields.

The dozen Malvegillian archers lined up along the ship's rail were far more skilled than the monks. Several Thothians went down with arrows through chest, neck, or belly. The others took cover behind broad crates and barrels stacked about the pier.

The remaining monks on the gangway backpedaled from Tug, spears extended before them in hopes of keeping the brute at bay. Whenever Tug drew close enough, his hammer battered away the spear-tips, sundered shafts, and shattered limbs. Not a man amongst them could stand against him for more than a single swing of Old Fogey.

The cluster of monks at the base of the gangway parted when at last their champion arrived. His brethren whooped and hollered at the very sight of him, relief on their faces, their courage renewed, their ground now held. Their hero swaggered forward, a giant even to match Tug.

Sarq, champion of Tragoss Mor, towered above his fellows, and was near as tall as Tug. Bulging, chiseled muscles defined him; arms thicker than most men's legs; chest as broad as a wine barrel; his face lined and stony, his skin bronzed, and pate bald as his brethren. His arms and torso, tattooed here and there, women, dragons, and bones. The scars that crisscrossed his face and body bespoke of a bloody, brutal life. Not the life of a soldier, but that of a killer. A creature that lived for battle, reared in blood, his skills honed in the pits of Tragoss Mor's arenas. He gripped the short-hafted spear in his right hand with ease and confidence. He lifted it above his head and his comrades cheered, their voices heard across the breadth of the docks, chanting his name, over and over. Sarq grinned and posed and flexed as they roared behind him and urged him on. His eyes wild, manic; his body shook with battle rage.

Tug grinned at the challenge. "Let's feed the fishes, boys," he roared. He charged and pulled back his arm, poised to launch an overhand swing of his hammer. Sarq braced for the rush, spear readied before him.

Not ten feet from Sarq, Tug halted midstride and his hammer arced forward. A throw! He let

Old Fogey fly, aimed at Sarq's midsection. A daring, even reckless move to throw his prized weapon when facing such an opponent. But perhaps Tug knew it was his best chance, for as quick as he was with the hammer, it was a ponderous weapon against an expert's spear. If he failed to crush Sarq with his first strike, the monk's spear may well skewer him.

The hammer sped in, too fast, and too large to dodge at that distance. Sarq sprang to the side with almost inhuman speed, spared of the deathblow. Fast as he was, the hammer caught him a glancing blow to the thigh. That and his leap took him from his feet. The hammer careened into other monks behind Sarq and sent several down in a heap.

Tug barreled forward, his tower shield braced before him, pinned with broken shafts. Sarq recovered his spear and made his feet, but before he was ready, Tug's shield barreled in and struck him a crushing blow that splintered the shield and brought Sarq to his knees, his face and arm broken and bloody.

Tug pummeled Sarq in the temple, once, and then again, knocking the Thothian unconscious. The other monks scurried back, shocked and terrified. Tug grabbed Sarq by the belt, hefted him overhead, and dumped him into the harbor, the Tragoss champion never even having struck a blow.

Seamen and soldiers swarmed past Tug, cheering, and waded into the fray, weapons flailing.

Slaayde slithered up against the ship's rail between where Guj, his half-lugron boatswain, and young Sir Paldor crouched. Both they and the monks on the pier were pinned down. Archers and crossbowmen traded shafts to little affect, as most everyone was now well behind cover.

"Orders, Captain?" said Guj, glancing over at Slaayde. Slaayde studied the scene as best he could, peeking over the gunwale.

"We've got to clear the pier," said Glimador when he crouched down beside the others, "or Claradon won't be able to get to us."

"Agreed," said Slaayde.

"Up and over?" said Guj.

Slaayde nodded.

"I'll go," said Guj. "You stay with ship."

"Agreed."

Glimador looked at Guj quizzically.

"We jump over side," said Guj. "Then kill all them monks."

"Oh boy," said Glimador. He peered over the rail at the gap between *The Falcon* and the pier. "That's a ten or twelve foot drop and at least seven feet across. You can't be serious."

"It's the only way," said Slaayde. "We're pinned down here and bottled up at the gangway. We have to hit them across their whole line at once. They'll break and they'll rout."

"Are you a soldier now, Captain?" said Glimador.

"I'm a lot of things," said Slaayde.

"You tin-cans best stay put here," said Guj to Glimador. "Too far for armor and I'm not fishing for you."

Glimador looked over the side again. A crossbow bolt whizzed just over his head. "You'll get no argument from me."

Word of the plan passed down the line in moments.

Guj sprang up. "Ready, you scum," he shouted. "Up and over." He stepped atop the rail and leaped toward the pier as he shouted a war cry. A good thirty crewmen followed him over in two quick waves, even the cook, the navigator, and one of the cabin boys made the leap, weapons in hand. The pier's planks screamed and crackled but held when the men crashed to the boards. Amazingly, every man landed on the pier, though one or two went down, either taken by crossbow bolts or some injury from the jump.

Glimador looked down the line of the deck. Only Malvegillian archers and a handful of House Harringgold's regulars remained.

The pier now hosted a wild melee. Tug's group had partially broken the bottleneck at the gangway and was fully engaged with a troop of monks and a squadron of Tragoss Morian soldiers. Soldiers and seamen still crowded the gangway with no way to join the melee until Tug pushed the Thothians farther back.

Guj's seamen fell like madmen on the monks arrayed along the pier. They hacked and slashed with no mercy or regard. Their wildness was both their strength, since it struck fear in their enemy, and their weakness, since they fought as individuals, not as a unit.

Even over the din of battle, Tragoss whistles blared, a claxon call to arms. The city rose against them.

"Where are they?" said Slaayde as he strained to look down the pier.

"They'll be here," said Glimador.

"The pier will be ours in minutes, but with those whistles will come troops," said Slaayde. "Not just more monks, but squadrons of Tragoss regulars, trained soldiers. If they come in force, we're finished. To save our necks, we would have to push off at first sight of them and even then, we might not make it. Where's N'Paag? I need—-" Slaayde's words cut off in a grunt.

From the corner of his eye, Glimador saw Slaayde violently wrenched from his feet. He turned and witnessed a horror unlike any he'd seen before. He gasped and banged back against the gunwale in surprise. "Dead gods!?"

A fiend, a thing out of nightmare that moved like the wind, dragged Slaayde by the leg across the deck, then pounced on him, teeth and claws. The thing had been a man but moments before — it had been Prior Finch, a monk of Thoth, but was no longer. Now he was a monster, a fiend. Finch's bronzed skin was now a putrid gray; his teeth elongated into wicked fangs, his fingernails now razored claws, long and sharp as small daggers. His eyes burned red, blood red, illumed with an unholy light. A stench of death, putrid and vile, hung about him.

Slaayde squirmed and yelled and tried to spin and bring his sword to bear, but the thing had him well-pinned. It clamped its jaws on his leg, its dagger-like fangs unhindered by pant, flesh, or bone. Deep into Slaayde's calf did it bite. Slaayde roared in pain and anger.

Glimador bounced to his feet, sword in hand. Without hesitation, he extended his arm and pointed the tip of his sword at the monster that had been Finch. He recalled and bespoke his secret words of power; words not of the new, modern magic taught him by the masters of the Knights of Tyr, but olden words passed down from his mother. These words held eldritch power beyond the ken of other knights, well trained or naught. They called up energies that dwelt beyond the pale, plucked power from the primordial ether, and channeled it to his purpose. At Glimador's behest, crackling blue fire engulfed his sword and bounded from its tip. It arced through the air like storm-fire, crackling and popping, and blasted into Finch's shoulder. It seared the monster's flesh, bored deep into muscle and bone, smoke and sparks flew.

But that arcane spell that would have incinerated most any man or beast barely fazed the wanton creature. It didn't even cry out, though its head shot up from its victim. Blood dribbled down its mouth and neck, bits of Slaayde's pant and flesh dangled from its teeth. An inhuman growl — deep and guttural escaped from its maw; its eyes afire, locked on Glimador and promised only pain and death.

The fiend launched itself at the young knight, and leapt the twenty feet between them in a single bound. Glimador's sword sizzled by, wisps of blue fire still licked its steel, but the creature avoided the blow and struck back. Its horrid claws raked along Glimador's shoulder-plate and greaves, and gouged deep rivets in the tempered steel.

Glimador backpedaled and spun his sword over and over to parry the flailing claws that rained in. A dozen murderous blows he deflected, though it took all his speed and skill. Then Paldor was there; two Lomerian soldiers with him. They assaulted the beast from all sides, but it ducked and dodged with inhuman speed, capered and leaped to and fro, and sidestepped sword and axe. Its claws were everywhere and took their toll as it cursed in some guttural tongue unknown to mortal man.

A metallic tinkling sound filled the air and heralded the death of one brave soldier. It was the sound of chainmail links severing beneath otherworldly claws, the flesh beneath shorn and ruined as blood showered the deck. Just as quickly, the sound came again and another man fell to the claws, his entrails spilled on the boards.

Bertha appeared and dragged Slaayde farther from the fray as a volley of arrows took the beast in neck, shoulder, and chest. No blood sprang from the wounds; the missiles creating but a momentary pause in the melee.

Glimador and Paldor stood shoulder to shoulder, breathing heavily, and braced for the beast's next rush. Much of Glimador's armor hung in tatters. Paldor winced and tried to blink away the blood that trickled into his eyes from a wicked gash in his forehead.

"My magic can't stop it," said Glimador.

"Our swords fare little better," said Paldor. "What do we do?"

"We fight," said Glimador, "until we put it down or death claims us."

"Victory or Valhalla," said Paldor.

Kelbor appeared at Glimador's side, sword at the ready. Ganton the Bull charged in, roaring and cursing, several soldiers in his wake.

"Just in time," said Glimador.

The knights and soldiers encircled the fiend and pressed their attack. They cut off all escape and all room for it to maneuver. Hack and slash, stab and whirl, sword, hammer, and axe. Blow after blow struck the undead thing. No mercy, no quarter given.

A vicious slash from Glimador's sword severed the fiend's arm well above the elbow, but still it fought on. Kelbor's thrust pierced its chest; the sword's tip exited the creature's back. Kelbor twisted the blade and held it fast, transfixing the creature in place. Paldor stabbed it in the abdomen just as Ganton's hammer crashed down on its head and mashed it to pulp. The fiend's broken body collapsed lifeless to the deck; the evil power that had held it, now no more. It was dead, again.

"What in Odin's name was that?" said Ganton.

Glimador dropped to his knees in exhaustion. Paldor did the same.

Kelbor ran to the gunwale and looked out across the docks. "We've taken the pier," he said. "The monks flee."

The battle was over for the moment, though the cries and screams of injured and dying men filled the air, and Tragoss whistles blared all the louder, all the nearer.

"They're here," said Kelbor.

"Claradon? He's back?" said Paldor.

"Not Claradon," said Kelbor. "The Thothian army," he said turning back toward the others. "We're finished."

"You brought this on us," yelled Slaayde, his voice weak and crackling. The men turned towards the forecastle. Slaayde sat on the deck, his face deathly pale, his legs outstretched before him, a pool of blood expanding about him. Bertha was on her knees and tears streamed down her face. Awash in the Captain's blood, she desperately tightened a tourniquet about his leg. "You stinking Eotrus," said Slaayde. "You brought this evil to my ship, you bastards. You brought this death." His voice grew weak and his eyes closed. "Damn you, damn you all."

4
THREE MINOR EDICTS

The walls of the High Council chamber in old Tammanian Hall reverberated from the tensions that filled the air. Broiling tempers, shouted warnings, subtle threats, and dire predictions consumed the place these last many hours and all but continuously for several days.

Three days previous, with barely a quorum present, the Vizier — the Royal Archwizard of Lomion and recently anointed Grandmaster of the Tower of the Arcane, invoked a little known and less used point of order called Fastr that required the High Council to remain in continuous session until its present business was concluded. Matters could not be tabled and breaks were limited to mere minutes every few hours. No recess for meals or sleep. A grueling process that inevitably led to resolutions voted up or down, for good or ill.

Three diverse and controversial edicts were put forth for the Councilors' consideration. First, Chancellor Barusa proposed, of all things, that the government provide daily meals to Lomion City's needy, the treasury to foot the bill. Second, the Chancellor proposed that the Council extend Lomerian citizenship to Thothian immigrants residing within the borders of the Kingdom of Lomion. The council made no headway on either measure, the Chancellor having insufficient votes to press his measures until he and the Vizier went off for a time in private conference. When they returned, the Vizier proposed that the Council appoint a tenth High Magister to the Tribunal, the realm's highest judiciary body. The Vizier then called for Fastr, which Barusa and his faction curiously supported. Together they had sufficient votes to bring Fastr into play given the limited attendance at the time. Runners notified the absent Councilors and those in the city arrived to assume their seats, angry and insulted at the Vizier's tactics. For three long days and two nights they argued and debated and threatened, reaching no agreement. The hour grew late on the third night of debate before progress was made.

As customary, the High Council was assembled on the Councilors' Mezzanine, high above the audience floor where the courtiers and various petitioners lurked and whispered, though at this late hour only the most die-hard politicos, sleepy sycophants, and pathetic toadies haunted the lower hall, the bulk long fled to their beds or other more entertaining pursuits.

The councilors reclined in ornate, high-backed chairs better described as thrones. Their expressions varied one to another, running from dejected, to angry, to befuddled. All looked exhausted and to varying extents, disheveled.

Prince Cartegian, unkempt and wild-eyed as usual, squatted atop the center seat, capering and gibbering. At his right hand sat Barusa of Alder, Chancellor of Lomion, the most powerful man in the realm. Nearby, Bishop Tobin snored loudly, chin on chest. Arch-Duke Harringgold was there, as was Guildmaster Slyman, the Vizier, Lord

Jhensezil, Lady Dahlia, and the rest of the august body, save for Lords Glenfinnen and Aldros, both away, as their duties took them. The areas behind the Councilors brimmed with their personal guards, all armed to the teeth. The petitioner's hall below, and the stair leading up to the Councilors' Mezzanine were guarded by a squadron of Myrdonian Knights in dress uniform, arms and armor gleaming.

Guildmaster Slyman stood, crumbs tumbling down his stained satin tunic. So rare was it to see the guildmaster stir from his seat before session's end that his colleagues quieted and ceded him what remained of their attention. "These debates have gone too long," he said. "Each matter at hand must be decided once and for all. I call again for a vote."

"On which issue?" said Chancellor Barusa, his hand playing with an empty goblet, his eyes downcast.

"The Thothians," said Slyman. "They are good people. Hardworking, proud, and productive. They deserve the same rights and privileges as all Lomerians. It's time we grant them full citizenship."

"They're not Lomerians," said Harringgold. "They loathe Lomion and our very way of life. To grant them citizenship is madness. Some of them don't even want it and those that do only seek free services, benefits, and rights not available to foreigners. They want to use us, not join us."

"You've spewed that hate one too many times," said the Vizier. "Your prejudices are unbecoming a member of this esteemed council, and I'll hear no more of them. Continue on that course at your own peril."

Lord Jhensezil jumped to his feet, his jaw set, his face beet red, arm waving and pointing at the Vizier, though no words escaped his mouth.

"No hate lives in my heart, Councilor," said Harringgold. "Nor is it I making threats, it's you. If you will hear no more from me, then leave. You will not stop me from speaking the truth."

"You're so filled with hate, you no longer know what the truth is." said the Vizier.

"Is it hate to repeat the Thothians' stated goals," shouted Jhensezil, "using their own words, not ours? They admit that they plan to foster a revolution against our government, against this very council. They boast that they will transform Lomion into a theocracy under the rule of Thothian Law in the model of Tragoss Mor and Tragoss Krell. Is that what you want?"

"Free speech and liberty is the law of the land in Lomion," said Chancellor Barusa. "The Thothians are free to proselytize all they want. By naming them enemies, you betray yourselves as malcontents and harbingers of hate. You can't see beyond your misguided and outdated prejudices. And those miscreants that follow you are little more than mindless, toothless fools. It's you and your narrow-minded followers that should be silenced and censured by this council, not the Thothians."

The Vizier stood. "Councilors, this has grown too heated and far too personal. We all know the merits of the issue and have our own opinions. None of us will be swayed by further debate, therefore, such debate is a waste of all our time. We must vote. I call for hands. Citizenship for the Thothians, yea or nay?"

"The treasury cannot sustain the cost of feeding half the city," said Harringgold. "The realm is already far too deep in debt. We cannot afford this folly."

"Folly, Councilor?" said Chancellor Barusa. "You think it folly to feed starving citizens? Starving children? Let the poor go hungry while you sit fat and happy in your keep? You're a heartless bastard, Harringgold."

"How could anyone of good conscience withhold food from the needy?" said Slyman, his girth and the stains on his shirt proclaimed that none had ever been withheld from him. "As leaders of this realm, no, as human beings, we have a responsibility to care for others, to help them whenever and wherever we can. To do any less is simply inhuman and uncivilized. For you to advocate that we turn away and ignore their suffering disgusts me. Shame, Councilor, shame. We *can* feed the hungry, and so we must. It's as simple that. Don't you agree, Bishop Tobin?" Slyman nudged the bishop awake with a poke to his ribs.

"What, ho?" went Tobin, opening an eye. "We mustn't let the commoners starve," he said before his lid slid closed again. "That just won't do at all."

"Few citizens in Lomion are truly in need," said Jhensezil. "And there's no one starving. Most of those few that go hungry are foreigners too lazy to work or citizens that waste their money on wine, tobacco, or carnal pleasures. They're responsible for their own predicament. The rest of the realm shouldn't have to pay for them."

"I challenge every point you've made," said the Vizier. "Who are you to say who's lazy and who isn't? How would you even know? This is just more of your xenophobia, your bias, and bigotry."

"It's more than that," said Barusa. "Councilor Jhensezil steadfastly refuses to support levy reform. He knows that he and his wealthy supporters don't pay their fair share, and he seeks to keep the burden of funding the realm on the backs of the common people. That desire motivates every vote he casts on this Council. It's despicable."

"The wealthy pay nearly all the levies collected, Chancellor, as you well know. The common folk pay almost nothing. It's they that don't pay their fair share."

"No matter how many times you repeat that lie, Councilor, it remains untrue," said Slyman. "We are for the people and you are out only for yourself and your rich friends."

Jhensezil shook his head, and stood for some moments at a loss for words.

"A vote is called for," said the Vizier. "Shall the government fund food relief for the needy of Lomion City or not? I call for hands. Yea or nay?"

"Let us finalize the matter of the tribunal," said the Vizier, "and close our business so that we may all enjoy some much needed rest."

"Lomion has long had nine high magisters serve on the Tribunal," said Arch-Duke

59

Harringgold, "throughout all living memory and beyond. To add a tenth is unprecedented and unwarranted. You seek advantage for writs blustered through this council that violate the Articles of the Republic."

"You say that with such strength and confidence," said the Vizier. "Unfortunately, your thesis is entirely untrue and goes to pattern. The Tribunal has indeed numbered ten high magisters at times in the past. For many years, the Republic had but five, then a sixth was added. During the time of Potrades, four more were added to the Tribunal. For the past 150 years there has been but nine. There is no reason there cannot be a tenth or more."

"Might I remind the Council," said Jhensezil, "that King Gornon the Bold sought to add five High Magisters during his reign, all in an attempt to stack the Tribunal with his men. That measure was soundly defeated as should the one before us now. It is a slippery slope that must be avoided."

"Nevertheless," said Barusa, "this council has the authority to alter the number of High Magisters and if that be our will, we will do so."

"Garon Kroth's name has been put forth for the post of High Magister," said the Vizier. "I hereby call for a vote regarding his confirmation."

"Kroth is well known to have little regard for the Articles of the Republic," said Jhensezil. "He's publically stated on several occasions that our Articles are outdated and don't reflect the times. He's subverted them at every turn."

"He's well known to be a good and honest man with the best interests of the realm in mind," said Slyman. "That said, who cares what he thinks of the Articles? We have every reason to believe he'll do the right thing on the Tribunal. What more could we ask of any Magister?"

"Who cares?" said Jhensezil. "Upholding the Articles of the Republic is the very core of the Tribunal's charge. If we know he will not do that, we cannot appoint him. If fact, if he does not intend to keep faith with the Articles, then by definition he does not have the best interests of the Republic in mind."

"Outrageous!" spouted Slyman.

"You are out of order," said Chancellor Barusa. "This council will not tolerate such slanderous remarks. I'll caution you once again to tread carefully, Lord Jhensezil."

"It is for this council and the Council of Lords to make the laws of the land," said Jhensezil. "The Tribunal's role is to see that they're applied properly and to identify and strike down those edicts that violate the Articles. That is a cornerstone of the Republic. Without it, the Republic could fall into despotism."

"Your words insult every member of this esteemed council and those of the Council of Lords," said Barusa. "To assert that we would violate our oaths to serve Lomion, that any amongst us would act against the interests of the people, is scandalous, hateful, and borders on treason. Check your tongue councilor. I warn you, check your tongue."

***

Lord Harringgold entered his private chambers in the great fortress of Dor Lomion. His face was careworn and his eyes were downcast and red from fatigue. The usual spring in his step, gone, his energy depleted. He reverently placed his leatherbound copy of the Articles of the Republic on the sideboard by the door, dropped a thick clutch of papers beside it, and engaged the heavy deadbolt despite his picked guards that hovered outside. He doffed his heavy cloak, hat, scarf, and gloves and hung them on pegs beside the door. He could have dropped them all wherever — the servants would have collected them on the morrow and cleaned and folded them all proper, but he would rather do such menial tasks himself. That just felt right to him.

A long and stressful day, and a week to match — one of the most trying in memory. No sleep to speak of and not a decent meal in days. At least here, door secured, he was safe and free from disturbance. No one could enter without his knowledge or leave. He could put aside the cares of the day as best as his mind would allow. He would have a brandy by the fireplace. It would relax him. He would escape into a book, some fantasy to rouse the spirit and set sail the imagination. Once lost in such a place, the stress would fall from his brow and his muscles would relax. Soon he would think clearly again, reason ruling over emotion, fears, and doubt.

Then he would think things through until his mind quieted enough for sleep, if it did. He would sort out the meaning behind the maneuvers recent made in the Council chambers. He would set a plan. He had devised many stratagems of late to deal with the League and its machinations and been outmaneuvered at every turn, but whether by poor luck, happenstance, or superior guile, he could not yet be sure. He would adapt his plans, again, and again if need be. He would not let Lomion fall — not from within, no more than he would allow it to fall from without. Such was his duty. Besides, he was not a man to lose; he had no skill at it, and wouldn't learn now. He would think on things again when he woke. A good night's sleep always provided a better perspective. Perhaps things would seem less bleak in the morning.

He poured his brandy from the ornate decanter on the sideboard and turned toward his favorite chair. A cloaked figure sat beside the fireplace.

Assassin! Surprise filled his face, but not fear. The tumbler dropped from Harringgold's hand and faster than you would imagine he pulled a long dagger from his belt and assumed a fighting stance. The assassin's hand shot out nearly as fast, though it was empty. Strangely, Harringgold heard no crash of the glass and glanced down to see the tumbler suspended in midair.

"Be at ease, Duke," said the cloaked figure, his voice strangely familiar. "I'm here for council, not knifework." The figure pulled back his hood. It was Pipkorn, deposed grandmaster of the Tower of the Arcane.

"Magic," said Pipkorn.

"What?"

"You were about to ask how I got past your guards. We've weighty matters to discuss that can't wait and are best spoken in secret."

Harringgold's jaw was set, and his mood blackened further. "Grandmaster or not, you've no business stealing into my private chambers." The fact that Pipkorn could, likely meant others could as well. The very thought was frightening, almost paralyzing. His one bastion of safety and sanity was violated and proven woefully insecure. He knew full well that there were those about that desired his death. Knowing that there were ways past his security, how would he ever rest easy again? He couldn't. Not ever.

"I would have met with you tomorrow if you had sent word," said Harringgold. "Tonight, I've no energy for more council, best you get gone, and don't presume to enter uninvited again."

"The hour is later than you know, Duke," said Pipkorn, his voice as sharp as the Duke's knife. "My words can't wait, so seat yourself, and sip your brandy. Actually, if you don't mind, pour another. We've a bit of candle to burn, and I could use one too."

The tumbler sailed smoothly through the air and into Pipkorn's outstretched hand. He leaned back in the chair and took a sip while Harringgold poured his glass. "I need you to arrange an audience for us with the king," said Pipkorn. "We must meet with him tomorrow morning, which is why I couldn't delay speaking with you. We need to inform him of the events of today's Council meeting and discuss their ramifications."

"I didn't see you on the chamber floor."

"I didn't choose to be seen."

"Fine. Then inform him and leave me to get some sleep."

"The king holds little love for wizards, and less for me than most. He may not see me at all, and if he does, no doubt he'll make me wait for longer than the realm can afford. I need you to get me in."

"You seem to need little help in letting yourself in."

"True enough," said Pipkorn, "but Tenzivel's security is more . . . complex. A conventional entry would be best, I think. Otherwise, I wouldn't be here."

"I know that you've no love for the Thothians. I'm against their citizenship as I've made clear, but that resolution's passing is hardly a crisis. What is your urgency?"

"The matter of the Tribunal is the greater threat, as I hope you understand. I must have Tenzivel's thoughts on that. He must be made to see the road down which the realm is heading, before it's too late to change its course."

"Tenzivel is still the King, I grant you," said Harringgold. "But he's withdrawn from the government. Dead gods, he's withdrawn from the world. He spends most of his time drooling in his cups. Who cares what he thinks? Why bother meeting with him at all?"

"Wise council remains within him," said Pipkorn. "We need only extract it. One must never underestimate any man who has risen so far as he, even though he inherited the position."

"You think to convince him to resume his role in the government?"

"You don't have the power to stop what's coming, Harringgold. The king does, if he chooses to use it. We need his support."

"Then we should include Sluug and Jhensezil in these discussions, for they have strong opinions on these matters and their support is surely needed as well."

"Traveling in force to the throne room would not go unnoticed," said Pipkorn. "Little birds would sing of a conspiracy against the League. That wouldn't do, at least not just yet."

5
FLAME AND PARLEY

Shrill Tragoss Morian whistles, claxon calls to arms, blared from ahead and behind as Claradon's group limped toward the dock ward, two of their number left behind, dead in the street. Blood trailed from more than one of the survivors. Ob and Seran Harringgold trotted at the van; both spattered in blood, though most not theirs.

Artol hobbled along behind Ob, battered and bloody. He leaned heavily on Par Tanch whose face dripped with sweat and was frozen in a grimace of pain from supporting the huge soldier. Theta carried Claradon's limp form over his left shoulder, his shield in his right hand. Despite his heavy burden, Theta kept pace and even pushed the others. Kayla jogged beside him, her hand on Claradon's side; tears streamed down her face. Dolan followed closely behind, bow in hand and arrow nocked. He ran backward as oft as forward, gliding along easily, exhibiting no fatigue or emotion. Any monk or Alder man that pursued received naught for their efforts but one of Dolan's arrows in their chest.

The group smelled the dock ward well before they saw it, for a foul, fishy odor hung heavy in that quarter and spread over much of the surrounding environs with the afternoon sun. Merchants' Way, the wide avenue that ended at the wharfs, carried them in sight of the pier where *The Black Falcon* lay berthed. The last blocks before Dock Street, which usually thronged with street hawkers and seamen at this hour, lay deserted, shop doors shuttered, street stalls hastily abandoned, still stocked with wares.

"Hold up," said Ob as he signaled to Seran and came to a halt. The others stopped behind them. "Something's not right," he said, breathing heavily. "Where is everybody?"

Seran readied his shield. "There's movement in the upper floor windows," he said, pointing.

"Bowmen or lookyloos?" said Ob, a hand to his forehead to cut the glare.

"Can't tell," said Seran. "Too far."

"Shopkeepers and citizens," said Theta. "Let's move on."

"How can you possibly see that?" said Tanch.

"He eats his carrots, Magic Boy," said Ob as he looked back to check on Claradon, concern on his face. "Stop your whining. Theta, what do you figure drove them buggers inside?"

A troop of Freedom Guardsmen dashed down Dock Street, across the avenue's mouth, paid the group no heed, and turned onto *The Falcon's* pier.

Ob looked back at Theta. "There's my answer. They're headed for the ship. There's been trouble. That's why the locals took cover."

"Let's move," said Theta.

When they reached Dock Street, the wide wooden wharf that ran along the bay's edge, they spotted a squadron of Tragoss Morian soldiers and monks gathered at the next pier over. They were deployed, weapons drawn, around a group of Alder marines led by Blain Alder and his son, Edwin. Behind them, a large ship with black sails, which could only be the infamous *Gray Talon* that had long dogged their heels. The Alders spotted Claradon's group and shouted and pointed at them.

"Rat dung!" said Ob. "Now they'll have that lot on us."

Sure enough, half a squadron of Freedom Guardsmen and several monks broke off from their dispute with the Alders and charged Claradon's group, whistles blaring, shouting for them to stand down.

"Make for the ship," said Theta. "Run!"

"There are too many," said Seran pointing to the soldiers ahead who even now reached *The Falcon*. "We'll never break through."

"And with them others behind us, we'll not get out," said Ob.

"*The Falcon's* our only way out, so keep moving," said Theta as he sped up and took the lead from the others.

The group barreled down *The Falcon's* pier. The briny breeze that struck their faces carried the scent of blood. Other ships lined both sides of the long pier, gangways raised, sailors arrayed along rail and rigging, eyes fixed on *The Falcon.* Some shouted, some cheered, though what they yelled was lost in the general din. One ship pulled away from the pier in haste, its rigging not properly set; two others already sped away.

Near *The Falcon's* berth, the pier was in chaos. Freedom Guardsmen exchanged crossbow and bow fire with *The Falcon's* defenders. The guardsmen shouted for boarding planks and ladders; *The Falcon's* retracted gangway leaving them no easy way to board. Most of their troops scrambled for cover behind rows of barrels and piles of crates that lined the pier, cargo to be loaded aboard the ship opposite *The Falcon*. The monks attempted to board that vessel, a large caravel out of Minoc, suspicious of collusion with *The Falcon*.

Dozens of monks and a squad or two of Freedom Guardsmen lay dead, scattered about the pier, pierced with arrows, or cut down by sword or axe. Here and there lay a seaman from *The Falcon*, slain by some monk's sickle.

"Wizard," said Theta to Tanch. "If you've any magic that can clear our path, now would be the time."

Tanch looked aghast. "There are far too many. My magic cannot avail us here."

"Lord Angle," said Dolan. "They're on us from behind."

"What do we do?" shrieked Kayla. "We're trapped!"

"We fight," said Ob, axe in hand.

"Dolan — hold them," was all Theta said.

"Aye." Dolan's hand and bow moved in a blur. Hand to quiver to bow, pull and release and back to quiver, smooth and so fast the eye could barely follow. Arrow after arrow skewered charging guardsmen. Six men went down in as many seconds; each pierced through head, neck, or chest. A score more came on in their wake, shields upraised.

The guardsmen in front noticed Claradon's group and decided at a glance that they were in league with *The Falcon* or at least that they would be the ones to pay for the dead monks on the pier. A full squadron broke off and charged the group, yelling battle cries, their weapons poised to strike. There would be no parley or surrender. They were out for blood and would settle for nothing less.

Theta's voice was stern and strong. "Pipkorn's ring," he said. "Use it."

Tanch looked confused.

"Use it," shouted Theta. "Quickly!"

Tanch's arms glided in a fluid, circular motion, then pressed together, palm to palm, fingers extended and spread. He pointed his fingertips at the squadron of monks that charged from the front. "Dead gods, let this work." He spoke his magical words, and with them, the ensorcelled Ring of the Magi, preserved through the long ages, glowed a sparkling green, brighter and brighter as the arcane words of power echoed on the wind, gathering strength, drawing energy not only from the weave of magic that filled the ether, but from Tanch's innermost core, from his immortal soul.

The spell completed, a stream of emerald fire erupted from Tanch's fingertips. It roared, sped outward and expanded in a conical pattern; a vortex of whirling flame from the beyond. Tanch fought to hold his arms and his gaze steady as the power of the incantation threatened to overwhelm him, mind and body. A dry heat scorched his hair and cheeks, and squinted his eyes; the roar of the fire oppressed his ears. A metallic odor filled the air and Tanch tasted iron on his tongue; some strange byproduct of the ancient sorceries.

The cone of sorcery engulfed the pier in an emerald inferno of death. It blasted through the ranks of the approaching guardsmen, incinerating them, and roared on — enveloping not just the squadron that charged toward them, but the whole of the troop. Most died instantly, burned to cinders. Barrels of fresh water stacked along the pier boiled, burst, and caught fire. Barrels of oil exploded and blasted decking to ash and kindling, fiery oil spread and splattered in all directions.

Those guardsmen farther away were not fortunate enough to enjoy a quick death. They shrieked as the ravenous flames devoured them, their cries so loud, so pitiful, as to shake the pier itself and soften the hardest heart. Men rolled on the decking in agony and wailed for deliverance that would not come, for mercy not to be found. Others dived burning into the water, their only escape from the merciless fire. Some ran about in a frenzy, burning and shrieking before they collapsed to the deck. A few just stood there, unmoving, as the flames consumed them, body and soul.

Tanch gazed in horror at the destruction he had wrought. His strength was sapped, and his hands, upraised before him, shook uncontrollably and stung as if afire. The finger that bore the ring throbbed and swelled. He dropped to his knees, face locked in agony and shock as he looked back and forth from his hands to the gruesome death scene before him.

"Odin's beard!" spouted Ob, his eyes wide.

Artol and Seran wore looks of shock. Kayla stared at Tanch in awe and fear.

"When the flames clear, we make for the ship," said Theta.

The magic's wake left multiple fires spreading about the pier, threatening to consume the whole structure; the air now thick with smoke smelled of burning oil and seared flesh. Small blazes burned on *The Falcon,* the caravel, and a nearby schooner. Men yelled from the surrounding ships. The crews of what ships remained at the nearby piers scrambled to set off, terrified by what they saw.

"Behind us," said Dolan. "They're still coming."

Theta turned. A score of Freedom Guardsmen warily dashed from barrel to crate. Behind them, obscured by smoke, more figures approached.

Theta grabbed Seran's arm. "I need you to carry Claradon to the ship."

"Ob," said Theta. "Get the wizard up. Get him to the ship." Theta, gently, but quickly lifted Claradon from his shoulder and placed him over Seran's. Seran winced at the weight, his arm injured during the battle with the Kalathens.

Kayla turned to leave with Seran but Theta stopped her. "Help Ob," he said. "Get the wizard back to the ship. All of you — move! Dolan and I will hold them here." Theta drew his falchion. "And tell Slaayde to get the ship moving."

Seran staggered forward, barely able to support Claradon's weight. Ob and Kayla pulled Tanch to his feet and the three plodded toward *The Falcon*.

"I'll stand with you," said Artol.

Theta looked over the battered warrior for a moment. "I need you to help young Harringgold. Get them back to the ship quickly. We'll be right behind." Theta turned away and Artol complied.

Dolan moved close on Theta's right, under cover of his shield. Theta glanced at the quivers strapped to Dolan's back. One was empty. The second held but a few standard arrows, the rest were the Vanyar arrows gifted him by Pipkorn.

Dolan caught Theta's glance. "Six left, then it'll be sword and dagger unless I regift Pipkorn's arrows."

"Hold the ensorcelled arrows in reserve," said Theta. "We need only hold them for a moment; just until the others reach the ship."

"We may get cut off," said Dolan. "We can't fight the whole city."

"I have a plan."

"I thought as much."

A group of guardsmen charged, all war cries, wild eyes, and waving swords.

"How do they know we can't just burn them up like the others?" said Dolan.

"They don't."

"You think they're brave or stupid?"

"Stupid, I'd say. But in the end, there's not much difference."

Dolan plucked arrows from his quiver, aimed, and fired almost faster than the eye could follow. One man went down, an arrow through his forehead, another fell with an arrow through his neck, then one through the chest, and then another. Two men reached them, swords swinging wildly. Theta seemed barely to move. His left arm

74

whizzed from side to side, his falchion a blur, and as quick as that, two men lay dead at his feet, their bodies quivered as their blood showered the boards. The other guardsmen had seen enough. They turned heel and fled.

Theta smashed the lid from a nearby barrel, overturned it, and rolled it from one side of the pier to the other, dousing the decking with oil while Dolan stood watch, an arrow nocked. The smoke and the debris strewn about the pier made the clear oil all but invisible.

"I see now your plan," said Dolan. "A couple more squadrons are coming up." He looked over his shoulder. "They're almost back to the ship. I'll get a brand. We'll light the oil and be off and clear."

"No," said Theta. "Light an arrow, but hold it secret until my mark."

Out of the smoke, still some yards away, marched a group of men, Milton DeBoors at their van. On his left were Blain and Edwin Alder and a squadron of Myrdonian Knights. On his right, a score or more Kalathen Knights.

"Now come their best," said Dolan.

Theta stood his ground, his piercing gaze locked on Milton DeBoors. Ten yards from Theta, DeBoors halted. The others followed suit.

"Put down your weapons or die, you scum," shouted Edwin.

DeBoors' hand shot out and locked on Edwin's throat. "Shut your mouth, fool. You know not to whom you speak." DeBoors shoved Edwin back and he would have fallen, but Blain caught him and held him still as he struggled, bristling at the mercenary's insolence.

"How dare you—" Edwin began, his hand going for his sword, but Blain clamped one hand over Edwin's mouth and the other locked an iron grip on Edwin's sword arm.

"Be still your hand and your tongue, my son," he whispered, "or that one will take both and more."

"Parley," shouted Theta.

DeBoors turned to those beside him. "Stay here," he said quietly. "I'll speak with him alone." Blain grimaced. He clearly wanted to join in the parley, but was fully occupied in holding Edwin in check.

Theta stepped forward, halting just before the nigh invisible line of oil. DeBoors moved to within six feet of him.

"There's still time to divert from this path, DeBoors," said Theta, his voice quiet, so only DeBoors could hear. "No good can come of it for we or for Midgaard."

"For Midgaard?" DeBoors shook his head. "Do you still think yourself so important? So grand? The Age of Heroes is over and long forgotten, Thetan. The people don't even remember what we did in those days, not the truth of it, anyways. Civilization is reborn. Brave heroes aren't needed any longer. To think anything else is delusion. We must make a life for ourselves in this world. We cannot wallow in dreams of past glories. After all this time, haven't you learned even that simple truth?"

Anger flashed across Theta's face and his voice grew louder and sharp. "Do not presume to

76

lecture me. What life is that of hired killer? Can you do no better? What became of the man that I knew? The man that served with me at R'lyeh? What of your code? What became of your honor?"

DeBoors shifted his feet and tensed — subtle movements, but plain enough for any trained to see such things. He was poised to explode into motion as a cobra preparing its strike. "It is for honor that I stand against you now. I will not have my honor questioned — not even by you. I have a contract, sworn and paid. My word is my life. I must keep it sacred; my honor demands it."

Theta's voice grew calm, its cadence slower. "There is much of which you know naught. Much you must consider before you pursue this course. The veil betwixt Midgaard and Nifleheim has grown thin of late. Worse, it has been breached. Creatures of Nifleheim have crossed over. I've seen it. I've fought them. Gabriel Garn fell in battle against them, as did many brave souls. This news is new; it may not have reached you; not the true tale, anyway."

"They say Gabriel fell to trolls in the mountains north of Lomion City. I found that tale unlikely, but I find yours the more so."

"I speak the truth as I always have. Our old duties have returned, like it as not. The veil between the worlds must remain sealed now and forever. Otherwise, Midgaard will crumble and mankind will be wiped from the world never to rise again. I've taken up my sword against this darkness. You must take up yours as well. Stand with me, DeBoors. Midgaard needs you."

DeBoors paled at these words. "Your truth,

Thetan, I pray is not mine. Yours is a truth too horrible to contemplate. Better that your mind be muddled and mad. Better that your tongue weaves lies for your own ends. Any truth is better than what you're peddling."

"Denying reality doesn't change it."

DeBoors paused, thinking. "What proof do you offer?"

"The proof is on the ship that I follow — *The White Rose*. Follow it with me. See the truth for yourself, then stand with me."

DeBoors paused again, his eyes locked on Theta. "I cannot breach my contract," he said shaking his head, though his voice lacked some of its previous conviction. "No matter what perils await. I cannot deny my honor, for without it, I am nothing."

"Your contract is of little import compared to the fate of the world. You've a higher calling now as in times past."

"A moment ago you asked after my honor and now you advise me to shove it aside. Your contrariety reveals you. Perhaps the fell stories that still linger about you hold more truth than I once thought. I fear you walk in darkness, Thetan, a weave of lies and deceptions spinning about you. I always suspected as much, but now it becomes clearer. I'll not walk that path with you."

Theta paused, and took a deep breath. "Think on what I've told you, long and hard, and keep your eyes open for the truth. There is time yet for you to decide. Another day . . ."

DeBoors hand moved purposely toward his sword's hilt. He glanced down and noticed the wet decking between him and Theta. He saw its straight line and pattern and knew at once what Theta planned. The coiled energy almost visibly drained from him. His expression, one of relief. "Another time then," said DeBoors.

Theta's eyes were hard and cold and bored into DeBoors' very soul. "Make the right choice, old friend, or when we next meet, it will be for the last time." Theta signaled to Dolan, and his flaming arrow struck the oil-doused boards and set them ablaze, engulfing the pier in flame.

6
MOTHER ALDER

The din in House Alder's dining hall was as loud and chaotic as ever, the immense table filled to capacity with immediate family. Voices chattered, men, women, and children, glasses clinked, silverware clanked. Food was served, then eaten, rejected, or spilled in near equal proportions. Servants bustled about striving to keep flagons filled and the mess in check. How many conversations both friendly and heated competed for attention was anyone's guess. Yet this was no holiday celebration, seasonal feast, or family reunion. It was just dinner, same as any other in House Alder.

It was Thorsday, so as usual Chef served roast boar. Large and meaty enough to satiate the entire clan, Chef broiled it whole on a spit in the Alder kitchens. Expertly seasoned, the meat moist and tender, its skin blackened and crisp but not burnt. With it came assorted vegetables, breads, and cheeses, homemade and imported. Potatoes from Kern — not the common white variety, but the large brown and yellow ones from the Northlands that tasted pre-buttered and fluffy. Choice local greens from Sanderson's farms, corn and apples brought upriver from Dover. Biscuits baked in the kitchens, sourdough and whole-wheat, both made that morning and drowned in fresh butter. The tasty gravy poured over most everything was spiced with red peppers and tomato and sweetened only Chef knows with what.

The feast was served on heavy earthenware plates, square and colorful, a specialty of the Lomerian kiln-masters. The diners ate with silver forks, knives, and spoons, one set to each, polished so thoroughly they cast a reflection. Some of the men forewent the family cutlery and carved their meat with personal knives, some exotic, others utilitarian, almost all made of some variety of steel. Each diner had a water cup and a glass flagon for wine or mead. Pitchers filled with clear water from one of the Alder wells and chilled with shaved ice brought down from the mountains lined both sides of the table. A long sideboard held an array of desserts, homemade, local, and imported, ranging from delectable pastries and choice, fresh fruits, to whipped cream and assorted pies.

The matriarch of the House, Mother Alder, as everyone called her, perched at the table's head, bejeweled at neck, wrist, ears, and fingers with baubles, pretentious and gaudy. A shapeless black silk gown engulfed her slim form, which always seemed to smell of mothballs, though none were present in the house. Her coloring and features, subtlely different from most Lomerians, marked her of far eastern origin to those of sharp eye and worldly ways, and her sultry twang confirmed her foreignness to all but the most dense. Where most Lomerian nobles would labor to lose such an accent, she took pride in it and dared anyone to look down on her for it. Marriages to foreigners were as common as dirt in the cosmopolitan city of Lomion, but scandalous amongst the great Houses, excepting for arranged nuptials with properly placed nobles of other realms. Whether hers was arranged or not was not commonly known, perhaps due to the passage of years, though unlikely tales abounded, one more scandalous than the next. Thankfully, her brood inherited few of her foreign traits, so they appeared properly Lomerian as noble folk should.

She glared at once with pride and disapproval at her progeny as she sat her throne, a ponderous oaken thing that nearly swallowed her. The massive armchair was an ornate affair, adorned with hand-carved engravings and cushioned with soft, tufted leather pillows stuffed with goose feathers imported from Ferd. The dining hall's other chairs, though smaller and less ornate, matched it in style and color, and complemented the room's decor, accoutered as it was with its thick-top, oaken trestle table, antique sideboards, glass curio cabinets, gleaming wood planked floor, tray ceiling, and fresh painted walls abounding with ornate mouldings and exquisite tapestries.

Mother Alder's brother, Rom, sat at her right hand, tall, gaunt, and sullen. He was the younger sibling by some years, but looked at least twenty years her senior. Mother Alder's youngest son, Bartholomew, overlarge and vacant, slouched at her left. Sundry other descendants and in-laws lined the lengthy board for the evening's repast. Two highchairs confined the youngest grandchildren in the brood to exile in the room's back corner where their carrying on barely reached Mother Alder's ears and hardly annoyed her at all.

At the table's far end sat the Chancellor of the Kingdom of Lomion, Barusa, eldest son of Mother Alder, though he too looked some years her senior. Oblivious to the din that surrounded him, his attention focused on the pile of choice meat stacked high on his plate where no vegetables dared venture.

Mother Alder picked up the silver bell devoid of any trace of tarnish that resided beside her place setting and rang it in practiced fashion. Before she set it down, the room went silent, its occupants still, even the children. A wooden gavel sat by her other hand; the tabletop gouged from its use, though she spared it that night. An uneasy tension filled the air and grew by the moment as Mother Alder silently judged each face in the room.

Though the servants kept their eyes downcast, those of each family member shifted to Mother Alder as she spoke. "As we have each ten-day since their departure, tonight my dears we bow our heads in solemn prayer to the one true god," she said, her voice haughty, sultry, and strong, though a bit gravely, better hinting at her years than did her youthful, comely face, "and beseech the safe return of Bartol, Blain, and our dear Little Eddy."

"Lift now your flagons to drink their health," she said, making a holy sign across her chest, "and may the good Lord forgive our transgressions in so doing."

"Here, here," said the family.

"Edith," said Mother Alder, addressing one of

the grandchildren, a slim girl no more than twelve. "Stand and recite the prayer."

Edith bounced to her feet and pulled a small leaf of paper from her pocket, wrinkled and discolored from years of service. She held it before her. "Dear Lord," she said, carefully enunciating each word, "bless House Alder and all those who dwell within. Bless Mother—"

— A sharp intake of breath and a startling groan of pain burst from Mother Alder. All eyes flicked to her. Edith fell silent. Mother Alder's torso went rigid, and her hands crushed the arms of her chair, her knuckles white. She reached out to Bartholomew and met his gaze, her eyes wide, almost in a panic, a look wholly uncharacteristic. "Bring me the Alder Stone, now."

Bartholomew froze. He didn't seem to know what to do.

"Mother," said Barusa as he rose to his feet. "What is it? Are you not well?"

Bartholomew reached out a hand and gripped her forearm, but she swatted him away. "Go, now!" she said, glaring at him.

Bartholomew hefted himself to his feet and waddled from the room with as much speed as he could muster, several servants following.

Barusa arrived at his mother's side. "I sense contact," she said to him.

"What do you mean?"

"Another Seer seeks me, you fool," she said through grated teeth, wincing, her face white, sweat beading on cheeks and brow. "Someone of power and fueled by urgency. They're attempting to contact me telepathically. I know not who they are, but they lack control for the contact is jarring and painful. They know not their own strengths. I can't even tell for certain if this is meant to be a message or an attack."

"What can we do?" said Barusa.

"Nothing until Bartholomew returns. The spell she's using is too wild, I need the stone to help me focus and control it. Until then, I have to block it out."

Some moments later, servants opened the dining hall's door and Bartholomew gingerly stepped through carrying an ornate box — a cube, more than a foot across, plated in gold and studded with emeralds, citrine, and obsidian. That box had housed House Alder's Seer Stone for years beyond count, handed down from mother to daughter through the centuries. The Alder Stone, a priceless treasure, rare and powerful. Despite its import, the true account of its origin had long faded from family memory, and if ever recorded was lost in the great fire of ten generations back.

Bartholomew gripped the box in both hands and pressed it tightly to his chest. Servants hovered on each side, pillows cupped in their hands and held low, ready to cushion the precious box's fall should it spill from Bartholomew's grip. Other servants frantically cleared the place setting in front of Mother Alder. Bartholomew carefully placed the box before her.

She looked up and nodded to him, a signal to remove the box's cover.

He fiddled with some concealed lever on one side and then the other, then carefully lifted the box. The top and sides detached from the base.

As the box rose, the scent of red cedar wood, the box's base material, filled the air.

Revealed within was a crystal sphere some nine inches in diameter, of emerald tint, transparent, yet cloudy and murky of depth, filled with swirling mists of green, yellow, and black. A Seer Stone. The Alder Stone. One of the rare few known, a survivor from the first age of Midgaard, the Age of Myth and Legend. An artifact possessed of powers deep and mysterious, its full potential rarely imagined even by its learned masters. Its surface, generally smooth and polished, though pitted and scratched here and there, but whether from age or careless use in times past, or marred by wild magics it had weathered, who could say? Something radiated from it — a strange thing. They couldn't see it, hear it, or smell it, but bizarrely, they tasted it. Those within twenty steps of the stone suffered a heavy taste of iron in their mouths, tinged with something bitter, not easy to define. It dripped from the inside of their cheeks and clung to their tongues, relieved only by cleansing the palate with salty or sweet food or drink. Those closest to the stone tasted it the strongest, those farthest barely at all. From the stone also emanated a strange underlying vibration that afflicted all those that came too near — an eerie phenomenon that churned the stomach and oft set teeth to chattering.

Mother Alder breathed deep the pleasant scent of the red cedar and even welcomed the familiar bitter iron byproduct of the stone's esoteric magics. She gazed deeply into the Alder Stone though she did not touch it. "A message," she said, relief in her voice. "Not an attack. Someone seeks an audience." She looked at the family, all standing about, concern on many faces, keen interest on all. "Best you get gone now, dearies."

The family and most of the servants filed from the room without discussion or protest, some eager to leave, practically fleeing; others stepped out only reluctantly. Barusa, Rom, and Bartholomew remained, though each stepped back several feet, giving the Alder Stone wide berth. Two servants remained as well and hovered nearby, curious jars and white towels in hand. Mother Alder motioned to one of them. "Prepare the stone, carefully," she said. "Miss not a single spot."

The servant opened one of the jars that he clutched, dabbed the end of a special towel inside, coating it in a thick, green, but translucent gel, which he then used to vigorously polish the Alder Stone as Mother Alder looked on. Strangely, the stone somehow absorbed the green unguent as quickly as he applied it. It made the stone shine brighter and somehow its depths appeared the clearer. The servant grew paler by the moment and sweat beaded on his brow. The gel expended, the servant staggered a step or two and violently vomited, dousing a wide stretch of the floor with his stomach's contents. Mother Alder shook her head in disgust and displeasure, though she didn't look at all surprised. The second servant rushed up and began polishing the stone, this time with a yellow salve, thick and pungent, smelling of fruit and sugar.

Mother Alder noted a flutter in a nearby tapestry. When she looked over, she saw shoes jutting from beneath its bottom edge. Someone hid behind it, a child from the look of the shoes. "Get out from there, now," she shouted.

The tapestry parted and Edith peeked out, terror on her face. "I'm sorry, Mother Alder," she said, her words barely audible. "I want to stay. Please let me; I'll keep quiet. I want to watch."

"Do you now?" she said, eyeing the girl. "That's a brave lass, or a foolish one. Which is it then, I wonder?"

Bartholomew put a hand on Edith's shoulder.

Mother Alder glared at him, then looked back at Edith. "Have you seen me use the stone before?"

"No, Mother Alder. Father says I'm too young."

"Perhaps you are, lass, but perhaps you're not."

"I've watched the soothsayers in the market use their stones plenty of times. I'm not afraid. Nothing to be afraid of, if you ask me."

"Ah, foolish then," said Mother Alder. "The market soothsayers are tricksters. They pronounce false predictions for money. Their stones are common glass or cheap crystal — they've no power at all."

"How do you know this?" said the girl. "They seem real enough. They foretell things."

"When you watch them, do the people crowd close to get a keen look into the stones?"

"Yes, always. People fight to get closest. I'm not usually able to get close at all. When I'm older,

I'll push through to the front, then I'll see everything."

"When the crowd gets close and stays there, that's when you know for certain that the stone is a fake. The magic locked in a real Seer Stone repels common folk. People inch away from it. It makes them nauseous if they linger too long or stray too close. You've just seen that for yourself," she said, gesturing toward the servant who still retched in the corner. "It makes one feel morbid. They feel as if their life, even their soul, is being drained away. People shrink from real Seer Stones."

"That's why you always send the family away."

"Aye. This girl has promise," she said looking to the others. "Must take after her mother."

The yellow salve expended, the servant stepped away and staggered to a far corner of the room, obviously fighting to keep his nausea in check. The first servant was back now, a jar of black gel in hand. He set to polishing the stone with it, a fresh cloth employed for the duty.

"I promise you, you'll never see a real Seer Stone on a street corner or in Lomion's market, deary," said Mother Alder. "There are very few true stones left in the world, if ever there were many. All are held by powerful Seers, great Houses, or Arch-Wizards. The Elves have a stone or two, legend says, as do the Svarts, if any of them even still exist. Some great kings are rumored to have one too, though I doubt the truth of that. No my dear, I'm afraid the Alder Stone is the only one you'll ever see."

"Have you ever seen another, Mother Alder?" said Edith.

"Not in all my years. That's why the Alder Stone is so precious. That's why we guard it so closely. It can never be replaced. It gives our House power that other Houses can only dream of. That's why they hate us, you know. Jealousy, envy, it drives them mad, the scum."

"So if the other stones aren't real, does that mean all the other Seers are fakers?"

"Not all of them. A Seer Stone doesn't make a woman a Seer; it merely enhances the powers she was born with. A true Seer catches glimpses of the future and can commune with others over a distance — no stone required. Some few can even use plain glass spheres or crystal balls, as the commoners call them, to aid their skills, though the objects have no magic of their own. Mayhaps a few of your market soothsayers are of that ilk. Lomion has its share of Seers of varied skills, though none of them can match an Arch-Seer equipped with a Seer Stone."

The servant stepped back from the Alder Stone, his polishing completed. A sickly green pallor hung across his sweating face; his eyes watery and bloodshot. He bowed stiffly to Mother Alder, turned, and took but two steps before collapsing face first to the floor.

The stone pulsed with a brighter light and more shine than ever, its original emerald color fully intact.

"Enough lessons for today," said Mother Alder. "The stone is ready, so it's time to begin. You'll feel sick for certain if you linger any longer.

Are you sure that you want to stay, deary?"

"I'll stay," said Edith. "I'm not afraid."

"Brave lass. That's good. We'll see if your courage holds."

Mother Alder's face drew into rigid concentration, and her brow furled as she reached out with both hands, fingers spread and crooked, toward the Alder Stone. Just before her fingers touched the stone, streaks of white light leapt from them to the stone's surface, and similar streaks erupted within the stone, in dazzling, undulating patterns interrupted by multicolored swirling mists. When her fingers grasped the stone, a shooting pain careened across Mother Alder's head. She jerked back and winced as it shot in streaks from her temples to the nape of her neck. She groaned and gritted her teeth, but mercifully, the pain soon passed.

Of a sudden, the room went hot; the air turned muggy and thick and reeked of old mothballs. A grating, high-pitched buzzing began, but whether it came from the stone or elsewhere was impossible to determine.

Barusa winced and stepped farther back, as did Bartholomew and Edith, though Rom held his ground, seemingly immune to the stone's affects. Edith went all green, doubled over, and vomit shot from her mouth, drenching her uncle's shoes, as well as her own. Mother Alder didn't notice, all her attention focused on the Alder Stone.

7
DEATH WATCH

Sir Paldor Cragsmere, a white cloth stained crimson tied about his forehead, his silver plate armor blood-splattered, his lip split and swollen, walked ahead of Theta and Dolan as they descended *The Black Falcon's* creaky stair to the Captain's Deck. The corridor at the stair's base was wood paneled, lamp-lit, and well-appointed as far as ships' corridors go. It was hot and smelled of wood and lamp oil. Even here there was no escape from the moans and cries of the wounded strewn about the main deck where they called, begged, and whimpered for whatever meager care and comforts their fellows could offer.

"Hard on the ears, such sounds," said Paldor.

"Harder on the spirit," said Theta.

"We gave better than we got. Slaayde's crew fought like demons. Tough men, every one."

"Good to hear," said Theta. "Better still had it not come to a fight."

"Aye, true enough," said Paldor. "They put Claradon in a big stateroom next to the captain's quarters. More comfortable and private than the Captain's Den."

A short ways down the hall, Little Tug and Guj stood guard at Slaayde's cabin door.

Paldor looked back at Theta. "Slaayde's hurt too," he said quietly. "Not sure how bad."

"What's the word?" said Theta, halting when

92

he reached the guards.

"Bertha can't stop the bleeding," said Tug, his eyes and cheeks wet, a handkerchief in his hand. "Lost a good chunk out of his leg, he did."

"Ravel learned up healing over Ferd way," said Guj. "He's trying some things."

"Yeah, some things," said Tug nodding. "The Captain is the toughest bloke I've known; he'll lick this," he said, though his eyes and expression displayed less conviction than his words. Both seamen stared at Theta hopefully, as if they expected him to whip out some magic something-or-other and fix Slaayde straight away.

Theta nodded. "A hard day," he said.

"Aye," said Guj.

"A hard day," muttered Tug.

Theta patted both men on the arm and moved on. Sergeant Vid and an Eotrus trooper stood guard outside Claradon's cabin. Vid nodded and opened the door as the three approached. Paldor stepped in.

Theta scanned the room before entering. It was dominated by a large, four-poster bed in which Claradon lay unconscious. His face was ghostly white. His chest heavily bandaged, blood already soaking through. A heap of blood-soaked linens lay discarded on the floor.

Ob and Kayla fussed over Claradon's bed and argued back and forth. They paid no heed to the new arrivals. Tanch trembled in a chair beside the bed, wringing his hands, his head down as he mumbled to himself. Claradon's knights were there: Glimador, Kelbor, the Bull, and Trelman. They huddled to one side of the room and perked up at Theta's appearance — each stood a bit taller, a bit straighter.

"A death watch," whispered Theta. He turned to Dolan and spoke quietly. "Since everyone's here, no one's minding the ship. Go to the bridge and keep an eye on things. If the First Mate has any bullyboys with him, get the other Eotrus sergeant and a trooper or two to stand the watch with you. Let me know if anything worth knowing happens, and watch your back."

"Right," said Dolan, and he was off.

Theta stepped into the room. Kayla bathed Claradon's head with cold compresses and wiped dried blood from his face and arms. Ob stood on a chair and leaned over Claradon, examining him. He turned to Theta. "We cleaned the wound and rewrapped it tight as we could," said Ob. "but it's still bleeding. A right bad wound." A dark red stain was slowly growing on the wrappings.

"Why won't the blood stop?" said Kayla, her voice quiet, her face pale.

"He needs a healer," said Tanch. "The best we can find, and quickly."

"Any healers hereabouts would be in Tragoss Mor," said Ob. "Case you didn't notice, we're running from there right now, our tails between our legs. Can't rightly go back and make nice now can we?"

"What's the next closest city?" said Theta.

"Too far," said Ob. "Minoc's five days northeast, up the coast. There are towns and villages closer, but all we could count on there would be bleeders, snake oilers, and the like."

"We should go back to Dover," said Tanch.

94

"No better care south of Lomion City."

"It's too dang far," said Ob. "He would be long dead afore we made port. Besides, we would have to slip past the Tragoss navy to get up the river. Wait!" Ob started and nearly leapt into the air. "Theta, give the boy some of that witch's brew of yours; the one what healed up me arm. That will fix him up straight away!"

All eyes turned to Theta.

Theta shook his head slowly. "Do you think an ointment can heal a heart hacked by a sword, gnome?"

The light dropped from Ob's eyes. "I — no, of course not."

"He'll live or not, as his strength allows," said Theta.

Ob glared at Theta and looked around the room at each man. He stepped from Claradon's bedside, motioned the others toward a corner, and lowered his voice. "There's nobody here what wants Claradon to live more than me. He's like a son to me, and always has been. Maybe the more so now that Aradon is gone. He's as tough as they come, but we've got to face facts. I've seen men wounded like this before. The truth is he should be gone already — up Valhalla way with Aradon, Gabe, and Brother Donnelin, tipping mugs with old Odin himself. No healer can see to such a wound. It's only because he's as tough and stubborn as he is that he's lasted this long."

"You're quick to give up on him," said Tanch.

"I've seen a lot of wounds, wizard. From a lot of battles. Many more than you've seen or ever will see, I'll wager. I know what I'm talking about."

"There must be something we can do?" said Kayla. "We can't just let him die."

"We can pray," said Tanch.

"Aye, Magic Boy," said Ob. "That we can. I've never been much for it myself, but it can't hurt, and Claradon would like it since he's prayed for us so many times."

"Do you pray, Lord Theta?" said Tanch.

Theta stared at him for a moment before responding. "Who would I pray to?"

"An odd thing to say," said Kayla, but whether she referred to Tanch's question or Theta's answer was not clear.

"The all-father, Odin, of course," said Glimador. "The king of the gods; the lord of strength and wisdom. Who better? Unless you're one of those that favor Tyr or Thor or Heimdall."

"Good old Odin may be surprised to hear from me, it's been such a time," said Ob. "Glimador, you know the words as good as any. You take the lead." And he did. The group bowed their heads respectfully and said their words with more conviction than most of them had in years.

Theta paid little attention to the ritual. Instead, his mind drifted back to that night in the Vermion Forest before the Gateway opened — to that time when he and Gabriel stood alone at the rim of the circle of desolation.

"All these years I've protected the line of kings," said Gabriel. "The bloodline must not be broken. If I should fall this night, this burden too you must bear."

"You've lived long, Gabriel, not likely this

night will be your last," said Theta. "Why bother to speak of such things?"

"Even we are not immune to death."

Theta smiled. "Close enough."

"Death can come at any time . . . from any source. Be on your guard tonight, my Lord. This will be a test unlike any we've faced since R'lyeh."

Theta's smile fell at those words and at the strange look on Gabriel's face. "You've more to tell. Spit it out and make it clear."

"Claradon must survive this, no matter the cost."

"The boy? Look out for him, of course, but don't play the hero to your folly. You've greater worth to this world. He has three brothers. The line of kings hinges not on him alone."

"I'm not speaking of the bloodline. I'm speaking of Azrael."

"Azrael? What has he to do with the Eotrus? Speak quickly and plainly for the hour grows late and tales of Azrael are oft too long and convoluted for my patience."

"Alright boys," said Ob, drawing Theta from his thoughts. "We're doing nothing standing around here except dripping more blood on the Captain's carpet. I want two of you five," pointing to the knights, "in here watching over Claradon at all times. That's in addition to the guards at the door. The door guards are to be Eotrus men only. No seamen, no Harringgolds and no Malvegils — no offense, Glimador. First shift will be Bull and Trelman. Glimador — you'll be coming with me to the Captain's Den. I want to hear everything what happened while we were ashore. The rest of you, clear out, get your wounds seen to right and proper, give a quick clean to your gear, and then get some rest."

"I'm staying," said Kayla.

"Of course you are," said Ob. "Stay, but cause no mischief. You men watch her too. Watch her close. We only met her today for Odin's sake. It's bad enough that she's part elf. She could be a darned spy too for all we know."

"Castellan," said Glimador. "Did you learn which way *The White Rose* went?"

"Yep. We're headed to Jutenheim."

Theta nodded to the two guardsmen stationed at the door to the Captain's Den before entering. Ob, Tanch, Glimador, Kelbor, and Paldor sat at the table in the center of the main room, an ornate ale stein set before each. All except Tanch looked over as Theta walked in. The wizard's gaze remained downcast. He was pale and looked exhausted, as if he were about to pass out. His hand shook as he raised the stein to his lips.

"Everything in order?" said Ob.

"Still no sign of pursuit and we're on course for Jutenheim," said Theta. He took a seat that faced the outer door and doffed his gear. "I doubled the guard on Claradon's door. I trust you've no objection."

"None," said Ob.

"I also stationed young Harringgold and a half-squad of his men on the bridge deck to ensure that we stay on course. I would have them stand a twelve-hour shift, with Paldor captaining another half-squad thereafter."

Paldor looked surprised and turned to Ob.

"Six solid men on the top deck at all times," said Ob. "That's smart thinking," he said as he leaned toward Theta, "but our men are not yours to command. I'll remind you not to forget that."

Theta nodded, albeit begrudgingly.

"I don't know how they do things where you hail from, but we Lomerians got a strict hierarchy. With the mix of men we have amongst us — that hierarchy gets a might complicated. As this quest is led by House Eotrus, Claradon, as Lord of the House commands. That makes me, as his Castellan, second-in-command. If we get Jude back and he's in sound shape, he ranks third. I trust everyone is with me so far," said Ob, looking to each of the knights in turn. "Now is where things get complicated. I should've gone through all this with you men at the start, but only today did it hit me how dangerous this stinking mission is, and how the hierarchy may come into play, like it as not. So I need to make sure everyone knows their place, so there's no grumblings in the ranks. We can't afford no stupidities or posturing. We all got to work together to get Jude back, to stop Korrgonn, and to get our stinking butts home. You men with me?"

"Aye," they said.

"Kelbor is the senior Eotrus knight and would normally rank next in line. But we're on wartime status here, boys, so things are a might different. In wartime, blueblood sometimes trumps rank, so fourth in line is Glimador, as he's first cousin to Claradon and the son of a Dor Lord. Next in line is Par Tanch, as House Wizard. Then comes, strange as it may seem, Seran Harringgold. Even though he's not an Eotrus, his standing as a nephew to Duke Harringgold trumps everyone else. His fancy pedigree notwithstanding, if he acts against the interests of the Eotrus, his commands need not be followed." Ob looked at each of the gathered knights. "You men understand that?"

They all nodded.

"Good. After Seran, comes Kelbor, then Bull, then Trelman, then Paldor, then Artol. After that is Sergeant Vid, then Sergeant Lant. After that, I really don't care. As a foreigner, Theta has no rank amongst us, and despite his skills, won't be leading while any one of us still lives. That said, if you find yourself in command, listen to Theta's council, value it, then make up your own stinking mind. Captain Slaayde has no rank amongst us, no matter the circumstances, and best you watch him and his bullyboys and keep them all at arm's length. Everyone understand what I've said? Any objections, voice them now — that includes you, Theta."

None were raised.

"Magic Boy thinks we ought to drop Claradon off at the first port we pass," said Ob as he looked at Theta.

Staring into his mug, Tanch said, "Claradon needs rest and a healer. He doesn't have either here. If there's no objection, I'll stay with him and a small group of guardsmen. He'll be a lot safer than on this ship."

"The Alders won't stop looking for him," said Theta. "Are you prepared to face them with only a few men at your side when they find you at

100

some island port?"

"I can handle myself well enough when need be." Tanch looked over at Theta, his eyes bloodshot and heavy-lidded. "I trust I proved as much today."

Theta nodded. "You showed your quality, wizard. Of that there can be no doubt."

"Always thought you were nothing but a dandied-up hedge," said Ob. "Not too proud to admit when I'm wrong. That's the gnome way, you know. You done good, old boy," he said, patting Tanch on the shoulder as he rose to refill his mug from a tapped half-keg on the sideboard. He poured one for Theta too.

"Much as I hate to say it," said Ob, "Theta, you done good, too — for a stinking foreigner. You boys should've seen it. When we got jumped in the street, Theta cut down a half-dozen Alder marines with that sword of his, but that wasn't the half of it. Few men can stand up to a Kalathen Knight and live. To fight and kill two at once and live is the stuff of song and legend. With my own eyes, I saw Theta take on six of them. He dropped four at least what I saw and came out without a scrape; his hair still combed all right and proper. Never saw skills like that in all my days. Never heard of skills like that. Had he not been with us, not one of us would have gotten out of that spot alive. The Eotrus are in your debt, Theta, and we'll not forget that." Ob stood and raised his mug. "To Mister Fancy Pants."

The others all stood and raised their steins. Tanch rose slowly to his feet, a pained expression on his face.

"Glad you're on our side," said Kelbor.

"Here, here," said the others.

Theta nodded appreciatively and drank with the rest.

"I need to take my leave," said Tanch. "The magic I threw today took more out of me than I can say. Never felt any aftereffects as bad as this before." Tanch turned toward the back room, but Ob placed a hand on his forearm.

"Give us a minute, boys," said Ob. "I need to speak with the wizard and Theta. The knights rose and stepped out, ale mugs in hand.

"No man can survive that wound," said Ob. "We've lost them all. Aradon, Jude, Claradon; only the young ones are left, and even Malcolm's hurt bad by some stinking beastie. We've failed them all."

"There's still hope for Jude," said Tanch. "And Claradon isn't dead yet; I'm not ready to give up on him." Tanch swayed where he stood and leaned on the sideboard to steady himself. "I need to lie down; we'll talk later if I'm still alive — my back is killing me." Tanch trudged off to his bunk, pale and unsteady.

Theta withdrew a metallic flask from a pouch at his belt and placed it on the table.

"Ain't that your witch's brew what healed me arm?" said Ob. "You said afore it wouldn't work on Claradon's wounds."

"It's for Slaayde." Theta produced a small metallic case and placed it beside the flask. "His leg is bad. His man Ravel plans to amputate and cauterize it. He might not live and if he does he'll be out of commission for too long."

102

"You figure we need him to keep his crew of cutthroats in line. I agree."

Theta carefully opened the metal case. Within the padded interior was a curious tube about two inches long and made of glass. One end of the tube narrowed to a tip, the other was capped with a very small bladder.

"An alchemist's tube. You're full of surprises, Theta. There seems no end to your bag of tricks."

Theta carefully opened the flask, tipped it slightly, and used the alchemist's tube to draw up a drop or two of the liquid. Theta gently placed the tube on the table, retightened the lid on the flask, and replaced it securely on his belt.

Ob stared over at the tube. "That brew must be worth its weight in gold."

"A thousand times that at least."

Ob raised his eyebrows. "And it won't work on Claradon's wound?"

"I answered that question already."

"You figure Slaayde's worth it?"

Theta lifted the lid of his ale stein and drank most of it in one go. "There's no more important thing in the world right now than us catching and killing Korrgonn. Keeping Slaayde in the game may help us do that. So yes, he's worth it." Theta emptied the contents of the tube into the stein, closed the top, and swirled the mixture around.

"So you'll have the good captain drink up," said Ob, "and it'll cure him good enough to live and to keep his leg and nobody knows nothing from nothing."

"Yes, except that Slaayde, Ravel, and Bertha will know, because I'll tell them. And they might tell other crewmen. That'll put them in my debt."

Ob paused for some moments, thinking. "Until now, to them you were just a soldier. Now you'll be more. That's unexpected. And it's dangerous — since anyone what can brew up healing potions can also whip up darker stuff, poisons and such, like as not. That'll get them to thinking. That'll put the fear in them." Ob took a deep drought from his stein. "That's crafty, Theta. Right crafty. If you weren't as big as a small mountain, I might think you were part gnome." Ob took out a cigar and lit it with a lantern. "There's an old saying back home what goes, "Nothing is as it seems in Lomion." You sure fit that well enough, Mr. Fancy Pants."

8
UNWELCOME GUESTS

"The Seer is not seeing clients today," said Rimel, his voice strong and unyielding despite the formidable array of sweat and steel that fronted him and Dirkben. Rimel smelled trouble at the first sight of that crew. They didn't just happen by for a spot of tea, a palm reading, or a toss of the bones, nor were they random rowdies or local yahoos out for fun or profit. Some were just guardsmen, but others were veteran soldiers, hard men, foreigners all, there for deadly purpose no doubt. That didn't bother Rimel much. He'd dealt with their kind before. Skilled but predictable, overconfident in their numbers, and too trusting of their shiny gear. That would be their undoing, it always was. If they wanted blood, he would shed theirs without regret. He knew he could. He'd proved his mettle time and again on the battlefield, in back alleys, and barroom brawls these many years. There was no more feared Freesword in all of Tragoss Mor than Rimel Stark, and he knew it. Maybe they did too, but probably not. That would be an advantage. Dirkben on the other hand was just pretty. Azura should've canned him months before, but she always took to the pretty ones. No matter, Rimel could handle these guests, or so he hoped. "Try again tomorrow or the next," he said.

"She'll see us," said Blain Alder, all broad-shouldered, plate-armored, and deadly serious.

"We're emissaries of the High Council of Lomion, here on official business." Edwin Alder stood beside Blain, hand on his sword hilt, anger and impatience on his narrow face, so like his father's save for the wicked scar that overshadowed his features. The Alder marines behind them stood tense and ready to spring. But the one Rimel marked the most loomed large at Blain's right and said nothing. DeBoors was as tall as Blain, but broader, harder, chiseled, his armor and gear of an archaic style, like something out of a museum's collection. The pall of recent battle hung over him, but not the others, though each reeked of smoke. Bloodstains and spatter marred DeBoors' tabard and his face. Curious that. Fire simmered behind his steel blue eyes. Visible at the merest glance, they bored into Rimel, and dared him to stare back. He didn't; it wasn't worth the effort. Rimel knew he could best the others, but maybe not DeBoors. There was something about him, more than just the eyes, something that shouted danger, that invoked fear, something that made his stomach twist to knots and told him to run for it — run for it, before it's too late. But that wasn't Rimel's way. Nerves are a Freesword's constant enemy. They'd plagued Rimel same as the rest, but he'd never felt like this, not even when he was young and green, and he was long past both. There wasn't a man alive that Rimel feared. Not one.

"That right?" said Rimel, forcing his voice to stay strong and confident. "Lomion is a long, long way from here, and the Seer is a citizen of Tragoss, so your business can't be all that official, but official or not, she can't see you today. She's ill. I hope I've made myself clear," he said, a fake smile on his face. "Come back tomorrow. If the Seer is well enough, she'll see you then. That's all I can offer. Now be off with you and good day."

"Were the Eotrus here earlier today?" said Blain. He described Claradon, Ob, and Theta.

"All information about the Seer's clientele, including their comings and goings is private," said Rimel.

"If they weren't here," said DeBoors, "then they're not clients. In that case, you betray nothing by admitting you've not seen them."

"I cannot say one way or the other," said Rimel.

"That proves it as far as I'm concerned," said Edwin. "Else he would say they weren't here, if only to be rid of us."

"Tell the Seer that we're here," said Blain, his voice slow but sharp.

"We're not leaving until we see her," said Edwin, menace in his voice, the wild in his eyes. He was itching for a fight.

Rimel felt the pulse of blood at this neck and temple; his heart raced. Enough sparring, there was only one way this could go now. He stared the group down, took a deep breath, and glanced to Dirkben who'd gone all pale and sweaty. The spineless wretch would be of no use at all and Gorb was nowhere to be found.

"You're not listening," said Rimel as he moved his hand to his sword hilt.

Azura heard shouts, crashes, and clash of

arms. She didn't know whether it was real or a nightmare, and she didn't much care, so long as it wasn't that thing, Thetan, come back for her soul. She knew he wanted it, and her body too — he lusted for them. What she couldn't understand was why he didn't take both when he had the chance, and why he let her live after she learned his true nature. Maybe he thought her too insignificant, too common to bother. Maybe he wanted her to live in fear, to suffer. That's why he'd taken what was most precious — her youth, her beauty. He'd ruined her beautiful hair, and dead gods, not just that. She'd aged, withered, the vitality sucked from her veins, devoured in mere moments by wicked magic unheard of. She'd lost years, ten at least, probably fifteen, maybe more, stolen, the last of her youth and then some. Her face was lined now, and drawn; she could feel it, her skin all creased and puffy to the touch. Maybe twenty, dead gods, maybe even more. A glance in the mirror reflected a stranger's face, not her own. More like her mother now than herself. Please gods not more like grandmother. She was ruined, finished. A crone. She knew not how bad it truly was. She only dared to look for the barest moment — long enough to know her youth was gone, but not long enough to tell how far. She didn't want to know. She couldn't survive it, the knowing.

He had no right to do this, not to her or anyone. That's how he survived, it had to be. He was nothing but an inhuman fiend that sucked the life force from others, others of power, like her. He fed on them, stole their strength, and added

108

their energies to his own, preserving his life and his youth down through the ages. That must be it, but she would never know for certain unless he came back. But he wouldn't come back. He'd rejected her, cast her aside. He could have taken her with him, made her his woman, or his slave, but he'd left her, discarded her all broken and withered as if she were trash, or some petty commoner, not the greatest Archseer in all Midgaard, not a woman of beauty, terrible beauty, desired by most, envied by all. Beauty now lost and never to be again. How could he do that? How could he think himself above her? But he was, she knew that, and he knew it too. He was above everyone and she hated him for it, for everything. He'd gotten what he was after. She told him *The White Rose* was off to some accursed island called Jutenheim. She was too afraid to lie. That's what he wanted from her and she prayed he would never want anything more. And yet she prayed he would come back and claim her. He had too. He could give back what he'd taken if he wanted to. She would make him want to. She had her ways. There was nothing she wouldn't do to get those years back. Nothing.

More commotion interrupted her thoughts, this time closer. Now she knew it was real, not some dream. The unmistakable sound of steel weapons clashing in anger — a desperate melee within her very tower, her home. The nerve of some people. An irate customer, no doubt, that blamed *her* for their sad fortunes instead of themselves. Probably that skinny wine merchant with the cheating wife down Meadow Way come back with some bullyboys to get his pound of flesh. *It's not my fault if your life sucks. Blame fate if you will, or the gods if you must, but not me, I'm just a witness to fate's hand, nothing more. I don't guide it; I can't steer it. I can't even give it a nudge.*

Would they kill the town crier for shouting bad news? Of course not, but prophesy misfortune and its nooses and knives all around. The fools. Most of the time it was empty threats or spat curses, nothing more, so who cares? Sometimes Seers suffered a reckless slap or punch, maybe even a full-on beating if they got cornered alone by some malcontents. But now and again it went serious and one got murdered in misguided revenge. One old hag was chopped in pieces a couple of years back, her head hung on display from a pike in Freedom Square, and she was a fraud. Who could do that to someone?

Azura plied her trade openly as she always had — no one would deter her, not even the Thothians, not even after what happened today. She was an upstanding citizen — a lady of high society, such as there was in that backward city, with powerful friends, and coin, and influence. She would risk none of the craziness. She took prudent precautions. She had too. She bought the best protection Tragoss Mor had to offer. Not faceless guards, but named men — Freeswords feared and respected across the city.

Gorb and Rimel would deal with the malcontents; she had no doubt. She would waste no more thought on the matter. Unless . . . this time it *was* the Thothians. When they came into power they purged every last mage from the city. There was nowhere for them to hide. The monks rooted them out from castle to keep, tower to manor, hovel to home, and sewer to cistern. Not one was left as far as she knew, save the occasional disguised visitor like Par Sinch, that lying bastard. The monks even killed the card tricksters on the corners, and they were no more than beggars or showmen, of no harm to any save those who couldn't spare the coin they lost at their petty games.

But Seers were not wizards, even the Thothians acknowledged that and held Seers in high regard. But some of the shaved heads were so dense they couldn't tell a dog from a cat. And more than one Seer suffered for it and died wailing during the purge. Seeress Jel's house was raided not three months before, long after the culling, by a handful of young monks too blind or stupid to know she wasn't a wizard. They burned her and her household with her before their betters showed up and stopped them. Too late for Jel and her people though. *Maybe now they've come for me. I dropped enough coin and kisses in the right places to ensure that would never happen, but you never know.*

Let them have my coin or my life if they want them. Why should she care? After what she'd seen, she wasn't sure she wanted to go on living anyways. If it *was* the Thothians, what could she do? There were thousands of them. Not even Gorb, dear Gorb, could hold them back for long. He'd been with her six years, Gorb had. At first, just as a bodyguard but later, as more. He was huge and strong, didn't speak much, and did as he was told, which made him nearly perfect. What more could a woman ask for? Riches and title? Fine, so she made do, for despite her haughtiness, Azura was a realist. Gorb brimmed with strength, but not with power like Thetan. Thetan had to come back for her, and she would hate him until he did.

Gorb would protect her, just as he always had. Tears streamed from Azura's eyes, though she held them tightly closed and gripped a tangled mane of silver in her hand. Her auburn locks had been her identity as much as anything. Now they were gone forever, save if she smeared her hair with pigment in vain attempt to recapture what was lost. She could always tell when a woman's color wasn't natural. Not everyone could, but she could. Not everyone even cared, the fools. She always scoffed at those women. The uglies. The faded beauties. And those who just wanted to change themselves, searching desperately for happiness in a bottle of dye. Now she would be one of them. Faded. Beyond recognition. She was ruined. There was no fixing it. Best she should lie there and die. Get it over with. It wasn't worth going on.

Someone pulled back the chamber's curtains. Gorb had sorted things out. He'd come to check on her. Not now. Now she just needed to sleep — to forget the ordeal.

"Are you Azura?" boomed a voice.

Azura bolted upright at the unfamiliar voice and sharp tone, a tone that held menace. Her dagger was in her hand and as she raised her eyes at the intruder, he swatted her arm aside and the dagger tumbled away. The intruder clamped a powerful hand about her throat. He pushed her against the wall and pressed his arm tightly against her. She could barely breathe. There were others with him.

"Gorb!"

"Are you Azura?" repeated Blain Alder, his face battered, his breathing, heavy. Blood streamed from a cut on his cheek and from his nose.

"It's not her," said Edwin. She's too old, must be a servant."

"It's her," said DeBoors.

"How would you know?" said Edwin. "You said you had never seen her afore."

"It's her."

"Where went the Eotrus?" said Blain. "Where did your mumblings send them?"

Azura tried to look past him through her shock and confusion. The scene surreal. How could this happen? "Gorb," she said, though not as strongly as she intended.

"What did she say?" said Edwin.

"She calls for her guards," said Blain. "He cannot help you, Seer. But you can help yourself. Tell us where went the Eotrus and we'll leave you in peace."

"Peace?" muttered Azura. "I'll never be at peace again. Not after what I saw. Not now that I know."

"What do you know?" said Blain.

"Where is Gorb?" she said, still dazed, not fully there.

Blain studied her for a moment, her expression vacant. She looked through him. "Gorb will be back soon. You were telling us where went the Eotrus."

"Where?" said Azura. "Who?"

Blain turned toward the others. His hands gripped Azura's arms against any threatening moves. "Her mind is broken."

"Did you bang her head into the wall?" said Edwin.

"I didn't, and I wouldn't. Barely touched her. The damage was done before we got here, for certain."

"What's happened here, Seer?" said Blain.

"He was here."

"Who?"

"Right here in my tower," she said. "He was in my head. I saw things, terrible things." She shook from head to toe. Drool slid from her mouth.

"What did you see?"

"Never ask that! Never! I could never say. I could never think it; not ever."

"Who hurt you?"

"Him."

"Who? Name him."

"The devil, Thetan."

Blain looked back at the others, concern on his face. "Where did Thetan go?"

"Are you going to kill him?" said Azura. "Do you hate him too?"

"We're going to bring him to justice," said Blain.

Azura smiled. "Good, someone must. He's

114

evil. No one has ever been that evil. He's gone, thank the gods. My words sent him far away, across the sea. A land called Jutenheim."

"Why does he go there?"

"Why does he go anywhere? To destroy. That's what he does. It's all he does. He's going to kill everyone, everywhere. He's going to bring back the monsters. He's done it afore. He'll do it again. That's what he does, the evil." Her eyes closed and her chin dropped to her chest.

"She's bonkers," said Edwin. "How could some mercenary destroy the world? It's stupidity. There's probably no such place as Jutenheim, except in her wacky fantasies."

"It's a journey," said DeBoors. "But it's a real place."

"If there is truth to what she says," said Blain, "perhaps Theta has the Eotrus fooled. For all their faults, I doubt they've any interest in seeing Midgaard destroyed. That would be utter madness — a disease I don't know them to be afflicted with. Perhaps they do his bidding unknowingly."

"Perhaps," said DeBoors.

"Do we follow?" said Edwin.

"We may have to," said Blain. "Barusa tasked us with bringing Eotrus and Theta to justice. Do you want to stand before him, and before Mother Alder, the job only half done?"

"I'm not in charge of this mission," said Edwin. "You and Uncle Bartol are."

"That's helpful, son," said Blain shaking his head. "As soon as we get the rigging repaired, we'll set off," said Blain. "We should have stopped him on the docks. We could have ended it there."

He gently set Azura down on the bed. "Let's go."

"Wait," said DeBoors. "Rumor and story claim she has a Seer Stone — a real one by all accounts. It will be here, somewhere."

"Unlikely," said Blain. "Real Seer Stones are very rare. I doubt there's a score of them in all of Midgaard. If there's a stone here, it'll be common glass or cheap crystal. Not the real thing, just a toy for show. Even if she had a real one, I'm no thief."

"Last I heard," said DeBoors, "House Alder had a Seer Stone. A real one."

"Bunk and bother, what of it?" said Edwin. "We're wasting time. Mother Alder is an Archseer — the best in all Lomion, so of course she has a Seer Stone. What does it matter?"

"If we had use of a Seer Stone, we could contact her, and through her, Barusa. Unless you geniuses see no need."

"They can do that?" said Edwin. "The stones?"

"If one knows how to use them," said DeBoors.

"Perhaps we can convince Uncle Barusa to give us leave to go home," said Edwin.

"Worth a try," said Blain. "With Eotrus dead, I'm not certain there's a good reason to keep chasing his minions, unless Theta is truly what Barusa fears he is. Even then, Jutenheim is too far from home to worry about." Blain gently lifted Azura's chin. She opened teary eyes and met his gaze. "We require your services, Seer."

"You fools know nothing about Seers," said Azura, disgust on her face, her eyes more focused than before, her manner more lucid. "It's true, we can communicate through the stones, but distance and familiarity make a difference. I've never met the Alder Seer and Lomion is hundreds of leagues away. That is much too far. It can't be done."

"Then we're wasting our time," said Edwin, "and the Eotrus get farther away by the minute. Let's leave her be and be off."

"We would be on their heels already," said DeBoors, "if you hadn't let a saboteur slip on board to cut our rigging. And no one saw him? Were you all asleep or drowning in your cups?"

"How did you know we would pick up their trail by coming here?" said Edwin.

"Deductive reasoning," said DeBoors. "And a knowledge of the city."

"What kind of reasoning?" said Edwin. "What does that mean?"

DeBoors turned back to Azura. "So you don't have the skill to contact the Alder Seer," he said.

Azura's eyes narrowed and filled with hate. "I'm as skilled as any Seer you will ever meet, mercenary, but even on my best day, over that distance, all I could do is project a feeling or an emotion, not words, not a discussion. Even then, the contact must be with another Seer that knows me well, or it won't take. You fools expect me to strike up a conversation across the continent and have you join in." She shook her head and rolled her eyes. "If she was in Tragoss, I could do it, easily. No matter that we've never met, I would reach her, I have the skills, the power, but across hundreds of leagues, it's impossible. I can't help

117

you even if I wanted to, and I don't. Look what you've done here, you scum. Look at the blood on my floor. The blood on you. Look at me. Look at what he did to me," she said screeching. "You killed them all, didn't you? You killed my Gorb. Get away from me and get out of my home. Begone and let me die in peace. Just let me die in peace."

"We're done here," said Blain. He turned to leave, his face red with shame.

"No, we're not," said DeBoors. Blain stopped in his tracks. "You will try to make contact, Seer. Put your hands on the stone and try."

"No."

DeBoors' palm impacted Azura's cheek, a wicked slap that sent her reeling. He grabbed her arm and dragged her into a chair that faced the Seer Stone. He had a dagger in his hand. He placed it against Azura's ear. Edwin smirked, but Blain looked stricken, as if he wanted to intercede, but he didn't, and he said nothing. "Make contact, Seer, or I'll take your ear," he said, his voice soft and icy cold, "then I'll move on to other parts. Some you'll miss more."

Azura's hands shook. She reached out to the stone. Different from Mother Alder's — this one was brown in hue with jagged cracks that crisscrossed its pitted surface. Its texture was rougher, more weathered. The mists within, so thick and dark, the stone nearly opaque. When her fingers touched it, her body jerked and shook as if shocked. Her fingers stuck to the stone's surface and Azura moaned in pain. The room grew warm, then cold, then warm again, in rapid waves, the source of the temperature changes

118

wasn't clear, though they didn't emanate directly from the stone itself. A cloying, putrid smell filled the air. Edwin and Blain both stepped back, their faces going green. They looked as if they were about the retch.

"I should smell the flowers. It's always flowers when I touch the stone," said Azura as she pulled her hands back. "Dried flowers, fresh and sweet and beautiful. Now it smells of death. Death. Just like me."

"Focus, Seer," said DeBoors. "Reach out with your art and make contact with Mother Alder. You can do it. You still have the power."

"He even ruined my stone. He took my flowers. He's left me nothing," said Azura as tears streamed down her face. "Please help me," she said.

"Dead gods, stop your whining, woman," said Edwin as he moved farther into the room's corner, his back pressed against the wall.

"Concentrate, Seer," said DeBoors. He stood beside her, seemingly unaffected by the nausea generated by the stone. "Reach out and contact Mother Alder. Do it."

Azura reached for the stone. When her fingers were still an inch or two away, she jerked forward, as if the stone pulled her, and her fingers clamped to its surface. The room buzzed, a high-pitched keening sound and Azura shook. Her eyes rolled back showing the whites. Edwin puked in the corner.

"Something's wrong," said Azura. "I can't control it. It's not supposed to work like this."

"Concentrate," said DeBoors.

Vapors swirled within the Seer Stone. After a goodly time where nothing more happened, at last the dark mist coalesced and formed images, black and white, and a scene took shape in the stone's depths, clear enough for DeBoors to see as well.

9
THE POINTMEN

Lord Gallis Korrgonn, the son of Azathoth, the one true god, stood beside the ship's wheel on the bridge deck of *The White Rose*. His right hand gripped his battered ankh, that ancient relic of mystical power that once belonged to Sir Gabriel Garn, late weapons master of House Eotrus. At Korrgonn's side was Father Ginalli, high priest of Azathoth and Arkon of the League of Shadows. The hulking warrior Frem Sorlons and his lanky comrade Par Sevare observed the two from across the deck.

"The big boss is using that ankh thingy again, ain't he?" said Frem.

Par Sevare leaned over the ship's rail and spit a mouthful of tobacco juice into the sea, his cheek puffed out with a full wad of the stuff. "Probably to set our course. Somehow that talisman knows which way we're to go."

"It gives me the creeps. Stinking sorcery and such. No offense."

Sevare nodded.

"Must not be working so well," said Frem. "We're supposed to be headed due south to Jutenheim, but best I can tell we're sailing east and have been for two full days."

"We're to make a stop at some island."

"What for?"

Sevare hesitated before responding. "Lord Korrgonn doesn't see fit to share his plans with

121

me."

Lord Ezerhauten, gaunt, pale, and menacing as always, stepped up beside the two, his black armor, adorned with magnificently etched dragons, glistened despite the overcast sky, and contrasted sharply with Frem's plain silver. "The island holds an ancient token what Korrgonn needs for his mystical gobbledygook," he said.

"To what end?" said Sevare.

"To get us past the guardians of the temple in Jutenheim," said Ezerhauten.

"The who of what?" said Frem.

Ezerhauten turned toward Frem. "Is there anything between your ears, Sorlons? Anything at all?"

Frem put his right hand to his ear and tugged, then put his little finger in each ear canal and felt around for a bit. "No," he said, "nothing," a blank expression on his face.

Ezerhauten shook his head and failed to suppress a grin despite himself.

"We're headed to another temple," said Sevare. "A temple of power, like the one in the Vermion Forest. Only at such a place can another Gateway to Nifleheim be opened. That's why we're going all the way the Jutenheim, remember?"

"I remember that the old elf in Tragoss Mor said something about that," said Frem.

"Sorlons — did you think we were on holiday?" said Ezerhauten.

"I figured the elf's Orb was probably all Ginalli really needed," said Frem. "I guess I was confused. I get that way, sometimes. Isn't opening a magical Gateway a dangerous thing? Wasn't Ginalli lucky the last time that it didn't open in the wrong place and that something nasty didn't come through?"

"Last time," said Ezerhauten, "Korrgonn made it through from Nifleheim to Midgaard and so did Mortach, or so they claim. The League's plan would've worked perfectly but for Theta, or Thetan, whatever he's called. If they'd gotten us involved earlier, we could've stopped Theta, but, as it was, we weren't there and he mucked things up."

"Korrgonn says that when he and his knights passed through the gateway, they expected to be welcomed as heroes. Instead, they were ambushed by Theta and his henchmen. The portal was shut down afore Azathoth came through, and Korrgonn got jumped so bad he had to use some mystical whobittydo to take over Gabriel Garn's body just to survive."

"That just never sat right with me," said Frem. "Seems an evil thing to take a man's body. Taxes and tithes are bad enough, but that's just too far. Especially a man like Gabriel. I've heard stories about him for years. A true hero they name him — what even fought dragons, trolls, and such. Admired by fighting men from one side of the kingdom to the other. There may be more to it than I know, so maybe I shouldn't be talking."

"That's probably best," said Sevare.

"Don't believe everything you hear," said Ezerhauten. "Besides the praise you've heard, there are dark stories afloat about Gabriel Garn — always have been. Things that would make your skin crawl."

"Like what?"

"One tale from way back marks him a baby snatcher, though I don't recall the particulars. Another says he had a habit of hanging about the dead — doing who knows what with them, if you get my meaning. If that don't make your skin crawl, I don't know what would."

"I heard that one too," said Sevare. "If it's true, he had a sick mind."

"Another story oft told goes that some years back he got stuck wintering up in the Kronar Range with a bunch of folks after the snows trapped them up there. When food got scarce, dark things that best not be spoken of went on. Come spring, Gabriel was the only one what walked out of those mountains alive."

"I heard some story like that way back," said Frem. "I didn't know it was Gabriel though."

"Well, I'm afraid that he wasn't the great hero some folks made him out to be. A villain if you ask me, to do them things. Disappointing, I know, but that's the truth of it."

"Maybe so, but sometimes there's more than one truth, I figure," said Frem. "Since Gabriel's body is still walking about, where went his soul, his mind, his memories, and everything what made him, him?"

"Who knows," said Sevare.

"So is he dead for real," said Frem, "or stuck in there somewhere, all crowded up and cozy with Korrgonn?"

"Korrgonn says he's dead," said Ezerhauten. "So I guess he took over his corpse."

"So he's the walking dead?" said Frem.

"Undead, they call it," said Sevare, "but I'm no necromancer."

"Me great-grandmum told me stories about them undead fellows," said Frem. "Kept me up all scared many a night, and kept me in line when I was up to the mischief, fearing they would come for me if I was bad. I've never forgotten them stories. Great-grandmum named them fellows duergar. She said they caused a pack of trouble way back when, and we would be in the deep stuff if ever they came calling again. Pure evil she marked them. Mindless evil, best stay well clear, and then some, she told me."

"There's no such thing as duergar," said Ezerhauten, "except in fairy tales and ghost stories. And even if there were, Korrgonn is not one of them. Possession might be a better word to describe it, if there's a word for it at all. In any case, Korrgonn's adamant that Azathoth's reign on Midgaard must be reestablished. He says that opening a portal to Nifleheim is the only way, and only with Azathoth back in the game can Theta be stopped. That's what he tells me anyway, and that's a lot more than our clients usually tell. What the truth of it is, who knows."

"Stopped from what?" said Frem.

"Good question," said Ezerhauten. "Not really clear on the answer, other than they want him dead."

Sevare shook his head in disbelief. "This is a dangerous game. The risk is—"

"—none of our concern," said Ezerhauten. "The League is paying us better than anyone has in years, so we'll see this through, like it as not. Besides, the priest got the gateway opened right and proper last time, and with Korrgonn's help I expect it'll be that much easier the next. But you're right; it's a risk, a grave one. But the decision's been made and that's the end of it. I've no interest in trying to talk Ginalli or Korrgonn out of it."

"What guards the Jutenheim temple?" said Sevare.

"Korrgonn's not saying, but it's got him worried, so he must know. It must be tough as nails, whatever it is, to have the likes of him on edge. If he thinks we need some magical thingamajig to get past it, we best find it on this island."

"What if the island has guardians too?" said Frem.

"If it does, we'll deal with them," said Ezerhauten. "That's what we get paid for."

**

Breathing heavily, Frem pulled the longboat's oars with all his vast strength, sweat pouring down his face. Two lines of Frem's Pointmen: a mixture of robust lugron warriors and armored men of Ezerhauten's Sithian Mercenary Company, some rough-and-tumble veterans, others knights of aristocratic descent — third or fourth sons that would never inherit their family's fortunes, worked the oars behind him and struggled to match his pace; all equipped with full battle gear. The glistening, polished, red armor of the knights and the dragon-crested maroon tabards of the soldiers contrasted with the bare-chested, hairy bulk of the lugron warriors. The lugron wisely doffed their thick hauberks of heavy leather when they stepped aboard the longboat, but the sithians' chain and plate armor took too long to put on and off, so they wore it and suffered the heat.

The sithians usually worked alone, but at Ginalli's insistence, Ezerhauten agreed to integrate a troop of lugron into his mercenary squadrons. Frem was gifted almost half a squadron of scouts to bolster the Pointmen's numbers and replace the losses suffered during the company's last campaign. To Frem's surprise, they integrated easily with his team and followed orders. Skilled, surprisingly disciplined, yet hampered by strange and varied superstitions, they so far gave a good account of themselves. That said, they were a bit too bold for Frem's liking. You didn't get to be an old soldier if you were too bold and Frem aspired to old age. If he didn't get there, he would never see Coriana grown. Assuring that she was well-provided for, safe, and happy was more important to him than all else in the world. It motivated everything he did and seemed to affect every choice he made. Yet every day he suffered knowing that to provide for her properly, he had to remain a soldier and that kept him on the road, away from home. It was his only skill; his only way to earn a good living. It made him miss so much of her life. So much, it made him ashamed.

With each stroke, masses of noxious seaweed

piled against the oars, weighed them down, and threatened to snap them from the strain. So thick was the heady muck, rarely did the men even catch glimpse of the water. The cove was eerily quiet; the water calm save for strange popping and bubbling sounds that came and went here and again, and the occasional slithering movement of one stringy clump of seaweed over another as the waves gently buoyed the whole mass.

The nauseating fumes that rose from the decaying weeds were too much for Frem; his labored breaths sucked the foulness deep into his lungs. Fifty yards from the black sand beach, he dropped his oars and coughed uncontrollably.

The Pointmen looked to the longboat's stern where Sevare manned the rudder; their expressions pleaded for relief. Sevare stood up. "Alright men, oars down, let's take a break."

Oars dropped stem to stern, the Pointmen sweaty and flushed from the sticky heat and the grueling effort to keep pace with Frem. Several men collapsed in exhaustion; the rest coughed, cleared their throats, and spit phlegm into the muck. One man leaned over the rail and vomited. All drank deep from their canteens.

Sevare cut strips of cloth from a large towel, wet them with clean water from a jug, and passed them to the men. "Tie one over your mouth and breathe through it. It'll cut down the vapors."

Frem spat into the muck. "We should've thought of that before we left the ship." He upstoppered his canteen and swallowed a mouthful of water to clear his throat.

"It didn't seem like it would be so bad," said

Sevare. "Who would have thought a couple hundred yards would take so long and be such tough going?"

Frem scanned the cove. But for the modest black sand beach ahead, the cove's perimeter was barren and stony. Far to either side of the longboat rose huge, angular slabs of basalt and granite, black and dark-gray, ancient rock — stone born in the very core of Midgaard, thrown up from the depths in time immemorial. "Couldn't the captain have scared up a better spot to lay anchor? This stinking cove is clogged of seaweed from tip to tip and nothing but stone beyond."

Captain "Rascelon sailed us around the entire island," said Sevare. "There was nothing but jagged rocks, heavy surf, and fierce current that pushed the ship straight at the rocks. This place wasn't our best choice, it was our only choice."

"Well, it was a lousy one anyway," said Frem. "We would make better time walking this muck instead of rowing through it. I can't even see the water."

"If Ginalli had his way," said Sevare, "we would have rowed *The Rose* in here and anchored by the beach."

"I'm no sailor," said Frem, "but that don't make no sense to me. We wouldn't get a good depth reading through the muck — the ship would've gotten hung up or run aground. Then we would be fixed good."

"That's what the captain told Ginalli, but he wasn't listening. Rascelon didn't know how to deal with that — he's a hothead, if you ask me. Things started getting ugly and Korrgonn had to break it up before they came to blows."

"Then it was lucky for them both that Korrgonn was around," said Frem. "The captain is a tough man. He would have made short work of the priest in a straight-up fight, but I think he would have come to regret it. Ginalli's the sort to hold a grudge — a bad one, I would wager."

"You're wrong on that, buddy," said Sevare. "Ginalli's a holy man — he's not like that."

Frem didn't seem convinced. "What do you figure happened to the patrol?" he said. "sixteen men. Good fighters every one, yet not a sign for hours."

Sevare's gaze fixed on the two empty longboats that lay abandoned on the black beach before them. "I expect they're dead."

"Probably torn to pieces," said Little Storrl, a beardless youth that sat behind Frem. Storrl was by some years the youngest of all the Sithian Company, and the only one of lugron descent. "Maybe taken by lions or swallowed whole by some giant wyrm. I hear they have them out this way," he said as he looked around fearfully.

Seated beside Little Storrl was Sergeant Putnam, a grizzled soldier that commanded the Pointmen's first squad. "Clean the weed from your oars men," shouted Putnam, "and push that log aside," he said, pointing to a large piece of driftwood that floated amidst the seaweed heaped against the front of the longboat. He leaned forward and spoke quietly so the men behind couldn't hear. "Cannibals is what I hear haunts hereabouts," he said, his voice deep and gravelly. "We'll find their sorry skulls mounted on pikes by

130

the beach, all the flesh stripped off, white bone kissing the breeze. You mark my words."

"I was bent when Korrgonn picked that squadron over ours to scout the island," said Frem. "How could he pass us over? Scouting the point is what we do."

"Better than anyone," said Putnam. "And Korrgonn knows it; he's seen our work."

"Ezerhauten's head practically popped off when Korrgonn countermanded his orders and replaced us," said Sevare.

"But if he hadn't, we might all be dead now," said Frem. "Boiling in some cannibal's stew. I'm surprised Ezer let him do that."

"The commander is too smart to lock horns with Korrgonn," said Putnam, "even if he's not what they claim him to be."

"You think Korrgonn knew the danger?" said Frem.

"My guess is, he suspected," said Sevare.

"And held us in reserve?" said Frem.

"Why not send his best?" said Little Storrl.

"In Mages and Monsters," said Sevare, "when you're probing your enemy to test his strength, do you move your best pieces into action first?"

"That would be stupid," said Little Storrl. "You could lose your champions and then you would be done before the game even got started."

"He sacrificed his pawns," said Putnam.

Sevare nodded.

"So he's got some meat to him, does he," said Frem. "Some strategies and what not, all smart and tricksy. That's good, since the priest has got no sense at all, not for battle anyways, and nobody bothers to listen to us."

"The top dog values us," said Putnam. "That's worth something, I expect."

"Until he runs dry on pawns," said Frem. "We're back in the deep stuff boys, and this time it really stinks," he said, flicking his hand to knock off some clinging seaweed.

"That's not the only thing what stinks," said Little Storrl, wrinkling his nose at Frem.

Frem shook his head and messed the lad's hair, which set him giggling.

"You keep sweating like that and you'll swamp the boat," said Little Storrl.

"You're dripping near as much, boy," said Frem.

"True enough, but easy to fix." Little Storrl pushed aside the seaweed with his oar, dunked a bucket in the water, and upended it over his head to cool himself.

"Ugh," went Frem, wrinkling his nose and leaning away. "That water stinks worse than the air."

Little Storrl lifted his arm to his nose and sniffed. A look of disgust filled his face. "Well, since I stink already, I might as well be cool." He leaned over to fill the bucket again. "Aargh!" he yelled and jumped back from the longboat's rail.

"What?!" said Frem.

"Sit down, boy," said Putnam, "afore you end up in the drink."

"Something is in the water," said Storrl as he pulled a wicked dagger from his belt and pointed. "An eye looking up at me. It was huge."

Frem tentatively leaned over the side, a long

132

dagger in hand. "Nothing there now. Sure it wasn't just your reflection? Or some stinking fish?"

Storrl narrowed his eyes. "I saw something. I'm not sure what. Best we move on from here, I think."

Sevare looked back toward where *The White Rose* lay anchored at the mouth of the cove. The squadron of longboats that carried much of the ship's compliment was slowly gaining ground on them. "Agreed. Let's get moving before Ezer has our hides."

Sevare stood on the strand and scanned the expanse of stone ahead while Frem and the others secured the longboat, their efforts hampered by clumps of seaweed that enwrapped their legs as they pulled the boat ashore through the light surf. The seaweed clung to them and threatened to trip them, almost as if it were aware and of ill will. After a few moments of contact, it stung their skin and burned like the bite of a jellyfish, though not as severe. The men scrambled out of the water as fast as they could.

"Stinking weeds," snarled Frem. "Get off me," he bellowed as he tore a clump of weed from his leg. "Let's get off this darned beach. I don't see no skulls on pikes, so we still got missing men to find."

"A lifeless rock," said Sevare to no one in particular. "Not a tree, bush, or bird in sight. Nothing but stone." While Sevare watched, Frem's legs shot out from under him. He crashed face down to the wet sand and was pulled toward the water, his eyes wide with surprise and panic. Thick seaweed that looked like corded ropes were wrapped about his ankles and dragged him toward a watery doom. Frem drove a huge hand into the black, rocky sand to little effect. With his other hand he plunged his dagger into the sand to slow his slide. It sparked against the rocks and scarred the rocky sand, a deep rut left in its wake.

Sevare dived toward Frem, grabbed his wrist, and strained to stay his slide. But it was a powerful pull, beyond the strength of mortal men. Sevare's feet dug deep into the sand but he could not hope to hold Frem back. "Cut him free," yelled Sevare to whoever was near. "Now!"

The weeds dragged them both inexorably toward the water;

Swords and daggers came out all around. Putnam, Storrl, Moag, and Sir Roard hacked the weeds that coiled about Frem. With each blow landed, the weeds emitted sharp, rhythmic sounds, unholy crinoid cries of pain, and mayhaps, calls for help. Even in death, the weeds wreaked havoc. Each one that they severed shot a small cloud of noisome, acidic mist into the air that choked the men and stung their exposed flesh before it finally went silent and still.

With alarming speed, more corded weeds slithered from the water and advanced like snakes across the sand. How long they were, none could tell, for one end of each remained in the water. They wrapped en masse about Frem's feet and legs, acting in concert, and ignoring all else. Frem rolled to his back, pulled a second dagger from his belt, and slashed the weeds that coiled about his torso.

Without warning, a volley of thicker weeds rocketed from the water. They screeched as they sailed through the air — a high-pitched, discordant wail, sharp and painful to hear. Their ends held toothy maws, small but wickedly sharp and ravenous. The barrage slammed into the Pointmen. Men dived, reeled, or were knocked from their feet.

One weed slammed into Sir Roard's breastplate. Its fangs bit deep into the tempered steel as easily as a snake punctures a man's flesh. Another did the same to Storrl's hauberk, embedding its fangs in the thick leather. It wouldn't let go. Storrl grabbed the thing even as it pulled him toward the water. A desperate series of slashes with his blade severed it and he turned and bolted back to Frem's side. Dozens more hellweeds deflected off armor and shield or crashed into the sand. They coiled, hissed, bared their fangs, and struck like cobras, sending the men scurrying up the strand. The Pointmen tried to form a defensive line but the weeds were too quick, chaotic, and unconventional in their attacks. The men were assailed from all sides and were nearly overwhelmed, their only recourse was to move farther back from the water's edge and get beyond the weed's range.

Only Little Storrl, Sir Roard, and Sevare remained at Frem's side, the surf now licking his calves. Little Storrl tore desperate at the weeds, hand and dagger, his weight on Frem's chest to stay him. Sevare was half buried in the sand up by Frem's head, his face red, and arms burning from the strain of holding Frem back.

Roard stood at Frem's feet and held more weeds at bay with sword and shield. Over and over the snarling weeds slammed into his shield and breastplate, but Roard was sturdy and strong and stood his ground. He beat them back as best he could, his expression determined and confident despite the inhuman onslaught he faced.

An angry coil of weed rocketed from the surf and slipped past Roard's guard. It whipped about his neck and knocked the big knight from his feet. Dazed, Roard's hands went to his throat and sought to tear the weed free even as it clamped down and cut off his air. Before any man could come to his aid, it dragged him headfirst and face up into the water, his desperate struggles and great strength were to no avail. As quick as that he disappeared below the muck. He was not seen again.

"What hell shit these out?" spat Little Storrl as he stared at the spot where Roard disappeared into the surf.

"Save yourself, boy," grunted Frem through clenched teeth. "You too, wizard. I'm done for."

"No!" said Storrl as tears welled in his eyes. "I'm not leaving you, boss."

"You got to," shouted Frem. "You must tell Coriana that I love her — you tell her that! Now get gone."

"No!" said Storrl.

"Help us," yelled Sevare over his shoulder toward the rest of the Pointmen. The others couldn't approach, though Putnam and more than a few others tried, beset as they were with the

136

hellweeds.

"What do we do?" said Storrl to Sevare, desperation in his eyes.

"I've a spell that I can try," said Sevare. "I just need a moment,"

"I've got him," said the young lugron. "But hurry."

Sevare stood, whirled his hands, and wove an eldritch incantation. Harsh guttural tones, sounds never meant to be uttered by the throat of man, escaped through Par Sevare's lips. Yellow fire, mystic brought, beamed from his hand, roaring like a thunderstorm, and impacted the evil weeds coiled about Frem's feet. The raw power of that arcane blast severed them one and all, incinerating the weeds at the point of impact, though it left Frem unscathed. An inhuman wailing filled the air and the masses of seaweed about the strand bucked, roiled, and roared, and then mercifully receded, sliding, slithering, or rocketing back into the water and out of sight. A thick covering of weed still capped the water's surface but what remained was common and quiet, the devilish things having fled. Par Sevare's arms shook. Smoke rose from his hands and pain racked his body. He fell backward to the sand, unconscious. Frem scrambled up and away from the water and stumbled to the rocks at the back of the beach, his legs numb and barely responsive, owing to the effects of the constrictive coils. He tore at the dead remnants of weed that still clung to him, even as many of the slimy coils still squirmed in their death throes. Storrl dragged Sevare by the arm across the strand until others moved in to help.

"Pull the boats back," said Frem. "All the way up the beach. Get everything away from the surf." The men did so and then joined him at the back end of the beach. Someone threw a helmet full of water on Sevare to bring him around. His hands still steamed from the magic he'd thrown.

"Roard served with me for six years," said Putnam. "A good man and a good knight. He has a fine wife and three young ones. What's to become of them now? He shouldn't have died like this. Drowned by a damned weed in the middle of nowhere. It's senseless. Not a way for a soldier to die."

"He died trying to save me," said Frem. "That makes him a hero in my book. What better way for a soldier to go?"

Putnam was quiet for some moments. "Aye, true enough," he said, nodding. "Then a hero's death we'll mark it. We'll toast Roard at the next feast."

Sevare joined them, wet cloths wrapped about both hands, though he looked a bit unsteady. "No need to worry about his family, the League will see that they are well provided for, I'm sure."

"You're always right quick to speak up for the Leaguers," said Putnam. "You're getting a bit too much religion, if you ask me."

"I didn't," said Sevare.

"You think that devil weed got our patrol?" said Little Storrl as he gazed up at the darkening sky, a storm moving in. Thunder pealed in the distance.

"We would have seen the battle from the ship," said Frem as he placed a hand on the young lugron's shoulder. "They would not have gone quietly."

"Couldn't have taken all of them, anyways," said Putnam. "Just the same, I figure they're dead, probably to a man, rest their souls."

"Something else waylaid them," said Sevare before he spit a wad of tobacco to the sand. "Something inland, back in those rocks. Something we haven't seen yet."

"Something we don't want to see," said Frem.

"Whatever it is, let's hope it got its fill already," said Sevare as the first drops of rain fell on his head.

"More likely, they've just developed a taste for us," said Putnam. "Stinking cannibals. We need to secure the area before the others land. "I'll see that the boys get to it."

10
SEERS AND STONES

Mother Alder gripped the stone with all ten fingers. Swirling mists, green and gray, yellow and gold, blue and turquoise, leaped and morphed about the stone's interior. The vapors slowed, images appeared, rich in color, realistic and sharp, and slid into focus.

And there sat Azura, disheveled, drained, and aged. Blain stepped up behind her, no closer than necessary to see the stone's sights.

"Blain?" said Mother Alder, her voice somehow projected through the stone as clear and sharp as if she were in the same room. "Is that you?"

"Good to see you, mother," said Blain, his voice slightly distorted as it passed through Azura's Seer Stone.

Mother Alder smiled from ear to ear for a moment, then resumed her cold scowl. "Where's my little Eddie?" she said. "So help me, Blain, if you've let another hair on that dear boy's head get harmed – I'll have you and Bartol both hung from the rafters by your feet."

Blain sighed. "Edwin's fine, mother. He's right here, just a bit green about the gills."

"The stone will do that," she said. "A cup of hot tea — chamomile with honey will fix him straight away. Your brother?"

"He's well, but not here at the moment."

"Where in the Lord's name did you find a Seer Stone to contact me with, and when did you arrive back in Lomion? Why not just come home? Are you in trouble? Is someone after you?"

"We're not in Lomion," said Blain. "We're in Tragoss Mor."

"That far?" said Barusa.

"Impossible," said Mother Alder, her brow furrowing as she spoke. "No common Seer can initiate contact over that distance, stone or not. It would take an Archseer or a master oracle to make such a contact. Even then, over that distance, a two-way conversation is not possible. Who sits the stone before you? I don't know her face."

"Mistress Azura of Tragoss Mor," said Blain.

"Hmm," said Mother Alder. "The only Seer called Azura that I know of is from Dyvers, if memory serves. I met her years ago, but she would be much younger than this woman."

"I am Azura du Marnian of Dyvers and yes, we've met."

"Then the years have been cruel," said Mother Alder. "You use your stone recklessly, du Marnian. Now tell me, how did a second-rate soothsayer like you acquire a Seer Stone?"

"I see that your reputation and my old opinion of you were honestly earned," said Azura. "What is it they call you, the 'witch-mother?'"

Mother Alder cackled. "At least I have a reputation. I'm not the one hiding in some barbarian hovel of a city. Bandy no more words with me, du Marnian, once of Dyvers, and perhaps you'll yet see tomorrow."

141

Azura's eyes dropped and she made no response. She had no strength left for such sparring.

"Now tell me," said Mother Alder, "where did you get the stone?"

Azura glared at Mother Alder. "It has been held by my House for twenty generations."

"Has it now? I do seem to recall a tale or two about the du Marnian Stone." Mother Alder turned to Barusa. "A minor House of little consequence," she whispered, though loud enough to be heard through the Stone. "And how did you contact me over such a distance? Have you some token that enhances your powers or your Stone's? A bauble perhaps, dug up from some archwizard's tomb? Or did you sell your soul to some demon of the nether realms to acquire this skill? Tsk Tsk — did he take your youth in exchange? Is that why you've gone so gray, so lined, so decrepit?"

Azura's expression was bitter, but she was too battered to fight. "No tokens do I have, and I don't ally with demons. How it worked, I know not. They forced me to try, and somehow it just worked. I can't explain it, nor do I care."

"In any case, this contact is well planned and timed," said Mother Alder. "We've been eager for news. It seems at least some of my sons prove not quite useless after all," she said, glancing toward Barusa.

Barusa's jaw was clenched; his eyes firmly glued to his shoes.

"I suppose I should ask after your quest, dearies, afore your brother pees himself."

"Were you able to kill or capture the Eotrus?"

blurted Barusa.

Mother Alder spun about. Her hand snapped out and whacked Barusa hard across the face. "I gave you no leave to speak," she shrieked. "Stay your tongue until I do so, firstborn, or you'll regret it."

Barusa glared at her, but said nothing more.

"How fare the Eotrus?" said Mother Alder.

"Claradon is done for by all accounts," said Blain. "Skewered by DeBoors' sword — through the heart."

"His body?"

"Carried off by his lackeys."

"So you don't know whether he's truly dead?"

Blain looked to DeBoors who was only partially visible at the edge of the stone's field of view.

"Let the bounty hunter speak," said Mother Alder. "Have him move closer so that I can see him properly," she said, smirking. No doubt, she was amused by the thought that the great warrior would grow sick before her eyes from the stone's magic.

DeBoors stepped closer, leaned in toward the stone, and crowded Azura aside. He exhibited no reaction to the stone's emanations and took his time before speaking, making clear to Mother Alder that the du Marnian Stone had no effect on him. "No mortal man could survive the wound I gifted him. Even now he feeds the worms."

"So say you truly?" said Mother Alder.

"Aye."

"So be it or not, time will tell. What of the other?"

143

"Theta runs free, mother," said Blain. "He fights like no other. Our marines were no match for him and even the Kalathens could not stand against him. Five fell to his sword."

"That may prove it then," said Mother Alder. "I've prayed each night that the rumors about him were false, that he was just some puffed-up knight, but five Kalathens seems beyond the pale of mortal combat skills. What say you, firstborn?"

"He's allied with the Eotrus — that makes him our enemy. He killed Mortach who may have been more god than man. An enemy that dangerous must be eliminated, whether he's the Harbinger or not."

"A kernel of wisdom," whispered Mother Alder. "I'm overwhelmed."

"He's dangerous, there's no doubt," said Blain. "But he can't be the Harbinger of Doom. There's no such person, not in truth. The story is an ancient myth, a fable, nothing more. I'll not fall for such foolishness. I can't believe that you have, Mother."

"You can't deny he's a grave threat," said Barusa.

"Not in Jutenheim, he's not," said Blain. "It's halfway across the world. Let him go and good riddance."

Barusa nodded. "With young Eotrus dead, perhaps it is time to bring you home. But if Theta is the Harbinger, he may be a threat to us even in Jutenheim."

"Blain — if we believe in good," said Mother Alder, "we must also believe in evil, for they are opposites – perhaps they cannot even exist without each other."

"Then how did Theta come to Lomion?" said Blain. "Korrgonn and Mortach came through the Gateway from Nifleheim — called down by the League's mages. Or so they claim."

"You have your doubts, do you?" said Mother Alder.

Blain shrugged.

"Interesting. A skeptical mind is a keen one. Perhaps you are less worthless than you so often seem. As for Theta, perhaps he crept from some portal betwixt Midgaard and the nether realms. Some foul hole opened by an upstart what stumbled on an old tome of magic far beyond him. Or mayhaps he has been here all along — hiding in some dark corner of the world, biding his time, working his evil when chance permitted."

"You speak of the bogeyman," said Blain. "A vaporous spectre of fable and children's tale. I've seen him. He's a man of flesh and bone and blood. He can be killed, the same as any other."

"Can he now, deary? Seen his blood, have you? Does it run red like ours, or some other color?"

Blain had no answer.

"Are you the man what can bring him down, Blain Alder? Are you? No, for all your skills, you are not."

"DeBoors was hired to kill Theta," said Blain. "That's his job."

"You know nothing of Theta's nature," said Mother Alder. "None of us do, not truly. Theta has always been the primary target of your mission, not Claradon Eotrus; he's of no real import. You

145

know this — we discussed it at length before you set off. Nothing has changed. Pursue Theta no matter where he goes; no matter how long it takes, even unto the ends of Midgaard. You must also follow Korrgonn's ship, an easy enough task since Theta follows it too. I must know if the priest is successful in his conjuring. I must know if he opens another Gateway. And I must know what comes through. You must see this through, my dears, however hard it may become."

Blain took a deep breath before responding. "I'll see Theta dead then, but only if DeBoors and the Kalathens continue with us."

"Is that in doubt?" said Mother Alder.

"No," said DeBoors. "We've a contract; I'll see it through. I always do. My word is my bond."

"Good," said Mother Alder. "Duelist, the question remains, are you Theta's match?"

"I have the skills to bring him down," said DeBoors. "Though the task will not be easy no matter how well planned."

Mother Alder nodded. "You choose your words carefully, but your doubts bleed through. No doubt, you'll need your every skill to best him, but if your reputation is honesty earned, you may yet prevail. Be on your guard, my dears, for as long as you pursue Theta, your peril grows, be he truly man or beast. If he's the Harbinger, swords may not avail you despite the duelist's skills. You must use your wits to take him down — if you can uncover any. Now, what of your Seer?"

"What of her?" said Blain. "She's served her purpose."

"Ah, now more true to form," said Mother

Alder. "Without her and her stone, you fool, we can't communicate."

"You're suggesting we take her with us?"

"You must, and her Stone too. And when you're done with the quest, you will bring her and the du Marnian Stone here to House Alder — so that we can meet properly."

"I'll go nowhere with them," said Azura.

"You've no choice in the matter," said Mother Alder. "From this moment forward, you work for the Alders."

Azura's mouth hung open. "You plan to kill Thetan? That's what you said, right?"

"Yes."

"Fine. Then I'm with you."

"Good," said Mother Alder, seemingly surprised. "Oh, and deary . . ."

"What?" said Azura.

"Welcome to the family."

A servant frantically polished the Alder Stone with a soft cloth while Mother Alder and Edith looked on.

"Best you run along and get cleaned up, deary," said Mother Alder when she noted the girl's stained pant leg and shoes. The servants had mopped up her lost dinner and wiped down her pants and shoes, but the stains needed washing out, if they would come out at all.

"I will, Mother Alder, but I want to know more about the Stone, if you'll tell me."

Mother Alder raised an eyebrow. "Even though it made you sick?"

"Especially since."

"Well, well," she said, contemplating. "Edith, you're one of Blain's, aren't you?"

"First daughter," said the girl, nodding.

Mother Alder nodded. "Your father has always been a bit less dim than the others, so it makes sense that you are as well. You've promise, lass, not much perhaps, but some, and that's more than I can say for most of the rest. Sad that as a daughter you'll inherit next to nothing. Very well — I'll tell you some things. Not much, of course, since you're not capable of understanding much of consequence. But a little knowledge, perhaps, can't hurt and may make it through your skull. A Seer and her Stone are bonded to each other. The Stone will work its ways for no one else, unless the Seer dies or a more powerful Seer steals it out from under her."

"Has anyone tried to steal yours?"

"Not for a long time, deary."

"Are you going to steal the du Marnian Stone, Mother Alder?"

She raised her eyebrows. "Some promise, indeed," she said. "Yes, Edith, I am."

"No other House has two, do they?"

"Not that I know of, and I would know if they did."

"That will make our House stronger, won't it?" she said smiling.

"Aye, lass, it will."

The servant completed his polishing, folded the cloth, then produced a knife in its sheath from his pocket. He laid the knife across the cloth and held it before Mother Alder.

"The Alder Stone is not a toy, deary. It's a

useful tool, but such things come with a steep price. That's the way with magic. The risks are often worth it, but not always."

Mother Alder picked up the knife, unsheathed it, and sliced it slowly across the palm of her left hand, already crisscrossed with numerous scars.

Edith winced and pulled back.

Mother Alder made a fist and held it directly atop the Alder Stone. "The price I pay each time I use the Stone." Blood dripped onto the stone. The drops fell in slow motion. Each one made a distinctive "plop" as it hit the Alder Stone. Curiously, the droplets didn't bead down the Stone's side and fall to the table. Instead, the blood stuck to the Stone. A red stain formed and spread across its surface. Wherever the blood touched one of the pitted areas on the Stone's surface, a sizzling sound could be heard; smoke rose, and a burning scent tinged the air. Mother Alder opened and closed her hand again and again, and squeezed her fist tighter to keep the blood flowing. After a time the entire surface of the Stone was covered in a uniform film of bright-red blood. "Finally," said Mother Alder, sighing as she pulled her hand away. "I feared I would need a second cut. I hate it when that happens." A servant was there to tightly bandage her hand in practiced fashion. The Stone pulsed with an inner light casting the entire room in a reddish glow. When the glow dimmed, the blood was gone from the Stone's surface, and it returned to its normal aspect. "It was hungry this time. I wonder . . ."

11
DWELLERS OF THE DEEP

The day was dark as twilight; thunder pealed in the distance, but the rain eased. Frem Sorlons and Par Sevare stood in a dismal gorge of death — barbaric, brutal, and bloody, the air fouled of spilled entrails. To call the place a battlefield would have marked it too commonplace, too acceptable, too clean. It was none of those. Broken, mutilated bodies, the remains of *The White Rose's* missing patrol, lay strewn about the bottom of the shallow gorge. Stone steps led down some dozen feet to the gorge's rocky floor, which stretched no more than thirty feet across, though it was several times that long. Twenty steep steps carried one up and out on the other side. A trail through the stony landscape led *The White Rose's* shore party here via steps carved into the living rock and rugged pathways cut through giant slabs of granite.

"Perfect spot for an ambush," said Sevare as he surveyed the gorge's rim where six lugron Pointmen stood on guard, ostensibly looking outward to keep watch, though each glanced down again and again at the horrid scene below them. "They had nowhere to run."

From atop the stair, Sergeant Putnam signaled Korrgonn's imminent arrival. Within moments, Ezerhauten appeared at the rim with a squadron of sithians — Ginalli and Korrgonn in tow. The mercenary commander studied the scene and then ordered his men to spread out and bolster the guard along the rim. Soon Ezerhauten, Putnam, Ginalli, and Korrgonn descended the steep steps, made all the more treacherous by cascading water and slick moss. Sevare and Frem met them at the base of the stair, though Ezerhauten ignored them and walked past to examine the grisly remains.

"The whole patrol?" said Ginalli, his face grave.

"Hard to say," said Sevare. "The bodies are dismembered. Not sure how many there are."

"There's twelve heads," said Frem. "Counted them myself. They were chopped up right good, but there are twelve for sure."

Ginalli's face flushed red; his eyes narrowed. He winced and looked past Sevare, but with the darkness and a bit of distance, there was little to see. Korrgonn stood by, stoic and silent.

"Are you saying that someone cut them to pieces?" asked Ginalli through gritted teeth. He looked over at Korrgonn. "A ritual slaying?"

Sevare shook his head. "No, nothing like that. The bodies are torn and punctured as if by claws and teeth. It was animals. A pack of big cats, or wild dogs, or wolves, I would wager."

"Not eaten," said Frem. "Just ripped up and left to rot. Best way to count them up was by the heads, what's left of them anyways."

Ginalli looked about, alarmed.

"Be at ease," said Sevare. "They're long gone, whatever they were. We've posted a strong guard. If they come back, they'll not catch us unawares."

"Could it have been men that did this?" said Ginalli. "Maybe a pack of scavengers came in later."

"Checked for that," said Frem. "We found no arrows or bolts and no sword or axe wounds as far as we can see. Some holes though — could be spears, could be teeth — big teeth, like the fangs of a snow cat."

"Unless there's a forest farther on," said Sevare, "I don't see how this island could support a pack of big cats or wolves. Nothing to eat anywhere that we've seen."

"Nothing but rocks and some moss here and there," said Frem. "That's what has us stomped."

"Stumped," said Sevare.

"That's what I said," said Frem. "Stomped."

Ezerhauten completed his study of the remains and rejoined the group. "They died in a circle, fighting back to back at the end. A last stand. Too bad there's no one alive to recount the tale. It would be a good one for the annals. Putnam — you mark it down as best you can. Make sure that you record all their names, and spell them right. Those men should be remembered."

"Aye, commander," said Putnam. "I'll mark it good. Should I leave out the part about the heads?"

"No. We'll stand on the truth, just as we always do."

"What did this, commander?" said Ginalli. "Your men think it was animals."

"Unusual for animals to attack a large group of men," said Ezerhauten. "And there are no

152

carcasses. I don't care if it were cave bears, lions, or whatnot; our boys would've taken some of them down."

"So what are we dealing with?" said Ginalli.

Ezerhauten shook his head in frustration. "Can't say for certain. Maybe it was some backward tribesmen what still use stone spears, bone knives, and such. Had to be a lot of them though to best our men. Several score or more. They must have carried away their dead."

"Cannibals, probably," said Putnam.

"Maybe it was a dragon," said Frem.

Sevare rolled his eyes. "I expect we'll find out soon enough. There were sixteen men in the patrol. We've no sign of the other four. They either ran for it or were dragged off. If we find any alive, Ezer, you may get your tale yet."

"I assume the rain washed away any prints or blood trails," said Ginalli.

"Aye," said Frem.

"We'll need to stay in a tight formation," said Ezerhauten. "Sorlons — make sure you stay in sight of the main group at all times. We can't afford to lose another squadron."

"What of the bodies?" said Sevare.

"We can't bury them in this stone," said Frem. "And burning would get noticed."

"Have a detachment carry them back to the ship for a proper service and burial," said Ginalli to Ezerhauten.

"Hold on," said Ezerhauten. "We can't split our force. We may need every sword we have. We can pick up the bodies on the way back. It's not as if we'll find them in any worse shape later."

Ginalli glared at Ezerhauten. "Your compassion is overwhelming as usual," said Ginalli.

"Hard words, mercenary, but wise," said Korrgonn. "That's what we'll do."

"If you wanted someone kind and gentle, priest, you wouldn't have hired me," said Ezerhauten. "You would have taken up with the Blue Steel Company or the Wood Rats. Of course, those buggers would've already surrendered to whatever killed the patrol."

Ginalli looked insulted. "Assemble the men," he said. "We'll say a prayer for the souls of the fallen before we move on."

"A quick one," said Korrgonn. "We need to get to the center of the island. It's there that we'll find what we're here for."

"Which is what exactly?" said Ezerhauten.

"Don't overstep your place," said Ginalli coldly.

Korrgonn paused and took a breath, as if considering whether to respond. "An ancient talisman that will ease our getting past the guardian of the Jutenheim temple."

"Easing that passage has cost us sixteen good men already. Ten of them, my men. Some had wives and children and will be sorely missed. Are you sure this talisman is worth it?"

"I'm sure," said Korrgonn.

"Rest assured that the families of our fallen heroes will be well provided for," said Ginalli. "We take care of our own. All in accordance with our contract, of course."

"Good. I'll hold you to that," said Ezerhauten.

154

He nodded, turned, and marched up the stone stair to assemble the troops. "This is going to get messy," he said, but no one was close enough to hear.

Frem stalked cautiously at the van, making hardly any sound despite his metal armor and bulky physique. His eyes darted from side to side and took in all that appeared before him, though visibility was sorely limited. The rain had subsided, but the sky remained heavily overcast, the island dark as a moonlit night though it was still midafternoon; thunder and lightning came and went in waves. The brief flashes of lightning offered the only distant views of the stony vista. It smelled of rotting seaweed even here, far inland. Par Sevare and the Pointmen followed in silence closely behind Frem. The bulk of *The White Rose's* expedition trudged across the wet stones some one hundred yards behind.

Ezerhauten and a squad of soldiers broke off from the main group and moved quickly to catch up to the Pointmen. "Here comes Lord Sunshine," said Sevare.

The Pointmen halted and parted for Ezerhauten. "There's to be no magic thrown from here on out," said Ezerhauten to Sevare. "None at all. Korrgonn's orders."

"Except if we're attacked, right?" said Sevare.

"Not even."

"What? Why not?"

"He thinks it will give away our position to someone or something."

"If something jumps us," said Frem, "they

155

already know our position, so what's the risk?"

Neither Sevare nor Ezerhauten seemed to hear him.

"How am I supposed to fight beasts that can tear up our knights without magic?" said Sevare.

"Improvise," said Ezerhauten.

"Save up a good wad and spit in their eyes," said Frem.

"Worth a try," said Ezerhauten. "At least it'll give that swill you spit some purpose. Go argue with Korrgonn if you want. I'm just the messenger." Ezerhauten looked to Frem. "I'll walk the point with you for a while — I trust you've no objection."

Frem nodded his agreement.

Sevare choked down his frustration. "We'll want your sword close at hand soon enough, I expect."

"So how much does the League pay the families of our dead?" said Frem as they walked along.

Ezerhauten looked surprised at the question. "Two hundred silver stars went to the wives of our men what the Eotrus killed up by Riker's. Not so much, but it'll see to them for a goodly time. Why?"

"My daughter," said Frem. "I want to make sure she's taken care of, if it comes to it. What about the lugron what died?"

Sevare responded quickly, before Ezerhauten answered. "I'm sure their families got the same."

"They got nothing," said Ezerhauten.

"Ezer doesn't know what they got," said Sevare, throwing an evil glare at Ezerhauten.

"He's just pulling your chain. We're all treated equally, I'm sure."

Frem stopped and turned to face Ezerhauten. "What do you mean they got nothing?"

"I meant what I said," said Ezerhauten. "They got nothing."

"Why not?" said Frem, his voice sharp. "Their company got hired on by the League same as ours. Some of them are even believers. Why shouldn't they get taken care of the same? We're all equal, aren't we? All deserving? That's what the priests say at the services, isn't it? Why shouldn't the lugron families be treated the same?"

Sevare tried to step between the two warriors and pulled Frem by the arm. "We need to keep moving."

"Don't yell at me, Sorlons," said Ezerhauten. "You do remember that you work for me, not the League, don't you?"

"Aye."

"Good, because I've nothing to do with it. I'm just hired help, same as you." After they walked a while longer, Ezerhauten spoke again, quietly, so that only Frem and Sevare could hear him. "They got nothing because they're just lugron."

Frem stared at Ezerhauten for a moment. "So they're not good enough? Is that it?"

"The lugron are not in the club, boy, don't you get it? As far as the League goes, there are two kinds of folk. The elites — which are the priests, wizards, and noblemen. Then there's everybody else, the masses — the merchants, tradesmen, commoners, peasants, beggars and all.

Everybody is treated the same, just not the same as the elites. You won't hear that in any of Ginalli's sermons though. Heck, he wouldn't admit it if you held a knife to his throat. But that is the way it is all the same."

"Some folks having a lot when others have nothing is what the League is fighting against, isn't it? Isn't that what they're trying to change? Isn't that what the League is all about?"

"Of course it is," said Sevare. "Ezer's wrong on this one. Dead wrong."

Ezerhauten's smile was frightful. "Just be happy you're in the club and don't think too much about it." He looked back toward the main group. They had halted and no doubt wondered why the Pointmen weren't advancing. "Let's get moving."

Ezerhauten walked beside Frem. "You suspected the lugron got nothing, that's why you asked about them."

Frem shrugged.

"You're not as stupid as you look," said Ezerhauten.

"Oh yes, I am," muttered Frem as he stalked across the stony landscape.

***

Sevare froze when Frem stopped short and raised his hand, a command to his squadron to halt and go quiet, which they did at once; each man still and silent but poised for action within a single breath. The rearmost Pointman relayed the signal to the main group.

With the men still, the island went eerily quiet

despite the strange properties of the stark landscape that distorted and reverberated sounds, causing each word, step, or stumble to carry far and wide.

Frem turned his head slowly from side to side. Sevare knew he had sensed something. But what? And from which direction? Sevare heard nothing, and through the dark saw only stone. About them, nothing but an undulating expanse of bleak flat rock, curved stones, and tall, stark monoliths, upright sentinels that guarded hidden secrets unfathomed by man. Each block, boulder, and slab, weathered and curved, deeply pitted and eroded with age, not a sharp corner or knife-edge to be found. This was old rock, lifeless and barren, that harkened back to another age when the world was young.

Without thought, Sevare crouched, bent his knees, and tightened his grip on his staff for all the good that it would do. Some might take that old mahogany rod for a magical wand, a token of mystical power and esoteric energies that wizards of fable were wont to possess. Others would call it a weapon, for a staff held in skilled hands could oft match sword, spear, or axe. But to Sevare it was just a walking stick, a simple accoutrement, not an instrument of magic or a weapon for battle. He didn't even know how to wield it, save to swing it as any man would a club. Yet he gripped it all the tighter and drew from it what comfort he could.

Frem's hand went to his sword hilt and slowly pulled it from its scabbard. Sevare's heart pounded. He knew they were close — the things that had killed their men. He felt blind and naked without his magic, blast it all. He gripped the staff tighter.

Alongside Sevare, Ezerhauten tensed. His steely gaze penetrated deep into the twilight, his face etched with the sinister grin he always wore before a battle. He unsheathed his sword and held it at the ready. The other Pointmen did the same. The lugron sniffed the air, their broad noses keener than most men's. They caught a scent. They leveled spears; all their energy coiled, muscles and tendons poised to spring, ready to unleash the wanton bloodlust that ever consumed their ancient race.

A slight breeze passed from the north and now Sevare smelled it too. A putrid, fishy odor that fouled the cooling breeze that followed the rain ashore. A heady smell, a mixture of fresh and rotted fish; a scent of the sea; of life, but also of death and decay.

From off to the right came the creature's call. A sharp, startling, croaking sound that came not from man or known beast. It was full of menace, consumed of hate, old, dark, and deep. Ezerhauten, Sevare saw, looked left, while the others stared to the right whence the sound derived, though nothing emerged from the gloom. Now from the left came low-pitched, booming croaks, akin to the first call but louder, closer, even more menacing.

Sevare felt the hairs on his head stiffen, and a chill trickled down his spine. His hands grew icy cold. He'd never heard the calls of those things before, whatever they were, yet their cries were all too familiar, and with that realization a memory crept up from the depths of his mind and a fear took him. Something old, some primordial terror long dormant deep in his psyche. A gnawing memory buried within his bones, etched on his soul, passed down through the long years in his very blood. For somewhere in the grim and ancient past his ancestors knew well those sounds, and feared them, and that primal fear carried down through the ages as some racial memory that abided at the core of his being and called out to him through the veil of time, warning him to flee, to run, to live.

And then on they came, from the front and from the right and from the left; the denizens of the dark places deep in the bowels of Midgaard. Creatures left over from the old world, bygone days long sullied, withered, and best forgotten.

Each had two arms and two legs, but they were most assuredly not men. The smallest stood seven, perhaps eight feet tall; the largest well more than ten, though their size was deceptive for they bounded forward, croaking and gibbering, as much on four limbs as two; their uneven gate more batrachian than human.

Green or brown in color for the most part, their fronts lighter, white or gray, all scaly and glistening. Each had a large, ridged protrusion, some vestigial fin that extended from the crest of their heads down the center of their backs; their hands and feet webbed. But what struck terror in the hearts of the Pointmen were their heads — far oversized and narrow, dominated by expansive, toothy maws, and large, glassy eyes that moved independently and were rooted more to the sides than the fronts of their narrow faces. Their appearance was bizarre and alien and marked them part of some forsaken family tree long since lost, calling to mind an unholy union among man, fish, and reptile. Male or female, one could not tell.

But these were no mere beasts, no lowly animals pack-hunting prey — a spark of sentience, a semblance of civilization was theirs, for some carried weighted nets and bolos into battle; some held daggers of shell or stone. Others advanced with but teeth and claw. Most wore armor fashioned of seashell and stone strapped about their otherwise naked bodies with fibers of unknown make.

Knowing the carnage these giant beasts were capable of, normal men, sane men, would have fled howling, but Frem's Pointmen were no ordinary men. Rugged veterans of a hundred bloody battles with man, and beast, and darker things, their courage held, as it always held, and kept them to their duty. Only Frem's order to hold stayed the lugron from charging forward with their iron-banded spears. Par Sevare shuddered where he stood, but he would not run; he would not abandon his comrades; he would not shame his order, though on that stony ground he might meet his end.

Frem, Ezerhauten, and the sithians met the creatures as they came, swords blazing, fire in their hearts. The lugron lunged with spears and howled the same war cries as when they hunted the cave bear and the great cats in the high country whence they came. And when that wave of sea devils crashed down, the very stones of Midgaard shook and quaked. The powerful stench of the sea things washed over the men, a weapon in itself, for despite the boiling blood of battle, it was all they could do not to stoop and retch.

Tips of lugron spears shattered against the sea beasts' hides, but here and there, a weapon found its mark and impaled the things, sinking deep into their flesh, evoking high-pitched screams that were their death-cry, though these fiends met not their end with ease. They thrashed about, all flailing claws and gnashing teeth, they rolled, kicked, and clawed until they breathed their last and the spark of life finally fled. Their blood ran milky white and foamed up all bubbly when it tasted the air. Tempered steel clashed with primitive knife and claw, nets and bolos were thrown and men went down; claws raked, great teeth gnashed, and men died.

Severe ducked and spun, dived this way and that and evaded the claws and teeth. He felt the coward to not stand and fight, but he knew these were foes he could not match, not without his magic, not without disobeying Lord Korrgonn's orders. Severe feared Korrgonn's disapproval and his wrath, perhaps more even than death, though why, he did not know.

The battle lust full upon him, Frem roared and his sword crashed and thundered and pummeled the beasts with all the power of his mighty thews, but only the surest strokes pierced the scabrous hide of the fish-men, their very flesh as hard as the old stone of their isle. One great beast, the largest of the pack, a gnarled, thick-limbed one-eye, traded Frem blow for blow with a massive club of gray bone, until at last the creature blasted Frem's sword from his grip. Frem tripped it, and took it from its feet, but its huge webbed hands found his throat and clamped down with strength Frem had never felt before. Only Frem's steel neck guard staved off a quick death. Frem's iron grip found One Eye's throat and squeezed with all the strength that any mortal man did ever possess.

Lord Ezerhauten's swordplay dazzled the eye and kept the beasts at bay, but profited him little, for though his strokes carried great power, his style relied on swift, sure cuts and thrusts, and not on crushing blows. He could not easily pierce their hides, at least not fighting three to one as was his lot, so he wove a dance of death about him, moved and spun, and twisted and leaped to keep from their deadly clutches until aid arrived or his strength failed him.

Then above the din came a mighty roar. Mort Zag's great bulk bounded into the fray. Taller even than most of the fish-men and far broader than any, the red giant's axe crashed down with indomitable power and chopped through ichthyic limb and torso alike.

And then Lord Korrgonn was there. His great sword swung and thrust with inhuman, celestial power, his eyes wild as his blade bit deep in the fish-man flesh.

And then a wave of spears and swords crashed into the fish-men, the whole of *The White Rose's* shore party fell on them, the tide now inexorably changed. The fish-men croaked, hissed, and slavered as they fought, and killed, and died, but no words as we would call them ever passed their lips. They fought on until the last, without fear or hesitation, though their fellows died grisly about them. What ones escaped Mort Zag's and Korrgonn's weapons were pulled down by force of numbers, a dozen blades thrust into their eyes, necks, and groins, their hide elsewhere too hard to pierce.

The last of them was the great beast that wrestled with Frem, their digits still locked about each other's throats, the life fast draining from both. Korrgonn stepped up and grabbed One Eye's head, and swift and sure, twisted until a sickening crack was heard. The creature struggled no more and fell limp and lifeless atop Frem.

Ginalli picked his way across the bloody, corpse-riddled stone toward Korrgonn. "My lord," he said, "are you hurt?"

"No," said Korrgonn, his eyes and face still afire as he searched for more foes, his body quivering from the thrill of the battle.

Ezerhauten sank to one knee, breathing hard. "There could be more," he said hoarsely. "Keep alert."

Sevare and Putnam dragged One Eye's corpse from atop Frem.

Frem's eyes were open, and his chest heaved up and down with his breath, though he laid still, his face dripped with sweat. The upturned steel that served as neck protection at the top of Frem's cuirass was badly bent; the indentations of the fish-man's digits marred it, as a man's hand would leave an impression in clay. Blood trickled from

Frem's neck where the armor's edge abraded his skin. He lifted his hand to his neck and tugged at the armor. "Get this thing off me," he said. "I can't breathe."

"Roll over and we'll unstrap it," said Sevare. He did and Sevare fumbled at the cuirass's fastenings.

"Move aside, wizard," said Putnam. He had the cuirass off in moments. Frem took a deep breath and clutched at his throat, now a mottled black and blue. Blood dripped onto his padded shirt, yellowed from sweat and age.

Sevare checked on the other Pointmen while Putnam went to work on the cuirass, bending the neck-piece back with a pliers. "I'll have it serviceable in a minute. We'll fix it right as rain when we've time."

Frem sat up. "Never thought nothing could be that strong," he said. "My armor's solid Dyvers steel; the best there is and that thing bent it between its fingers. It would have crushed my throat in a second. In a second!"

"It's alright, Captain," said Putnam. "It's dead and you're not. Let's get this back on you before any more of them things show up."

Sevare returned, his face grave, Ezerhauten on his heels. The Commander looked them up and down. "Eight men dead," he said, "Par Landru amongst them, and two more will soon join them."

"Landru?" said Sevare. Shock filled his face for he knew Landru was as skilled a wizard as he, in some ways better.

"They took his head clean off," said

166

Ezerhauten. "Seems you archwizards can die the same as any man. Not so all-powerful after all, are you? Best remember that." Ezerhauten kicked the corpse of one of the fish-men. "We gave better than we got. Twelve of them are dead. Not one escaped. How many Pointmen do you have left?"

Frem and Putnam looked around uncertain.

"There are thirteen of us in fighting shape," said Sevare. "Two others are badly wounded."

"That's enough, I expect," said Ezerhauten.

"Who's dead?" said Frem, looking about. Concern filled his face. "Maldin, Moag, Royce, and Carroll look okay," he said, pointing at four of his squadmates that stood nearby.

"I sent Borrel, Dirnel, Wikkle, and Ward up ahead," said Sevare. "Lex and Torak are watching our left flank. Bryton and Jorna are sorely wounded. The rest are gone: Boatman, Held, and Storrl."

Frem started. "Storrl?! Little Storrl is dead?"

Sevare nodded; his expression grim. "Over there," he said, pointing. Some five yards away, atop a flat slab of stone, the young lugron's small body lay limp, his right arm missing below the elbow.

Frem lumbered to his side and knelt on one knee. The others followed him over. "Storrl! Storrl!" he said. He gently shook the lad, but he did not stir. He took the boy's remaining hand in his and held it tightly. "He was just a child," he said as tears welled in his eyes. "Stinking, fish-things! Evil beasts! He had no family left — there's no one even to mourn him, save us, and we ain't worth much."

167

"A good lad," said Putnam as he gently draped a blanket over the boy's body, leaving only his head exposed. "Always did as he was told. Mostly, anyways. I'll give him a good writeup in the annals."

"Had the makings of a fine scout," said Sevare. "Quick and brave, but not reckless. A good Pointman."

"Last of his clan, he told me," said Frem. "Some sickness took them all, winter before last. There's no one to remember them now, or him. No one to tell their tales."

"We'll remember," said Putnam. "Storrl and all the rest of our fallen."

"And toast them," said Sevare. "And not with any common ale or even Rebma Red. We'll crack a bottle of Everquist and praise our fallen Pointmen, one and all."

"Kernian brandy," said Frem.

"Brandy?" said Putnam. "The only time I saw you drink that was—"

"—up in Cinder Falls," said Frem. "After the battle, I gave the boy a sip from that bottle we liberated. He fancied it. Made him cough and turn a bit green, but he fancied it all the same. Made him feel grown, I expect, like he was really one of us, which he was after all. I told him I would buy him a bottle when he came of age. He liked that, he did. But now I never will."

"We'll drink to his memory," said Sevare, "If we ever get off this stinking rock and back to the world."

"What!" started Frem. "Storrl!" Frem bent close to the boy's face.

168

"What is it?" said Putnam.

"He squeezed my hand. He's alive. He squeezed my hand."

Sevare looked over at Putnam. "Get a tourniquet, you fool. Bind his arm before he bleeds full out." Sevare knelt down alongside Frem and held a small mirror to Storrl's nose and mouth as Putnam wrapped a belt about the boy's arm. "He breathes!" said Sevare, smiling. "Shallow and weak, but there's some life left in him."

Ezerhauten stepped up to the group.

"He's alive," said Frem. "We've got to get him and the other wounded back to the ship."

Ezerhauten leaned over and examined Storrl. "Aside from the arm, I don't see any serious wounds. He's lost a lot of blood, but he may yet live. The others are worse off. Most will be dead within hours at best. Moving will kill them outright."

"I need to get Storrl back to the ship," said Frem. "I'll carry him myself."

"We need every sword for what's coming, especially yours," said Ezerhauten. "Leave him here or carry him with us — as he's your squadman, you can make that call, but make it quickly, we've a mission to finish, and we'll be moving out forthwith."

"To Hades with the mission," said Frem. "If we're not headed back — we should track down and kill every one of these fish-things. They don't deserve to live. What in Odin's name are they, anyways?"

"The priest says they're minions of the

Harbinger," said Ezerhauten. "Some fiends he created or called up with dark magic; stationed here to stop us from finding the talisman."

"Then we've two reasons to see them things dead," said Frem, balling his hands into fists. "And another score to settle with the Harbinger."

"Now that's a good lad," said Ezerhauten smiling. "You couldn't have said it better had Ginalli put the words in your mouth. What a good little sheep you are."

Frem looked confused; anger flashed on his face. He looked to Sevare for support. "What's that mean?" Frem stood and faced Ezerhauten. "You making fun of me?" he said, menace in his voice.

"It means Ginalli's spewing more bunk," said Ezerhauten, "and you're all too ready to believe his humbug. That's most of what spurts from his mouth if you haven't noticed. Open your eyes and ears once in a while and it'll be clear enough. It's easier to blame your enemies for every misfortune. Makes it easier to hate them, doesn't it? These things were just animals, nothing more, same as a bear or a lion or a pack of wolves. Not minions of anything."

"You're a man of little faith and less imagination," said Sevare.

"Don't talk to me of faith," said Ezerhauten. "I—

"—Ginalli says what he says," said Sevare. "That doesn't change our quest. We're to help the League open the portal for Azathoth. To bring him back to us. To save the world. So what if Ginalli spews some humbug along the way. He—"

170

"—He's supposed to be the high priest," said Ezerhauten. "If you can't believe him, who will you believe?"

A tall figure appeared behind Ezerhauten and placed a hand on his shoulder. "You're supposed to believe me, Commander," said Korrgonn.

Ezerhauten turned and looked Korrgonn in the eye. Korrgonn kept his right hand firmly on Ezerhauten's shoulder; his other hand grasped his ankh.

"For I am the way and the path and the truth," said Korrgonn. "You and your brave company are my strong right arm on this quest. You are the sword to smite my enemies. You will stand beside me in a place of honor when the portal opens and our almighty father comes through to liberate the world."

A hint of a smile formed on Ezerhauten's face.

"For this, you will be rewarded beyond even your brightest ambitions," said Korrgonn, his ankh glowing softly in his hand. "But I must have your loyalty, and your obedience. It must be unquestioning. Will you follow me, Lord Ezerhauten?"

"Aye, Lord Korrgonn," said Ezerhauten mechanically, his eyes glazed over. "I will. To the end."

12

KING, COUP, AND CONSPIRACY TOO

"In Midgaard, nothing is as it appears. Nothing."
— Ob A. Faz III

The king's corridor was wide, as far as corridors go, and floored in gleaming white marble streaked with blue and black. The stone carried up the wall for three feet before transitioning to dark wood panels that kissed the coffered wood ceiling high above. Closely spaced marble columns lined one side of the passage and jutted from the wall, creating a series of alcoves. In each, was either a door or a marble shelf that displayed an ornate bust or a carving of a past king, legendary hero, or famed wizard of history, each piece more rare and majestic than the last.

Duke Harringgold walked confidently down the corridor, Pipkorn at his side, surrounded by steel; every booted step echoed off the hall's stark walls. "An entire regiment couldn't pass here if these men denied them," whispered Harringgold.

"I don't doubt that," said Pipkorn eyeing the dangerous-looking men that escorted them. The Dramadeens, the king's personal bodyguards, walked in front and behind, a dozen strong. Others lined the corridor before this door and that. They wore tabards inlaid with the Tenzivel coat-of-arms on a light-blue field, signifying their station, though beyond that, each was differently dressed and equipped. Each one, a named man of formidable history and reputation.

At one time, the Myrdonian order, commonly called the royal knights, guarded these ways, as was their duty far back into antiquity. The king had long ago lost faith in that elder brotherhood, believing them pawns and stooges for Chancellor Barusa. Instead, these past ten years or more, the king expanded the Dramadeens from what had been an honor guard of a handful of men, to a formidable core of stalwart warriors drawn from all parts of the kingdom and parts foreign, each one hand-picked by Korvalan of Courwood, their commander.

Each time Harringgold had audience with the king these last several years, he noted their numbers continued to swell. A fine strategy for without them, Harringgold knew the king would have long since been dead, his son, and nieces with him. As it was, they were virtual prisoners in the palace, leaving only rarely. Only Cartegian moved about reasonably freely — safe from most harm and intrigues due to his madness. He would never be allowed to assume the throne, so he was no threat — in fact, he often proved a useful tool in the Chancellor's machinations.

The Duke long sympathized with the king's predicament, now more than ever. The attempted assassination of Lord Theta in Harringgold's own fortress by some of his own soldiers had changed everything. His family, his fortress, and his very life were much less secure than Harringgold had always assumed. He knew that now, without any doubt, and that made him anxious, wary, and angry. Above all, angry. How many spies did his household harbor? How many assassins? Who could be trusted amongst his guards, his servants, his staff? Gods, even amongst the family? And if he couldn't trust his own, he certainly couldn't trust the king's men. But he had no choice — to meet with the king he had to leave his guards and his weapons behind. That made him feel naked and vulnerable, not feelings he enjoyed.

Pipkorn looked even more annoyed, for the guards made him submit to a search, doff his cloak, and answer brusque questions about its odd and varied contents. Threats to turn the guards to toads had no impact, instilling not the slightest hint of fear on their faces. In fact, thereafter, their searchings grew all the more diligent.

Though the corridor seemed to extend forever, eventually they reached their destination. The court herald, a nasally-voiced dandy, and the golden-armored and caped Commander Korvalan waited at the double doors that led to the throne room. The herald bowed at their approach. Korvalan didn't, but granted Harringgold a brief nod of respect before he pulled open the door without a word. Pipkorn received naught but a suspicious stare.

As the great doors opened, they saw the king seated on the fabled granite throne, hands on armrests, glinting crown atop his head. Prince Cartegian sat a smaller chair alongside and popped up as the doors fully opened. The room was otherwise empty. The herald stepped up beside them as they paused at the threshold. He struck a small gong before announcing each name. "The honorable Lord Harper Harringgold, Arch-Duke of Lomion City, Lord of Dor Lomion, and distinguished member of the High Council of the Kingdom of Lomion. Master Pipkorn, past Grandmaster of the Tower of the Arcane, and distinguished wizard of long standing." After a moment's pause, he whispered, "You may enter." They stepped forward and heard the heavy doors close behind them. The herald and the Dramadeens remained outside.

The relative unimpressiveness of the throne room never ceased to confound Harringgold. Considering the vast, ornate palace the royals lived in, you would expect the throne room to be monumental and majestic, with great, ornate pillars rising high to a domed ceiling adorned with some magnificent portrait of Odin floating about the heavens in his chariot. It was nothing like that. Perhaps thirty feet wide and twenty feet deep — large by any common standard but disappointing as the central seat of power of a country of millions. The marble floor tile from the King's hall continued in and extended throughout. Two lines of slender columns interrupted the expanse, each boxed out with mahogany panels. The walls were white painted plaster above rich walnut wainscot. Beautiful, rich, just not monumental or majestic. Save for one exception, the granite throne itself. Carved of a single massive block of stone, a deep emerald green with streaks of black and white and midnight blue, polished smooth to a high glossy sheen. Monumental it was indeed, with a tall back, wide breadth, and thick armrests, inlaid and fluted in impressive detail without joint or seam in sight. What army of men or mighty magics pulled it to its place atop the king's dais was unknown; the throne's origin lost to antiquity, though records proved it predated the founding of Lomion City itself. Many were the stories that surrounded the throne, creating a mystique that surpassed that of the kingship itself. People held it in reverence, even loved it in a way, though few had ever seen it firsthand. It was Lomion's symbol and some say its heart. More than one tale said it granted wisdom to he who sat it. Some said it granted power, which was obvious enough, or that it granted wealth, equally so. But what begot what was less clear.

As Harringgold and Pipkorn approached the king's dais, the ever-present smell of spilled beer reached them despite the masking scent of incense that burned in braziers hung here and there about the room. Cartegian scampered about like an ape, his tongue out, panting. Knuckles dragging, he charged the Duke, only stopping immediately before him. The Duke didn't flinch — he'd seen these antics before.

"Well now, what have we here, father?" said Cartegian. "A sorry lot of grubbers come calling, looking to fill their empty cups with our good wine or sample some smelly cheese, perhaps? What ho, but no, father, these aren't common beggars at all — it's old Mr. Boring himself and with him, Old Pointy Hat — where is your hat, by the way? Beware their speeches father, there's little chance of waking from the deep slumber they'll slip you into."

Harringgold ignored the prince, eyes affixed on the king. Pipkorn didn't seem to notice Cartegian at all. Insulted by the slight, Cartegian scrunched up his face. "Ah, no matter, Old Pointy's too scrawny a morsel, and Mr. Boring's hide is too tough for my troll anyway. Marinated for a full week and boiled all day he would still not be tender enough to chew, even if I hadn't pulled out his teeth. I have them on a chain beneath my tunic, you know," he said, patting his chest. "I would show you if you were trustworthy, but you're not, so I won't. I'll find a snack in the kitchens, instead. They've moldy cheese in a back cupboard that's quite tasty if you hold your nose and swallow it quick. It comes up even better sometimes. I sample it at will, as the fools leave it unattended."

"Cartegian," said the king sharply. The prince scampered aside, bowed and waved as if departing, a pathetic smile plastered across his face. Spittle dripped from his lower lip.

Tenzivel waved his visitors forward. He stood and stepped down from the dais. Harringgold was tall, but Tenzivel stood well taller. Lanky, pale of skin, bespeckled and lined. His height, distinguished gray hair, and booming, deep voice commanded any room he entered, though his voice was often slurred from excessive drink.

The king and the duke shook hands and held each other's gaze for a moment. Tenzivel shook Pipkorn's as well, though plain enough only out of courtesy. "What news?" he said, looking to Harringgold.

"Weighty matters of state for your ears only," said the Duke glaring meaningfully at Cartegian who squatted on the floor picking his nose.

"Leave us," said Tenzivel in a loud voice.

"I'm headed to the kitchens for second breakfast," said Cartegian as he bounced up. He held his chin high, a somber expression on his face. "That's why I'm leaving, and for no other reason." He dragged his feet, his arms limp, and head downcast until he pushed open the great doors and stepped out. Immediately, he popped his head back in. "Father, I've important matters to discuss with you about my cat and my troll. Matters of great and grave urgency, not to be postponed."

"Later, my son. Off to breakfast you go."

"Very well, I'm off," he said, a wild cast to his face.

"As far as this gateway business," said Harringgold, "we've done all we can until young Eotrus returns or sends word."

"Have you?" said Tenzivel. "You sent a boy and a foreign mercenary off to stop a Lord of Nifleheim — a creature purported to possess superhuman powers beyond our understanding. You gifted them a squadron of fresh faced recruits and a bag of goodies from Pipkorn's hall of surplus magic. Then you set them adrift on a pirate ship, and that's the last we've heard of them. Not a word for weeks. Is that how you've handled it? Was that your best tactics, gentlemen? Bungled it, you did. Badly. To our common detriment." The king took a long draught from his mug, not having offered any to his guests despite the tapped half-keg that sat beside the granite throne.

Harringgold's face went red. "We weren't sure that Theta's warnings about Korrgonn held merit — we're still not sure."

"The wizard was sure," said Tenzivel eyeing Pipkorn. "He believes the foreigner's words were true. If not, he would never have parted with his private stash."

"Merely some trifles to bolster their courage and raise their spirits," said Pipkorn.

"Humbug," said Tenzivel as he slapped his hand against the throne's armrest. The king emptied his mug and refilled it from the keg. "Don't lie to me, you sniveling turd. I'm still your king," he said, his voice slightly slurred.

"That goody bag held no jumping beans or marked cards, I'll wager," said Tenzivel. "Artifacts, talismans, or relics from some dark vault were they, for you turned them over in secret — to little boon for yourself as far as I can gather. No wizard would do so unless matters were truly grave."

"I had no idea your vision beyond this palace was so clear and expansive," said Pipkorn sardonically, "and your insight, so sharp."

"There is much you do not know, wizard. That's the problem with your kind; you think you know it all. You don't. You think yourselves the keepers of all knowledge, the custodians of all wisdom, to be parceled out in meager doses to those who kiss your behinds. Humbug, I say. Humbug."

Pipkorn glared at Tenzivel, his anger barely

constrained. "I may not know everything, Tenzivel—"

"—King Tenzivel," boomed the king as he smacked his armrest again.

The two glared at each other for a time. "I have news of the Eotrus expedition," said Pipkorn.

"Is that so?" said Tenzivel.

"How have you come by this information?" said Harringgold.

"I'm a wizard."

"Here we go again," said the king. "I've little patience for such answers. Have they returned or not?"

"Even now, they sail the Azure Sea," said Pipkorn.

"The Azure Sea?" said Tenzivel.

"Dead gods, that far?" said Harringgold. "How do you know this?"

"Via my command of magic, Duke. If you want more specificity than that, you will be disappointed, because I don't care to reveal my methods."

"Did they catch *The White Rose* or are they still in pursuit?" said Harringgold. "What of Korrgonn?"

"*The Rose* eludes them still. They sail in its wake to Jutenheim. Young Lord Eotrus has been gravely injured by a bounty hunter hired by the good chancellor. He may not live. Their pursuit has been foiled at every turn by matters mortal and more importantly, by those arcane. Someone is going to great pains to end their pursuit."

"Then Theta's warnings of Korrgonn's nature may indeed hold some truth," said Harringgold.

"Why Jutenheim?" said Tenzivel. "What is there of import?"

"That's not yet clear. What is clear is that Theta will not break off his pursuit, not even unto the ends of Midgaard."

"Do you truly believe that Korrgonn seeks to open another gateway to Nifleheim as Theta claimed?" said Tenzivel.

"I do."

"Then let's thank the gods they're as far away as they are."

"I fear it isn't far enough," said Pipkorn. "As grave as that threat is, there are other threats gathering of which we must speak, some closer to home."

"What next?" said Tenzivel. "Plague of toads? Rain of fire? Perhaps a gnome uprising," he said. "There hasn't been a good gnome uprising in these parts for centuries."

Pipkorn and the king stared at each other for some moments. "Thank you for the dramatic pause, wizard, you have our attention," said Tenzivel. "Now spit it out."

"I sense a darkness from the east and from the south, gathering strength, biding its time. Rumors of trouble in the mountains trickle down from the north — though its nature is equally elusive."

"Do not speak in riddles, wizard," said Tenzivel. "Straight talk is all I'll suffer in this hall."

"I've laid it straight as I can," said Pipkorn. "From the southeast I merely sense a disturbance — the nature of which I cannot yet discern. From the north, the hill people whisper of bestial calls in the night — calls not heard afore in this age. Some force is affecting the weave of magic. Something is out of balance. I can say no more."

"You've said nothing," said Tenzivel. "Babble, bunk, and bother gibbers from your tongue. If you've nothing more sensible to say, be off with you. Go practice your card tricks and sharpen your hat for I've no more patience for you. Harringgold — why did you bring this fool before me?"

"Master Pipkorn, don't spin us a tale of trolls," said the Duke. "That was fable when it fell from young Eotrus' lips, and it's more so now. He made it up entirely as you well know. He admitted as much to me."

"He didn't pluck the idea from the ether," said Pipkorn. "He merely embellished rumors already afoot."

"We can't concern ourselves with rumor when true enemies lurk in the Council," said Harringgold.

"They don't just lurk, Harringgold," said Tenzivel. "They control the Council."

"These tales I mentioned are more than rumor, I fear, or I would not have brought them up. Trolls do lurk in the depths of the mountains. Trolls and darker things too and they are stirring. Things not seen in generations. Perhaps they sense a gathering evil, or the opening of the gateway."

"Trolls are nothing but animals," said Tenzivel. "If any even still exist. Now you attribute to them powers to sense things from afar? These antics do not impress me."

"Perhaps the reported calls are from some

creature or creatures that escaped the Eotrus in the Vermion Forest," said Harringgold. "Some things that crawled out of the gateway."

"Perhaps," said Pipkorn.

"If a threat looms in the north or the south, or any other direction, we must know its nature and prepare for it," said Harringgold. "Master Pipkorn, you must reveal whatever else you know. This is no time for wizardly performances."

Pacing, Pipkorn considered for a moment. "The threat from the south is of a strange nature. I cannot define it for you; I cannot name it. All I can say is that it grows in power almost daily and its area of influence spreads. From the north, come the haunting calls in the night — whether troll, demon, hoax, or figment, I cannot say. Nor do I know if whatever it is could threaten the realm. I simply urge caution and diligence. Our borders must be monitored and protected. We must have time to react if the threat looms real."

"Your first sensible words," said Tenzivel before taking a deep draught of his mug. "Prudence dictates we not wait to react."

"Do you suggest going on the offensive?" said Pipkorn.

"A patrol of some strength at least is warranted," said Harringgold. "Equipped with ravens for messaging."

"If we give credence to the wizard's mumblings at all," said Tenzivel.

"And if the threat is real?" said Pipkorn.

"Crush it before it gathers its strength," said Harringgold. "Now we make progress, yet divert from purpose. We convened to discuss the

Council, I thought."

"A threat is a threat whatever its origins," said Tenzivel. "So long as we don't waste time or resources on rumor or figments."

"We cannot fight enemies on multiple fronts with the Counsel in disarray," said Harringgold.

"Sluug has stationed Rangers in Dor Eotrus," said Tenzivel. "Send word for them to ride out and investigate these noises in the night, if they haven't already."

"The men of Dor Eotrus will likely want little part in that, given their losses the last time," said Pipkorn.

"Sluug's rangers will handle it without them if need be," said Harringgold. "In fact, they may prefer it that way."

"And what of the South?" said Pipkorn.

"Send ravens to Dover and the southern Dors," said Tenzivel. "Tell them to send out patrols and to be vigilant."

"Do we tell the Council?" said Harringgold.

"If brought to their attention now, they'll think these matters some ruse and they'll block us," said Tenzivel.

"So we move without them," said Harringgold.

"Such is the king's prerogative," said Tenzivel.

"And what say you of the Council's machinations?" said Pipkorn after Harringgold had recounted the events of the recent council session.

"It's clear enough that Kroth's appointment

to High Magister strengthens the League's standing," said Tenzivel, "since he has long been rumored a member of their cabal. Three or four more such appointments would effectively secure the League's control over the Tribunal."

"To what end?" said Pipkorn.

"The primary function of the Tribunal, as you well know, is to assure that the Articles of the Republic are strictly adhered to, by striking down any edicts that contradict them. Ergo, by controlling the Tribunal, you can enact whatever laws you wish with impunity."

"That would be treason," said Harringgold.

"Aye," said Tenzivel. "But once they control the Tribunal, the republic will cease to exist. A despot will rise from the ashes. Barusa perhaps, or the Vizier, or some other, who knows. Lomion has stood a shining beacon in the world for a thousand years. Never yielding, never falling. And now, what could not be sundered from without, these bastards corrupt from within."

"Can their lust for power be so great?" said Harringgold.

"Envy and jealousy lie at the heart of this," said Tenzivel, "for within them reside the roots of evil. Power is merely an instrument used to acquire what they want most, and to deny others those same things. The republic must be safeguarded against this at all costs."

"Yet we must act within the law," said Harringgold, "or we would become as bad as they."

"And if they vote down the Articles of the Republic as readily as they cast aside all reason at

185

the last council session?" said Tenzivel.

"We work within the system and turn them back," said Harringgold.

"The only turning you will do will be in the grave, for you'll be dead, as will we all — unless the wizard escapes through some hidey-hole he conjures and slithers into. There's no coming back from where we're headed. If we fail, the only end will be a slow, simmering implosion of the realm over Odin knows how many years, unless outside forces destroy us first. Dictatorships and tyrants cannot stand forever, but they can hold out all too long, leaving much suffering in their wake. We can't allow that to happen to Lomion."

"We cannot halt or turn the vote in the High Council," said Harringgold. "That much was made clear in the last session."

"The Council of Lords is still in play," said Pipkorn. "The Lords can vote to block most any measure the High Council enacts, and they still control much of the wealth and military power of the realm."

"Someone must plead our case, lay it all before them," said Harringgold.

"Who shall have this burden?" said Pipkorn. "We must think carefully on this, my Lords, for the fate of the realm may well depend on our choice," he said, pacing. "Obviously, he must be a skilled orator, but also, he must not be a known enemy of the Chancellor or the Vizier, or that fact will tarnish his credibility and some who might otherwise agree with his points, may not even listen to them. That eliminates you, dear Duke, and me as well. He must also be a man of charisma, presence, and strength. A man known to the Lords. A man respected. A man who commands a room." Pipkorn looked to Tenzivel.

"It must be you, my Lord," said Harringgold.

Tenzivel shook his head. "It should be me, of course, but it cannot be. Another must stand in my stead, for if I appear before the Lords, the League will do all in its power to disgrace me, to discredit my words, and ultimately, to kill me. They have already made attempts."

"Attempts?" said Harringgold. "More than one?"

"More than a few, but my security is quite competent."

Harringgold looked shocked. "I've heard nothing of this. What has happened?"

"Recently?" said Pipkorn, looking as surprised as Harringgold.

"Last week my food was poisoned; that's happened twice before. A fortnight ago an assassin was caught climbing the outer wall. Two months ago, four foreigners made it into the corridor leading to this very chamber before my men cut them down. There have been other attempts as well. I've chosen to keep these matters quiet."

Pipkorn continued his pacing, seemingly deep in thought.

"If it were only my life at risk, I would not hesitate," said Tenzivel. "But it is Lomion's survival at stake. They will have plans in place to discredit me, pushing aside anything I say, if even I'm able to speak at all. We must put forward the right man, but a man unexpected."

There was a brief pause while Tenzivel and Harringgold thought and Pipkorn paced.

"Torbin Malvegil," said Harringgold. "He could be our voice. He's rarely seen in court, but he's well known and respected amongst the Lords, and he commands a room as well as any."

Tenzivel nodded; a hint of a smile on his face. "I had Malvegil in mind as well. I can think of no one better suited to the task."

"He may not come," said Harringgold.

"Convince him. The realm needs him. He must answer his King's call. Oaths have been sworn – and duty bound. Call him in my name and he must come."

"And if we fail to persuade the Lords?" said Harringgold.

"Then the Articles will be thrown down and replaced by writs less worthy. Writs that will remove our freedoms in the name of freedom."

"And if that happens?" said Harringgold. "Then what?"

"Then we must kill them all," said Tenzivel.

Harringgold's mouth dropped open, and his face went white.

Pipkorn halted his pacing and turned back toward the others. "Bold words from the King that hides in his palace."

"Do not presume to know my mind, wizard."

"Do not mistake me, Tenzivel," said Pipkorn. "Your words have wisdom to them, but they are shortsighted. That shortsightedness may bring us to ruin unless you see the larger picture."

"What babble is this?" said Tenzivel, his face scrunched up.

"Until now," said Pipkorn, "you've failed to see that it's part of the League's plan to force your hand. They want you to move against them. They will call you dangerous and stupid and all those that follow you, the stupider. They will name you malcontents and purveyors of hate. They will institute restrictions on free speech in order to protect the people and safeguard everyone from being offended by you and those like you."

"They can spout whatever stupidities they want in council chambers, as they did last night," said Harringgold, "but if they move beyond that and enact laws that remove freedoms, we will not stand for it."

Pipkorn smiled ear to ear. "Of course you won't. That's exactly what they're counting on. As I said afore, they want you and your supporters to move against them. That's one of their chief goals, for when you do, they will declare you outlaws and traitors, and they will crush you and yours, all the while hiding behind the law. They will use some charade to convince others, maybe even themselves, that they aren't in the wrong, and that you are. This is an old thing. It has happened many times afore and it will happen again. What's different here is that Lomion is the greatest city of the world — the greatest city since the Dawn Age and the time of Asgard and Odin. If Lomion falls, freedom dies, and may not arise and shine as brightly for untold ages. We must counter their maneuvers and we must preserve the republic."

"A devious plan, if true," said Harringgold. "But after what I witnessed in council session, I believe them capable of anything."

"And if we don't take their bait?" said Tenzivel.

"If the Articles are thrown down, they've won. That's their goal. Eliminating the opposition merely strengthens their position. I suspect if they succeed in overturning the Articles and you don't move against them of your own accord, they will find some way to murder you," Tenzivel, "and frame Harringgold and his supporters on the High Council."

"Such treason rises nearly to madness," said Harringgold. "But it's consistent with their maneuvers in council." Harringgold shook his head. "Such deviousness is beyond me."

"And that's what they're counting on," said Tenzivel, his voice quiet and somber.

"Indeed, my Lord," said Pipkorn. "These are the ways great nations fall. They must purge you from the leadership one way or another. The guile of the Alders runs deep; the guile of the Vizier is bottomless. They think many moves ahead. You must too, or outmaneuvered you will be."

"If Pipkorn is correct, my Lord, perhaps it would be best for you to leave the city. We can safeguard you —."

Tenzivel raised his hand to silence the Duke. "I will never agree to that, so let's discuss it no further."

"Then name Cartegian to the throne. Get the crosshairs off your forehead and have your son move on the League."

Pipkorn looked surprised at these words; Tenzivel the more so.

"They would kill him, almost certainly," said Tenzivel. "I'll not risk that. He may be mad, but he's still my son and I hold him dear."

"Then send him away and thereby protect your bloodline."

"No. The bloodline means nothing if a Tenzivel doesn't sit the granite throne. Harringgold — from this moment forward, I decree that your primary task is to resist the League's attempts to gain control of the Tribunal and amend or vote down the Articles of the Republic. Give this your full attention and priority above all else."

"Aye, my Lord."

Their meeting concluded, Harringgold and Pipkorn exited the throne room, leaving Tenzivel alone to his thoughts. Cartegian scampered up to them as they turned down the King's Corridor, a hunk of bread dangling from his mouth.

"Good day, Prince Cartegian," said Harringgold with a nod, though he continued walking past. Pipkorn ignored him altogether.

"Oh no, Mr. Boring, I'm not Cartegian. He was my great-grandfather. The poor old sot died years ago waiting for you and Old Pointy to get gone from the throne room. Has anyone ever babbled as much as you two? I think not. Not even my troll when he still had a tongue."

The prince hopped into the throne room, and continued hopping nearly to the King's dais. When he heard the throne room's doors close, he turned toward them.

"We're alone," said Tenzivel.

Cartegian straightened and wiped the drool from his chin.

"Were you able to hear?" said Tenzivel, his voice strong, no hint of a drunken slur.

"Almost every word," said Cartegian, his voice strong and sound as well, his eyes clear and focused.

"The wizard is wise," said Tenzivel. "He sees the League's plots and he's learned the lessons of history. He will be a useful ally in the troubled times to come, if he stays ahead of the League's assassins."

"I still don't trust him," said Cartegian.

"Nor do I, my son. Partly because he's more than he seems."

"Isn't everyone?" said Cartegian, a smug smile across his face.

13
SONG OF THE DEEP

Korrgonn stood silent and still as stone atop a flattened boulder of black basalt. That craggy rock, thrown up from the world's core in some nameless, forsaken epoch had never before felt the press of a man's foot, if the son of Azathoth could even rightly be called a man. It had lingered here through all the world's ages, untouched, unmoved, awaiting its purpose.

Korrgonn's eyes were shut. His ankh glowed softly in his right hand. A minute passed and then another, and still he did not stir.

The men of his expedition stood about the boulder, eyes locked on Korrgonn. They strove to be silent and still and barely dared to breathe.

The ancient stone beneath Korrgonn's feet began to rumble and vibrate, louder and louder, until at last it cracked asunder, fractured to its core. It crumbled to dust beneath Korrgonn's feet, its energy, its very essence drained to serve his need. But Korrgonn didn't fall as the stone collapsed — he hovered there for a moment, suspended in midair by means unknown, and then slowly sank until his feet again rested on solid stone. He opened his eyes and pointed. "That way," he said. "That way lies Dagon."

"That way goes where?" whispered Frem. "Did he say 'dragon'? I don't want to fight no stinking dragons."

Sevare looked at him, but said nothing, his

193

face gone all white and clammy.

Putnam responded quietly. "He said Dagon. That must be the name of some town or village. Probably a dung hole swarming with cannibals."

The troop reformed their lines, each man in his place, and resumed their trek — Frem and his Pointmen positioned well out in front of the others, as always.

Here and there as they traversed the barren rocky expanse, they came upon carved menhirs inscribed with likenesses of the fish-men engaged in all forms of wanton terrors, vile debaucheries, and grotesque blasphemies, sadistic or carnal. Torture and human sacrifices, even of children, were proudly depicted on those polluted stones, some painted in multiple colors, some mere primitive pictograms, some few lifelike in their skill and detail. The lines and strokes of most of the craven images were wide and clumsy — born of thick, inhuman hands.

As they traveled deeper inland toward the heart of the isle, the menhirs became more frequent and snaked a path through the barren, soulless sea of stone. The island was permeated with an overwhelming sense of age, of antiquity — in the carvings, the rock, even the very air itself.

After a time, they heard deep humming sounds, soft and distant at first, then louder as they marched on. When they neared the center of the isle, they discerned the din to be a chorus of hundreds of inhuman voices that chanted in some guttural tongue and called out to beings from the beyond.

Moag stalked back from the point, low and quiet. He expertly chose a path devoid of loose stone that could shift and give away his position. The task was easy enough for him, for lugron were at home in the high mountains, so careful movement over stone to him came natural. He signaled that more fish-men were ahead, and skulked back until he crouched before Frem and Sevare. "Two guards," he said in a thick lugronish accent.

"And the others?" said Frem.

"Can't see them. They be down some gully over the rise."

"Can we get to the guards?" said Frem.

"Their ears are on their kind, so we can make bow range easy, maybe get close enough to gift them with a spear or two. One volley is all we'll get, and if them shots go high, they'll land down the hill and we'll have the whole lot on us."

"Over there," continued Moag, "be an evil place. It don't feel right, and stinks something bad. There be two big pillars over there, bigger than any we've passed. They got some giant lizard thing carved into them, with the fish-men bowing down before it, like it was a god."

"Sounds like we're in the right place," said Sevare.

"Get the red giant," said Frem.

Two fish-man guards lay dead on the cold stone, their milky blood pooled about them, bubbling and foaming as was its wont. One lay on its back, Mort Zag's spear through his head. The throw took it through the eye and came out the back of its narrow skull; an instant kill. The other lay on its stomach, two steel tipped arrows lodged in its back, another in its leg, its head staved in by Moag and Royce as it tried to crawl away and call for its fellows.

Frem, Putnam, and Sevare lay on their bellies and peeked over the rise. Just beyond its crest began a wide stair that descended into a grand stone amphitheater that overflowed with the sight, sounds, and stench of the fish-men. The place, a vast expanse of narrow but steep stone terraces that served both as steps and seating, all arrayed in circular fashion centered about a watery pit at the very bottom. This black pool was more than thirty feet in diameter and ringed with a high altar of black stone.

Scattered around the seating bowl, the fish-men squatted and chanted unholy verses in practiced, rhythmic fashion; hundreds of alien voices rose and fell together, their bodies swayed and rocked in an inhuman, hypnotic dance. No doubt to them, their song held beauty, comfort, and depth of meaning, but to the human ear, it was a skirling, oppressive din, a cacophony of madness that caressed notes beyond the range of any throat or ear of man; their song all the more eerie for its echoes off the barren stonescape of the amphitheater.

"Dead gods, what a stink," said Putnam.

Sevare looked down on the scene before them and spit a mouthful of tobacco juice behind a stone. "Must be hundreds of them down there."

Frem took another quick peek. "Hundreds.

196

Oh, boy."

"A dozen were trouble enough," said Putnam. "If Korrgonn has us charge that lot, we're done for."

"Watch it, he's coming," said Sevare.

Korrgonn crawled up behind them. Putnam yielded his position without a word. Korrgonn looked over the rise and took in the scene below without reaction.

"You gaze now on the home of the dwellers of the deep," whispered Korrgonn. "An ancient breed, far older than any race of man."

"Never heard of them," said Frem.

Korrgonn turned to Frem, looking as if he'd never seen him before. "There's few of them left now, and they don't abide men. They prefer the cold dark of the deep sea and the depths of the earth, where it's quiet; where they still hold sway."

"Did you know they were here?" said Frem. "On this island?"

Korrgonn turned his attention back to the dwellers. "Those openings in the rock face down there," he said. "Near the bottom, do you see them?"

"Beyond the pool?" said Sevare.

"Yes," said Korrgonn. "Those lead to a warren of caverns and underground pools lit only by glowing lichen, if even that. That's where they live. Somewhere very deep there will be a passage that leads into the sea. What mysteries from the Dawn Age and beyond lurk in those warrens, no man will ever know. Like as not, no human has ever seen this view before and lived.

Mark it well," he said, "for after today, it will never be thus again."

A scream burst out, a pitiful cry of agony that for a moment eclipsed the roar of the dwellers' song. The men inched up the rise again and looked over.

"Dead gods," said Sevare. "On the altar."

"I didn't see them before," said Frem. "Oh, boy."

What struck the men's hearts cold was what lay on the grim stone altar that encircled the central pool. Atop that ancient basalt slab, stained of old with the blood of untold sacrifices, laid the mutilated bodies of the missing men from *The White Rose's* scouting party. Each wretched victim tied down and flayed open; the faces of three forever frozen in a mask of pain and horror; their organs extracted one by one by the deft knife-work of the dwellers' high priest. Their hearts laid beside them on the slab, as did their lifeblood, collected in large shells; their intestines extracted and laid bare on platters of flat shell. Lesser priests set to work carving up the innards with long, obsidian knives.

The greatest horror of all was that this atrocity was performed in part while the men still lived, for the fourth man, Sir Rewes of Ravenhollow, a young sithian Knight, still writhed atop the altar even as the stooped priest prepared to butcher him. Rewes fought with all his will. His jaw clenched, he struggled to hold back the screams, to deny the fiends the satisfaction.

Even as the men watched helpless atop the rise, the high priest sliced open Rewes' abdomen;

his stone blade cut deep and savage. The old dweller reached his clawed hand into the wound and pulled out a loop of Rewes' intestines. Powerless but to watch, at last Rewes screamed.

The old fiend, assisted now by two others pulled out the whole length of Rewes' innards intact, and placed them on a gruesome platter for chopping into footlong pieces. Their butchery completed, the platters were passed about and the dwellers each took a raw piece and began to eat of it.

Korrgonn motioned for the others to approach the rise. The troops scrambled forward, the last few yards on their bellies so they'd not be seen by the dwellers. The officers bunched around Korrgonn, awaiting orders.

The old priest turned and faced the gathered masses. He raised arms that still dripped with the blood of his victims and peered about with his glassy, soulless eyes. No emotion shone in those dead orbs, or across his stiff face, so alien were those dwellers. Their song abruptly ended and the place went still.

The high priest began to chant. Though old and stooped, his voice rose up over his fellows and boomed croaks of fealty and supplication, beseeching their dark god to grant his favor.

And then his tone and tenor changed, subtly at first, then more so. Each wizard amongst Korrgonn's group felt the mystic power of the high priest's words, though they were alien and incomprehensible. The weave of magic began to stir.

"Make ready your wizard-fire," said

Korrgonn. "When I give the word, and not before, blast them with your most powerful magics. Brackta to the left; Ginalli to the center, and Sevare to the right. We must kill as many as we can with the first strike."

"A creature will come from that pit," said Korrgonn. "A beast from the Dawn Age called Dagon. It's a thing not of Midgaard. Battle it not, for it is beyond you. I will face it; Mort Zag will assist me if he can. The rest of you are to keep the dwellers off me. That must be your only thought, your only purpose. Do not fail me, though your sacrifice be great."

"We can't fight hundreds of those things," said Frem.

"We won't have to," said Ginalli. "We have the high ground and it's wide open down there."

"So?" said Frem.

"We've magic that can deal with them," said Brackta.

"So many?"

"Two archmages of the League of Shadows can destroy a city," said Ginalli. "We have that, plus Par Sevare. We can manage them, though we'll need your swords to assist."

The dwellers joined in the high priest's incantation, and the ground shook from the power of their call. The lesser priests picked up the conch shells filled of blood and held them before the black pool. At the appointed time, they tipped the shells and poured the fresh blood, the blood of man, into the depths of that evil pit, their alien song droned on all the while.

After a time, the water in the pool began to

roil and bubble. At once, the pace and volume of the dwellers' song increased. The chanting reached a manic, dizzying pace. The sounds so loud, so pounding that the men covered their ears and prayed for its end. The dwellers' magic permeated the air. The men's bodies shook and vibrated. It was hard to breathe. Their heads felt as if they would explode. Soon the water sloshed over the altar, and then, at the very height of the skirling song, a geyser of crimson water burst forth and shot far into the air, far above the top of the rise, and a great black form followed in its wake, rising out of the well, propelling from the lightless depths. The creature rose up and up, out of the black murk, massive and dark, an otherworldly reptilian monstrosity, a thing of blackest nightmare and fevered babblings, higher and higher it rose, its bulk immense, and the world knew despair, for before them arrived the Old One, Dagon of the Deep.

14
DEATH OR TAXES

The envoy's footsteps echoed loudly in Dor Malvegil's great hall as he approached the Lord's Table with smug expression, rolled up parchment in hand. A small man, slight and balding, but not old. He was smartly dressed in the style of Lomion City bureaucrats, fabric rich enough to announce his noble birth to those who didn't notice his expensive perfume. He planted himself at least two steps closer to the Lord's table than propriety permitted; a fact not lost on the Dor's aged Castellan, Hubert Gravemare, who looked down on the little man with undisguised distaste.

"Your message?" said Gravemare, dispensing with the pleasantries reserved for more favored guests.

The envoy tilted his head and stared at the Castellan, amused, like an adult insulted by an upstart child. He turned his gaze to Lord Malvegil who sat before him, stoic and silent, his exotic lady at his side, silent as well. She rarely spoke in court; she didn't have to. After audience with Lord Malvegil, most men couldn't recall what he looked like, little less what he said, having spent all their willpower on not staring at his stunning consort's matchless curves and near flawless features. Less refined guests stared openly. Either way, their distraction gave Malvegil good advantage in any negotiation. And he used it. This envoy, however, didn't seem to notice her.

"Greetings, my Lord Malvegil," said the man, his casual words appropriate only for a high-placed nobleman on par with a Dor lord. "I am Brock of Alder, duly appointed envoy of the Crown, here on official business of great import."

"Of course you are," said Gravemare, sardonically. He rolled his eyes on hearing the envoy's name, as the Alders were not favored by the Malvegils, the feeling being mutual. "What is your business?"

"A small matter of funding," he said, eyes locked on Lord Malvegil. "The Crown has authorized additional levies." He presented his scroll and made to step closer but the point of Gravemare's walking stick poked his chest and held him back.

"No closer," said Gravemare. "Hand me the scroll and get back in your place, Alder."

Brock fingered the walking stick aside and held his ground. He handed Gravemare the scroll but avoided his gaze.

"It bares the King's seal, my Lord," said Gravemare, "the wax unbroken." He stared down at Brock. "If the Crown petitions for additional funding, House Malvegil will of course consider the request and respond appropriately in due time. If there's nothing else, good day to you, Sir."

Brock shook his head dismissively. "This levy is not optional, my lord," he said, a hint of distaste dripping from his mouth. "The High Council passed the edict, ratified in due course by the Council of Lords and signed into law by his royal majesty Prince Cartegian on behalf of the Crown."

"The kingdom's levy has stood at five percent

for generations," said Gravemare.

"Now it stands at fifty."

"Fifty?"

"And will likely do so for as long, unless the Council sees fit to raise it the higher."

"Ridiculous." Gravemare tore open the scroll and scanned its contents, disbelief on his face. "This must be a jest."

"The Crown does not jest," said Brock, his tone now all too serious. "You noted the King's seal and now see the prince's mark. All is in order, I assure you, but examine it as closely as you will. Take all the time you want. It will change nothing."

"What crisis provokes this?" said Lord Malvegil. "Is the Council raising a war chest against some enemy?"

"My Lord," said Gravemare, "the writ implies this is a permanent levy."

"Permanent?" said Malvegil.

"No Dor can operate under such a tax," said Gravemare.

"Sheer madness. Robbery," grunted Malvegil, his knuckles white against his chair's arms. "The Crown has no claim to these monies. This is Malvegil revenue right and proper."

"Legal decree gives the Crown the right to the revenue."

"What is the purpose of this, Alder?" said Malvegil.

"It's quite simple, actually. The Lomerian treasury requires substantial additional funding and you and the other Dor lords have the funds."

"Funding for what?"

"I should think that would be obvious even here in the provinces. There are many needy people to care for throughout the realm — the poor, the old, the infirm, the sick, not to mention the foreign workers trying to establish themselves, good people come to Lomion seeking a better life for their families. There are many worthy segments of society long neglected and underrepresented. They need the Crown's support and they shall receive it. It's the right thing to do. It's the moral thing to do. And this edict makes it so."

"By stealing my money?" said Malvegil.

"Not stealing, my Lord. These measures are being enacted completely aboveboard and within the law. The redistribution of revenue will be performed fairly and honorably. Every Dor will bear the same burdens, excepting those that themselves have been historically disadvantaged. In any case, my Lord, I'm certain you will understand that I'm not charged with debating the merits of these points with you. I'm here merely to inform you of the edict, to give you time to gather the funds for collection next month. No doubt, you will elect to sell various holdings to raise the sums. We understand that such matters take time. We wouldn't want to catch you unprepared."

"We will confirm the efficacy of this writ with Lomion City," said Gravemare.

"By all means," said Brock. "I would expect nothing less from the Malvegils."

"The Dor lords will not stand for this," said Malvegil. "Not one will give in to this madness."

Brock looked amused. "So I've been told by a number of other Dor Lords. I will tell you what I told them. The Crown will not suffer any defiance on this. Any lord that fails to present the required funds will be stripped of his title and his holdings. All his property will be sold at auction, the proceeds deposited into the Lomerian treasury."

"The Council has neither the stomach nor the strength to do such stripping," said Malvegil.

"You people actually think the funds you collect are yours. They're not. The council and the Crown grant you title and charter without which you're nothing. By all rights, the tax should be one hundred percent. You should be grateful at fifty. . ."

"Grateful?" boomed Malvegil as he smashed his hand on his armrest. "I should be grateful?"

"You Malvegils have wallowed in wealth and extravagance all too long while the people starve and suffer. Look at this place," he said as he gazed up at the high rafters and around the large hall. "Such a waste; the decadence. How dare you live like this when there are people starving, when there are people out of work for months, some for years? When I walk the streets and see the poor, the disadvantaged, and then I enter a place like this, it disgusts me."

Malvegil's voice went slow and icy. "No one is starving on Malvegil land and any unnatural suffering is of their own making, not mine. Look around my streets — find me a beggar — there are none. Everyone has a job that wants one and is fit to work. Any man or woman that works hard here can make a good life for them and theirs."

"And the rest are ushered out, disposed of like so much refuse," said Brock.

"A man must take personal responsibility. He can't just sit back and expect to be taken care of by the Crown or by others."

"And why not? You think a hard worker is more entitled to live, to eat, to have a family or a roof over their heads than someone who isn't? They're not, they're just different. And who are you to judge anyway? You think yourself better than the lowliest tradesman on your docks? You're not. All people have equal value and worth, no matter their skills, or station, or bloodline. Your blue blood means nothing in Lomion any longer. Times are changing, Lord Malvegil. The old system of Lords and peasants will soon be a thing of the past, a relic best forgotten. This is your one chance to do the right thing and change with it, or else be swept aside. Open up your halls, Lord Malvegil, and let the people in. Let the common folk dine at your table. Let them enjoy the comforts of your castle. It's their right and due as much as it is yours, perhaps more so. After all, it was their sweat and blood that built these walls."

"What? Are you suggesting I host a feast and open the Dor up to the public?"

"You're as dense as a doorknob, Malvegil, and only half as interesting. I'm telling you that if you truly cared for your precious people you would abdicate your position and let the people govern your Dor as equal partners alongside you."

Malvegil's jaw was set; he gripped the wooden arms of his chair so tightly they threatened to break off.

"You have given us much to think on," said Lady Landolyn as she reached out and put a hand over her husband's — a gesture that at once comforted, calmed, and restrained. "When will your auditors arrive to review our ledgers?"

"Within a fortnight. The collection of levies will follow one to two weeks thereafter, if all is in order. Shall I assume that on further consideration you intend to comply with the edict, Lord Malvegil?"

Malvegil took a deep breath and leaned back in his chair, his expression stoic once again, his voice now devoid of emotion. "The Malvegils have ever been loyal to the Crown and that will not change, edict or not. We will comply, under protest, but we will comply."

Brock looked surprised, then smiled. "A wise decision, my Lord. Follow through with it, as I'm certain that you will, and we will enter a new age of peace and prosperity together." Brock turned to leave, then spun back again. "I trust you will have no issue with the honor guard that will accompany the auditors and the levy collectors."

"Who and how many?" said Gravemare.

"Irrelevant. Merely a squadron or two. Such is necessary in these dark times — the Crown's monies must be safeguarded along the road."

***

"I was about to order the guards to seal the door," said Malvegil, tapping his sword hilt as he spoke. "I would have killed him. I would have cut him down right in our audience hall, in our home, but for your hand and your words that broke my fury and gave me the moments I needed to think better of it. You've served me well, my love, as always."

"It would have meant war," said Landolyn.

Malvegil nodded. "Had I killed him, Barusa would've dispatched an army to siege us. They may even have tried an assault."

"And now? What of his promised honor guards? Do you think they'll send only one or two squadrons as he said?"

"It will be a full brigade at least. It would be too easy for us to deal with fewer than that, and they know it. They will infiltrate us with spies and with their regulars, if they can. Once they do, it will be hard to displace them. If Barusa intends to seize control of Lomion, he may even send a full corps behind them. They will attack after their infiltrators disrupt us or commandeer the lifts."

"What do we do?"

"We do the only thing that we can do, my love. We let them in with a broad smile and open arms. Then, when the time is right, we kill them all."

Landolyn's eyes went wide. "We can't, Torbin. That will force Barusa's hand. He'll have to send an army against us. He may go after Glimador too. We can't take that chance. If we wipe out a brigade of Lomerian Soldiers, the High Council will back him, even the Lords may take their side. There will be no safe place in all of Lomion for us, and one way or another, we will lose the Dor."

"Most every path I see leads to war or to us

losing the Dor," said Malvegil. "These walls have stood unbreached under Malvegil rule for four hundred years. They will not fall under my watch and we will not be displaced."

"We can't stand against the Lomerian army."

"Aye, but mayhaps we can hold the siege long enough for them to lose their stomachs for it."

"I don't want to live on the run."

"Nor will you. I will not abandon this place. If it comes to it, the Malvegils will make our stand here, on this ground, our ground. Woe to any who try to take it from us."

"There may be another option," said Landolyn. "Take the fight to them. Go to Lomion City and plead our case before the Council of Lords. Many will stand with you."

Malvegil nodded. "That has merit. It's bold. I like it. But it may be exactly what Barusa wants. He can't break these walls, but if he can lure me out, into the city . . ."

"Dead gods, do you think they'll . . ."

"— try to kill me again? They don't like me any better now, so yes, I imagine Barusa will try again, assuming he was behind the other attempt, which I'm not certain of."

"Just forget what I said. I wasn't thinking. Your place is here."

"If I don't go, more than likely we all die."

"Not if we give them what they want. Pay the tax."

"Never."

"Not even if it means our lives?"

"Not even."

"As your wife, that makes me angrier than I

can say, but as Lady Malvegil, that makes me more proud than I say. You must go to Lomion. You must speak to the Lords if there's any chance at all of undoing this edict."

"There's a chance. Not much, but a chance."

"And if you fail? Then what?"

"Then I suppose I'll finish what my nephew started."

Landolyn looked shocked. "You mean to kill the Chancellor?"

"A duel, fair and honorable, though I'll not show the mercy Claradon did."

"I'll not hear of it. You're not a young man anymore, my love. Duels, if for anyone, are for the young."

"I'm not as young as I was, but I'm not old either. Don't treat me like some stooped graybeard. I'm still in my prime."

Landolyn raised her eyebrows and shook her head, her mouth open to say something, but she thought better of it. "I'm sorry. You're right. You're not old."

"Barusa is older than me by ten years at least. And I'm fit. Fitter than I've been in years."

"He'll never fall into such a trap again."

"His ego won't allow him to avoid it. But if it does, then I'll do what needs be done."

"What does that mean?"

"That means, if the edict isn't overturned, one way or another, I'll see Barusa dead. I'll bring down the whole High Council if I have to, but I'll not stand by and let Lomion fall to the Alders and their like."

"Dead gods, has it really come to this?" said

Landolyn.

"They've brought us to this brink," said Malvegil. "If they want what we've built here, they'll have to take it. I'll not hand it over, edicts be damned."

"They'll try. One way or another, they will try."

"And they'll swim in blood for it."

15
SUMMONING

Though he struggled to appear calm and natural, Bire Cabinboy walked stiff-legged and white-faced through the shadowy corridor of *The Black Falcon's* cargo deck, his demeanor announcing to all, or so he feared, his undeniable guilt, but since no one was about, his fears mattered naught. The deck was quiet — as quiet as a big sailing ship packed with soldiers and seamen was wont to be. Nevertheless, each moment that the ship's alarm bells failed to toll, surprised him. Each step that he didn't hear his name shouted in angry voice shocked him. Surely, every man aboard knew by now what he had done — his disloyalty, his wanton betrayal.

Not yet. His black deed only lately completed. They couldn't know yet, could they? Were they waiting for him even now in the rear storage hold, swords and axes drawn; a sack ready to drop over his head? Was the navigator already trussed up and squealing, or skewered and dead — an Eotrus blade through his heart? Perhaps his head already adorned the mast — food for the gulls. Would he end up there too, or was he too small, too worthless, to warrant even that dubious honor? They would probably just run him through and dump his corpse into the drink.

Foolish thoughts. No one knew what he had done. Not yet. The plan may yet be successful; then it wouldn't matter who knew what.

The hardest part was behind him. He'd sauntered past Claradon Eotrus' tin-cans, all upturned noses and spit and polish like all their ilk, and entered the Captain's Den, ostensibly to go about his duties as he did each day. Low as he was, it fell to him to sweep the floor, clean the soiled plates and washbasins, scrub the water closet, and endure every other menial task unfit for men of higher station and better breeding.

Alone in the Captain's Den, Bire carefully arranged mop and bucket, broom, brush, and bristle, like actors in a play, ready to emote his innocence and proclaim his punctiliousness at a moment's notice. His stage set, he focused on weightier deeds than his daily toils.

Until last week, each time that the room was clear when he entered, he would search its every nook in methodical fashion, just as he'd been instructed. The Eotrus had walked in on him more than once, but he shifted to cleaning so quickly that no one paid him any heed. Sneak-thievery was easy when no one noticed you, and few noticed Bire — short, scrawny, unkempt, and none too pretty with his crooked nose and blotchy complexion.

After searching the place time and again, Bire concluded that if his charge was here, it could only reside in Theta's locked trunk and nowhere else. Big and bulky, the trunk rested in a back corner covered by a fancy blanket far cleaner and plusher than the one Bire slept under on cold nights. The blanket's deep color and intricate pattern screamed *made in Ferd,* which bespoke high quality and even higher cost. The Captain had a

Ferdian blanket about as good, if faded from use, though he'd never waste it as a dust cover. Theta must be stinking rich to treat such a treasure so.

Same as most common folk, Bire held little love for the rich. They looked down their noses at him when they bothered to look at all. They thought themselves his betters. But for the fortunes of birth, Bire could've been one of them. Should have been. He was clever enough. He worked hard when it suited him. He deserved better than his lot. That's why he fell in with the navigator. Darg Tran told of how the League was out for the regular folks, not the nobles, and not the wealthy merchants and knights always favored by the government. Doing this deed for the League would put him in good stead. He wasn't sure how much they would pay, since Darg was vague on the particulars, but it would be a lot, he was sure, enough the set him up in a decent cottage in Lomion City, or so he hoped. He would have a bedroom, a separate sitting room, and a kitchen, like proper folk. There would be an outhouse just a stretch down the way so he wouldn't get too cold or wet in the bad weather, but far enough so as not to stink up the cottage too much. That would be nice. He deserved it as much as anyone, didn't he?

Bire stared for long minutes at that chest, daydreaming of things that could be. What treasures resided within besides what he was sent to find? Together with the League's payment, would there be enough for a truly better life, the life he deserved, the life he longed for? Enough for a ship of his own? For servants, women, and who knows what more? A smile crept across Bire's face. He would suffer no sleepless nights for having liberated the chest's contents from Theta. What had Mr. Fancy Pants ever done to deserve such riches anyway?

For a full week, Bire had worked the trunk's lock, employing every trick he'd learned growing up on the streets of The Heights in Lomion City. The lock stubbornly refused his every advance. Theta must have paid dearly for such craftsmanship, especially since the trunk was also said to float. Handy that, for sea travel. If your ship went down, your clothes and baubles pop to the surface all dry and dandy. Of course, you would likely be dead or drowned, but at least your drawers would carry on.

Bire both dreaded and craved defeating the trunk's lock, for he had some little sense of the consequences. This morning he finally managed it — all quiet, clean and proper — no damage done. With the lock's opening click, Bire's heart raced; his pulse pounded at his neck. He glanced again and again at the door, expecting someone to walk in all angry and accusing. He expected to get caught. Even if he made it clean from the room, getting nabbed was a real concern; one that had kept him up for several nights, for without the key, Bire likely couldn't relock the trunk. Next time Theta checked the chest, he would know at once something was amiss, and suspicion would quickly fall to Bire, for no one but he and the Eotrus men had access to the room. They probably wouldn't even suspect their own, all high and mighty, every one. They would come straight for him, nooses and knives.

What if Theta checked the lock a dozen times a day, knights and nobles being all wary and suspicious by nature? Or maybe the oaf hadn't given the trunk a thought since he came aboard. Who could say? This whole venture was reckless, but living reckless always gave Bire a thrill, which was half the reason he sailed with Slaayde. Too bad there was nowhere to run to at sea or he would slip them for certain. He ran like the wind and dodged better than a gnome when he needed to.

Darg said the stuff would be in a small sack or a metal vial or flask or maybe a small box, plain or fancy. Not much help that. He would search and see what was what. The trunk's pleasant scent struck Bire first. Cedar, leather, and clean linens. Bire inhaled deep and savored it. He let his breath out and took another. It would be nice to have a trunk like that. He didn't have stuff worth putting in it, but it would be nice to have all the same.

Bire rummaged about the trunk's depths, quiet and careful, always an eye to the Den's door, the fear and thrill of discovery never far from his mind. Dried food of expensive taste; carefully wrapped weapons; fancy clothes; leather-bound books and miscellaneous gear; strange devices, gadgets and contraptions, metal and wood, most of which he couldn't identify, though they looked rich, populated the chest, filling it to its brim. Hard things to sell and to pocket they were, so Bire left them. He hoped for coins or jewels but found none. Near the bottom, Bire found a small locked metal box and knew instinctively his quarry hid inside. Despite its size, the box was weighty. He hefted it from the trunk with two hands and set it on the floor. Its lock was common enough and yielded quickly and cleanly.

Within was naught but a leather pouch drawn together at the top with a leather cord — the type the rich oft used as money purses. Bire didn't open it. Not because Darg had warned him that a single touch of the stuff would likely kill him. Bire didn't believe such hogwash — not much anyway. It was all bunk and bother. Touching stuff didn't kill you, except for certain poisons what slip in an open wound. Even then, you would probably survive — maybe lose a hand or arm if it got bad enough and went all septic. This stuff wasn't poison, was it?

Bire lifted the pouch and marveled at its weight. A bag of lead ore weighed less. He cupped the underside of the pouch and gently squeezed. The contents felt loose but stony, like a bag of sand and gravel, though it couldn't be anything so common. Bire's heart raced and his eyes flicked to the cabin's door again and again as sweat dripped down his neck.

But he'd made it. He closed the box and placed it back in the trunk. He tried to arrange the trunk's contents exactly as he'd found them, though he realized he hadn't taken close enough note of what went where. No matter, the deed was done. There was no going back.

Bire made it out undetected; the stupid guards paid him no heed. He traversed the main deck unmolested, though he felt like every eye was on him and a placard that read *guilty* was nailed to his forehead.

When he arrived at the stern's storage hold, he used the special knock the navigator had taught him. A faint grunt was the only response. His hands shook and his brow dripped with sweat. He fumbled for the key Darg had given him. He unlocked and opened the door, tentatively, his pulse still pounded, not knowing what to expect.

The room looked different and so did Darg. All the barrels and crates were crowded to the corners and piled high, leaving the room's center clear. Despite his age, near enough to sixty, Bire guessed, Darg was sturdier than most, even for a seaman, but those barrels were heavy. How he managed them on his own, Bire couldn't fathom.

The navigator stood in one corner adorned in a ridiculous robe, gaudy, bright, and hooded. Where he had stowed that thing, who could say? Well hidden for certain, for in it he looked like some wannabe wizard dressed up for the bizarre. The more serious sight lay at his feet. Inscribed in chalk on the deck boards was a peculiar, geometric pattern of wavy lines and strange angles that was hard to look at without going all dizzy. Bire couldn't focus on it, though he tried and grew weak-kneed and nauseous for his efforts. He'd never seen its like. Maybe there was more to Darg Tran than he knew.

"About time you found it," said Darg. "Were you followed?"

"Got here clean. How did you know I found it this time?"

"Show it to me."

Bire pulled the pouch from his waistband and

held it up. Darg stepped close and took it from him.

"I'm to get my reward, right?" said Bire.

"You'll get what you deserve. We all do in the end."

"What do you mean by that? You're not going to pull something are you?" said Bire. He tried to sound menacing but fell well short.

Ignoring him, the navigator raised the pouch and felt its weight. "More than enough."

"Enough for what? What's in there and why didn't you tell me before?"

"You didn't look?"

"I didn't want to get dead."

"Smart thinking."

Darg carefully opened the pouch and peered in. He angled it so Bire could see inside. It contained nothing but black gravel and dust.

Bire's eyes widened with alarm. "It's not my fault, I thought that was it." Bire started to back away, his hand fumbled for his knife as panic crept over his face. "I'll go back. I won't stop until I find it — just give me another chance."

"Not so fast, boy. You did your job well and good and you've earned some truth. These broken bits and pieces might look like sorry rubbish but they're what we're after. They've got a power in them; even the littlest bits. They're holy — all that's left of something called an Orb of Wisdom. It and others like it came down from Nifleheim in olden days. The orbs got the power to open a doorway back to Nifleheim itself — to where the Lord Azathoth holds court; from where he watches us even now." Darg glanced up at the ceiling, a hand placed over his heart.

Bire stood blank-faced for some moments. "Are you serious? A doorway to Nifleheim?"

Darg nodded.

"That should be worth a lot, shouldn't it? Something what can do that must be rare."

"That power got busted with the orb by that no-good Theta — curse his black soul. But even these bits got some use. They can pull open a portal — no grand gateway that Lord Azathoth would ever use — but a small hatch fancy enough for one of the lord's servants. It won't stay open long, but long enough."

"Is that what this business is about?" said Bire as he pointed to the strange pattern on the floor. "You're giving it a go, yourself?"

"Yes."

"Some servant to Azathoth, you say? You plan to conjure up a chambermaid or butler to the gods? Maybe Azathoth's cabin boy and I can exchange notes? Have you lost it? Magic is not real, Mister. It's all bunk. And what do you know about it, anyways? You look ridiculous, by the way."

Darg narrowed his eyes. "You saw what the Eotrus wizard did in Tragoss Mor. You saw the fire what came from his hand and fried crispy more than a hundred men. No bunk was that, boy. That was power, raw and deadly. That bugger's got the juice and old Darg — I got some too."

"Everybody knows he used some ancient gizmo gifted him by Old Pointy Hat, Pipkorn himself. Probably a one-shot deal. Unless you've got some old magic thingamabob from who knows when hanging about, there'll be no mystical doors opening hereabouts anytime soon."

"I know what I'm doing, and now I've got everything I need to do it. The orb shards are the catalysts I need for a summoning."

"The shards are what? You're no tower wizard, Darg Tran. You're just an old seadog. Have you lost all sense?"

"Tower wizards don't hold all the power, boy. I've been trained up good with the magic, just as my father was before me, and his before that. The old power runs deep in my family. Just because I chose a seaman's life don't take away from that. Besides, I've done a deal of conjuring afore today. You saw my handiwork not long ago."

Bire looked confused.

"Them two creepies what attacked the Eotrus over by the Dead Fens. They were Einheriar — holy warriors out of Asgard. I called them up and I'm proud of it. Biggest conjure what I ever dared by a long stretch. I hoped they would have the juice to take out Theta."

"They almost took out the captain."

"Bad luck that was, but the captain is still kicking, praise Azathoth. Tough bugger, he is. Now, if you know what's good for you, you'll not talk against me again," said Darg, menace in his voice.

Bire took a step back. "I meant nothing by it," said Bire as he poised to run for it.

"Forget it, boy, you knew no better, but now you do. I've work to do and your help is welcome. I'll not be calling up no cooks or maids or other common folk from Nifleheim, if even they have

222

them there. I'll be bringing over a Brigandir. Ever heard tell of them?"

"Nope."

"They're mystical warriors what serve Lord Azathoth. Top troops, even by Nifleheim reckoning. Far and away beyond the power of two Einheriar. Only one as tough as that can stand up to the Harbinger. And if we're lucky, our boy will best Theta and Midgaard will be free of him at last. Once he's gone, we'll mop up his men, though even that will be a close fight. Bloody lot of knifework it'll be, but if the crew stands with us to a man, we will see it done."

"Theta doesn't seem no worse than the rest of the Eotrus lot."

"Well, he is. They're just greedy, stupid fools with mixed up heads. He's something else altogether. Not a man at all is he. Some kind of demon held over from the Dawn Age, or so they say. Looks rarely tell the whole tale, lad. That one is the most evil thing what ever set foot on Midgaard. We've a duty to take him down or die trying. And if we die, at least we'll go down as heroes. What old seadog or snot-nosed cabin boy could ask for more than that? So are you with me?"

"Aye," said Bire as he wiped his nose with his sleeve. "What do we have to do?"

"We've got to go slow. There's more to this summoning than any I've done before. One mistake, one slip-up or bungled word and the whole thing will be botched. If that happens, something else may hear my come-hither and come calling instead. Some thing from the black depths of Gehenna or the icy wastes of Archeron. A monster or who knows what. We don't want no part of that, lad. Believe me, we don't."

"If it's so dangerous, maybe best we leave things be," said Bire. "Maybe take down Theta some other way. A dagger in the back or the throat works well enough, I hear. But I'm not saying I'm the one to do it."

Darg shook his head. "Better men than us have tried that on Theta and come up dead for it. Olden magic is the only way with the likes of him. If something wicked comes through our doorway, like as not it'll try to kill all aboard and maybe even sink the ship. That would be the end of us and our mates, but Theta would get dead too. In the end, stopping him is more important than us, or the Captain, or even *The Falcon* herself. That's the hard truth of this whole business, but truth, nonetheless. If the Brigandir comes through as planned, he will go after the Harbinger and best him, the lord willing. Either way, Theta might end up dead and that's all we're after."

"It's just that we might end up dead too."

"It's not easy being a hero, lad." Darg knelt, pulled out a piece of chalk, and added to the pattern on the floor planks. "That's why heroes get famous. Some folks may even sing songs about us in days to come. They might know our names from Lomion to Ferd and beyond."

Bire's eyes brightened. "Us, famous? A song with us in it? That would be something. You think maybe someday they would put our names down in a book?"

"Who knows, lad, maybe someday, hundreds

of years from now, some folks will read about old Darg Tran and Bire Cabinboy, and how we stood up to the Harbinger and put him down or got dead trying. Either way, heroes they'll name us. That would be something, wouldn't it?"

"That would be something," said Bire, beaming.

"Now, stand by the door and keep a good watch. Not a peep from you except to warn me if someone comes."

"And if they do?"

The navigator pulled out a long knife from beneath his robe and handed it to Bire.

Bire paled. "I never killed no one," he said as he wiped his nose again. "I stuck one of the monks good back on the docks, but I don't think I killed him. My knife was small and maybe not as sharp as it could've been. What if two or more of the Eotrus come? What if it's one of our boys?"

"Improvise."

"What? What if Theta comes? What do we do then?

"Pee ourselves, pray he slips on it and cracks his rotten head. Now be quiet." When his chalking was completed, the navigator set to murmuring strange words. He placed various mystical paraphernalia about the pattern's perimeter: a stone idol of a rotund woman, naked; a flask of spirits — rum, spiced; a vial of quicksilver; the foot of a rabbit; and the mummified hand of a gnome.

"Everything's ready," said Darg.

"You sure we shouldn't do this later?" said Bire. "Maybe we're rushing into something what there's no coming back from. Maybe give it a bit more thought?"

"No, we're doing this now. It's time, I feel it," he said, a strange look in his eyes. "Now keep your teeth together and don't step inside the pattern or you will come to a bad end."

Bire stepped back into a shadowed corner as Darg began his invocation. The navigator's voice was strong and melodic. He chanted in standard Lomerian instead of one of the strange wizarding languages mages were often wont to use, though many of his words were big or old and incomprehensible to Bire. Darg carefully extracted orb shards from the pouch with a long-handled metal spoon. With each stanza chanted, he broadcast a spoonful across the pattern. Strange, soundless sparks erupted when the shards hit the deck's surface. As the spell progressed, the room grew colder and the light from the candles diminished and flickered, threatening to plunge the room into darkness. The navigator's breath steamed; icy droplets formed on his face but his chant continued unabated to completion.

> By power words and runic script
> bound of ancient oaths,
> And shards of wisdom from magic's
> weave, lately spared by fate's
> reprieve,
> I do bid the heavens' heed
> And blessed boon, turn celestial will to
> my behest.
>
> By Loki's luck, let lock be loosed,

*Of Surtur's sigil shall seal be
sundered,
By Hildskjalf and Odin's grace
Lift the sacred veil betwixt the nine
and clear the elder paths.*

*For a hero of heroes is needed now in
olden Midgaard land,
So blessed stir from sleep a warrior
born in beloved Nifleheim,
Holy and proud, fearless and strong,
righteous and golden, the elite of
Odin's hand is he,
Come now forth, oh Brigandir,*

*For without your hand we hath no
hope
To stand the minions of the dark,
For this, we beg you, champion of
Azathoth's divine spark,
Come now to your journey's end, your
trek across the worlds, from Nifleheim
to Midgaard,
Appear, appear, honored Brigandir.*

When Darg completed the last stanza, the deck beneath the pattern dissolved and fell away, though the chalked pattern hung in place, suspended in the air by means unfathomed. It hovered, not statically, but shimmered and vibrated from side to side, a high-pitched hum spewed from it. Below the pattern, nothing but blackness, an abyss impenetrable.

The navigator tossed a last spoonful of orb

dust across the pattern. The shards of wisdom glinted as they fell, slower than they should, as if nature itself sought to repel them. When they struck the pattern, a high-pitched crack rang out, akin to a shattering pane of glass. With that sound, the veils betwixt the worlds abruptly dropped. The pattern vanished and in its place, a void; blacker than black, opaque to the eye, though a flood of hot, acrid air rushed from it, scented of smoke and sulfur and odors unknown. Darg resumed his chanting; this time he mumbled a verse in some forgotten tongue nigh unpronounceable, filled of sounds short, sharp, and harsh. The only recognizable word, "Brigandir," he repeated now and again through his casting.

After a time, the blackness stirred. Its surface rippled like water. Some thing from beyond its horizon sought to pass through. Bire's heart ran cold; his breath caught in his throat. Comes now a Brigandir of the heavens or a fiend of the nether realms, none yet could say. Sweat poured from Darg's brow. He held his ground and continued his chant though his voice quaked.

From the void's depths slowly emerged a hand. But it was not the hand of a man. Long black claws extended from spindly, boney digits, seven in number on a hand of reddish brown hue. The arm whence it sprang crept behind, heavily muscled, rough in texture, more hide than skin, more beast than man. A musky, bestial odor and waves of shimmering heat came with it, flooding the room.

Bire shrank into the corner and begged the

shadows to conceal him. He thought he should pray, but knew no prayers. As he watched, transfixed, he quivered in terror, too afraid to flee. The thing crawled up and out of the pit. A head, two arms, two legs; its body, a tall, broad-shouldered mass of harsh muscle, reddish brown in color, head to toe to black barbed tail. Naked save for loincloth and swordbelt. Its eyes a fiery gold. From amidst its wide forehead extended a single thick horn of black. Its teeth, yellowed and large; its mouth the larger. Its tongue, forked, thick, and black. Incisors extended over and past its lower lip even with closed mouth.

The creature sprang fluidly to its feet despite its bulk. Startled, Darg took a half step back, and then braced himself and rooted in place. His arms gesticulated wards of protection, but whether they were naught but feeble wisps of hope or steely mantles of magic, only time would tell.

The creature extended its arms downward and to its sides, as if stretching. From its back now unfurled great wings, black, membranous, and bat-like. Its eyes, uniformly golden; no whites to them at all. The turn of its head the only tell to which way it gazed.

Heat poured off the creature like an oven. Wisps of smoke escaped its mouth and ears. Brimstone fouled the air and set Darg to coughing.

Bire pulled up his shirt, pressed it tightly to his face, and breathed through it, hoping it would stave off any coughing and keep his presence unnoticed.

"Well met," said Darg between stifled coughs, his voice quaking. "Do you understand my words?"

"Aye," said the creature after a time, its voice husky and strong. Its head turned this way and that, scanning the room; its golden eyes no doubt penetrated the room's darkest depths.

"I'm Darg Tran, son of Karn, of the old House Elowine. Great deeds need doing, so I called you down to help us set things to rights. What are you called?"

The creature turned fully toward Darg; its eyes bored through him. An expression, half smile, half leer, came across its face. "Brigandir," it said as it took a step closer to the outer edge of the chalk pattern, within arm's reach of Darg. Its hands met the unseen barrier raised by Darg's protective magics and it halted. It pushed the barrier, but could move it not. Its smile grew wider. "I care little for your purposes, magling," it said in a strange accent, wisps of smoke trailed its words, "for I have my own."

Confusion covered Darg's face. "You're only hereabouts by my come-hither — so what other purpose could you have?"

The Brigandir paused, apparently gathering its words. "Your summoning was but one move in a game far older, wider, and more dangerous than you can know, magling of the Elowine." The Brigandir straightened and expanded its chest, towering over Darg. "I am charged with ending the great dragon's existence — with sending cursed Thetan at long last to the void and freeing Midgaard of his evil. That is my purpose — so commands mighty Bhaal, Lord of Nifleheim. You've served the great lord's purposes, though you knew it not, and you will continue to serve . . ." Smoke rose from about the creature's feet; the floorboards scorched and smoked wherever it placed its feet.

"Then we have common cause," said Darg. He held his ground and trusted to his wards. "If your Thetan is the same tin-can what we call Lord Angle Theta."

"The beast goes by many names," said the Brigandir. "I will know him when my eyes gaze upon him, for evil such as his cannot long hide despite its guise."

"Good. Then by the celestial powers, I command that you do my bidding until our deed is done. Then you will be off again home, doing me no harm or foul," said Darg, taking care to keep well outside the pattern.

The Brigandir laughed — a frightful sound that grated on the ear as a wayward fingernail across a chalkboard. "You think me your creature? Your tired prattle and sorry scribbles cannot contain me, nor can your babbled magic control me. I am wrath. I am vengeance. I am justice. I am the Hand of Bhaal. I've walked these worlds since the Dawn Age, long before your lauded line began. Insult me not again, magling, or be it to your peril."

Darg's face went white; his mouth dropped open but no words fell out.

The cabin rocked as the ship swayed in the waves. "We're aboard a ship?" said the Brigandir; concern now on his face.

Darg took a deep breath before responding. "*The White Rose* out of Lomion City."

"No matter. Where hides the traitor Thetan?"

"Aboard," said Darg. "With him, a contingent of forty or so soldiers, several knights, and a wizard."

"Who lurks in the corner?" said the Brigandir, gesturing toward the shadows within which Bire hid.

"A scrawny cabin boy what works for me."

"What aid can you offer me against the Harbinger and his men?" said the Brigandir.

Darg was taken aback. "I didn't think you would need nothing to get this done. But you've my magic and my sword if you want them. No disrespect, but I need to ask — your look is not as legend tells. Not by a long stretch, I would say."

The Brigandir laughed again, as frightful as the first. "The journey betwixt the worlds is not as simple as stepping through a doorway, magling. By Lord Bhaal's grace, this form he did provide me to safeguard my journey."

Before Bire's eyes, the creature instantly transformed into the shape and likeness of a normal man — plain and undistinguished save for a tall height, wide breadth, and golden tint to his eyes. "Just as this shape better suits my purposes now, as I would take the Harbinger unawares, if I can," said the Brigandir, his voice still husky and deep.

"Smart that," said Darg, staring at the transformed Brigandir. The Brigandir's features were smooth, with little texture. The varies of skin tone, blemishes, and small lines and wrinkles that mar the aspect of all men did not afflict him. "With a hood about your head, no one will mark you," said Darg. "If we're lucky, you will get to walk straight up to Theta and stick him good and quick."

"Pray Bhaal it be that easy. But even if not, I'll see the deed done."

16
DAGON

Dagon heard the call, the age-old chant of his worshippers, his dwellers of the deep. They begged for his favor and his blessing and prayed for his presence. Merely to look upon him, they would kill, they would die, they would give all they had and ever would have; such was their devotion.

But he was tired; he would not answer their call this time, just as he had ignored it the last, and the time before that, and so often over the last age. He had neither the energy nor the desire to endure the hardships of the surface world. Each time he ventured to that alien place, he felt vulnerable and blind. It was so hard to see in the bright light; his hearing and sense of smell sorely diminished. On the surface, he drifted in a fog, only half-aware of the world around him. Even moving was a labor, all his bulk supported only by his legs. He hated trudging through wide-open spaces, exposed on all sides to whatever unknown horrors lurked about while he struggled to breathe the rarefied gas that abided there.

Not a place for Dagon was the surface world. It didn't suit him, mind or body. He was a creature of the depths and the dark. He preferred the comfort of his watery tunnels whose ways he knew so well — where nothing could venture without his notice or leave. In the depths he was king; he was god.

Better to slumber there, quiet and still, in the cold dark beneath his tiny island, his one refuge on this pathetic little sphere. Better to go unnoticed. That had kept him secret and safe down through the lonely years of his long exile. Too much time on the surface invited notice — and notice would eventually attract the ancient enemy, a dreaded man-thing that lived only to hunt and destroy his kind; a fiend whose armies shook the world and ravaged all not in their image. That creature was called the Harbinger of Doom — for in his wake came little but death and despair.

Dagon had hid for ages beyond imagining. He would not risk revealing his location now. He was too weak to fight, too tired, much too tired, devoid of energy and will.

Then something changed. He smelled the essence of life drift through his water. Blood — manling blood, the sweetest elixir in all the infinite spheres. His beloved children, always faithful, always true, poured it even now into the well of worship, foregoing their own enjoyment to gift it to him. Not just some token measure, buckets of it, fresh and strong and pungent; the living essence of multiple manlings. Not in years had his children made such an offering. His dwindling minions, still devoted, still loyal, and still strong, not like of old, but still strong.

When he absorbed the living essence of the blood, even diffused and afar, Dagon felt his old strength return. His heart beat faster, stronger. The water pumped through his gills again. The taste and scent of the sea brine mixed with savory blood ignited a fire in Dagon's belly — a hunger for manling flesh. An irresistible longing for blood and souls.

With this, his fatigue ebbed. His energies simmered and grew and this stirred something in Dagon. Feelings; emotions he hadn't felt in long years. His minions' devotion, after all this time, made him feel alive again. He hadn't felt alive in so long. He had slumbered too long. For this awakening he was grateful. And such favor should not go unrewarded.

He would honor his followers with his presence. He would relish in their prostrations, and enjoy their melodic song. He would delight in partaking of their human offering, and relish devouring the human souls and absorbing their immortal energies.

Dagon reached out with outré senses and knew at once that his labyrinthine tunnels remained sacrosanct from the well of worship's rim to the nethermost tunnel's most stygian depth, to the long passage between his solitary lair and the open sea. Nothing had dared venture into his domain — not a single fish, not one lonely mollusk, not even the older, stronger things of the black and gelid depths. Dagon could as yet sense almost nothing of the sea and surface world beyond his demesne. It would take time to fully awaken; to be himself again.

Dagon's limbs moved slowly and stiffly at first, barely responding to his will as the tug of gravity challenged and strained his muscles. But after a few moments, they became again as they were of old, strong and supple and powerful.

Dagon swam toward the ululating sounds, toward the song of his children.

The cold of the watery depths did not assail him, nor the pressure, how could they, for had he not traveled the interstellar ether and endured the nigh-endless void among the spheres, an abyss colder and emptier than anything? Had he not traversed the frozen wastes of Nifleheim, the fiery depths of Gehenna, and the ruins of fabled Archeron? In truth, these dark tunnels were a minor pleasure, a relief, a joy in their way, or so he told himself.

Soon, he glided effortlessly through the network of dark caverns and dismal tunnels that were his home beneath the isle, though in truth, the isle was ever more prison than home. He swam and swam and pulled himself through passages wide and passages narrow, through the icy depths, up, up toward the thin air and stinging light, toward the dreaded surface world.

Upward he swam. The light came into view, the blood scent grew stronger and the chanting louder. His followers gathered en masse for his glory. He heard their voices; he sensed their beating hearts pulsing blood, though they had no more soul, no more spark of divine essence than did the cold stones of the deep.

A pitiful gathering it was compared to the vast throngs of old when his children roamed Midgaard and built, warred, and thundered in his name. In days of yore, they gathered daily in the thousands, often by tens of thousands, and time and anon, by the millions, row after innumerable row as far as he could see, all for his glory, all shouting his name. Long gone those days of glory, long past. The hundreds gathered now would serve him well enough in these sad times, or so he told himself.

Dagon reached the bottom of the well of worship, the long vertical shaft that connected his chthonian depths to the audience hall that his children had constructed on the surface world to honor him. He raced upward faster and faster, eager for his children's supplication and ravenous for the sweetmeats and sweeter souls that would soon be his.

He thrust up out of the well and into the blinding light, up and up and up through the air until his feet landed atop the altar of sacrifice that was the well's rim. He squatted, perched over the well. His gnarled toes found the ruts his claws had scraped in the well's rim over the ages and anchored securely to the stained stone. He tasted the air as he purged his gills of water. He felt the hated sun on his face and cringed.

Dagon could barely see as yet, blinded by the bright light that had not plagued his eyes since the last offering, his more esoteric senses overwhelmed by the abrupt change in atmosphere. Squinting, he barely made out his beloved children arrayed on stone seats. A great cheer rose up the moment he appeared, though so few were left, the vast stone temple nearly empty. His eyes would adjust soon and he would mark them well. He would search out his favorites, the young high priest that exhibited such devotion, and the one-eyed youth — foremost warrior of the clan, though he could not now recall their names. No matter. He coughed and coughed again, and spat up more water from his lungs. He hated that choking feeling — another reason to shun the surface.

Then it happened. The unthinkable. The world exploded in fire and lightning and death. Concussive blasts burst about him, buffeted him from side to side, and nearly threw him from his perch. Waves of heat assailed him and tongues of fire singed his legs and torso. His ears rang from the blasts and were bombarded by his children's screams. His nostrils flooded with the acrid scent of their burning flesh; his vision still blurred; all his senses still dim and sluggish.

A lesser creature would have fled down the well to safety, but Dagon of the Deep feared no mortal creatures and held his ground. He heard the clash of weapons and the battle roar of men — puny monkey things that wielded metal swords, axes, and hammers. They rained down on his children, offering only death, as was ever their wont. They hid behind petty shells of steel, or shields of wood, the cowards. So tiny, so fragile, so ephemeral was man — yet so enduring, dangerous, and determined; their evil, boundless; their lusts, insatiable. On they rushed — how many, Dagon could not discern. Not many by the sound, but the timing of the attack told him all.

A cunningly laid and long-planned trap, launched only as it was at his rare appearance. To set events as this took guile, trickery, and treachery, the traits, the very signature of the ancient enemy. There could be no doubt, the Harbinger of Doom was here at last to seal his fate and send him screaming to the void. But his life would need be won; it would not be freely given, not to the Harbinger or any other. He would fight unto the last beating of his hearts.

Dagon's anger became rage, and with the rage his old strength returned, his confidence surged. He felt powerful again. He was powerful again — far beyond the ken of any mortal creature, any petty manling. He was Dagon of the Deep — he who uncounted millions worshipped of old. He who drank the blood and devoured the souls of millions more. He who slew the great wyrm Tyfus of the Hyades; who basked at Cthulhu's side and swam the murky tunnels beneath long-sunken R'lyeh; who devoured Dhak of the Lorthran, laid waste the Trigron, extinguished the Fordisnon Imperium, and exterminated to the last soul the ancient empire of Misel Tarm. He need fear little in all the innumerable spheres. Where his brethren, great and small had failed, he would not. He would crush the Harbinger and his manling armies. He would put the Harbinger down at last and send him wailing back to whatever hell spawned him.

Through the anguished screams of his children, he heard the grunts and roars of some warrior born. As his vision focused, and his other senses attuned to the alien environs, Dagon saw him. A hairless, red-skinned creature — puny, but larger than a manling, larger than many of his children. He bounded down the stone steps, cudgel in hand, and tossed aside the children that sought to bar his path. The arrogance of these mortals. The profound stupidity. Dagon would crush him.

Dagon could not name the red creature's race, but no matter, for he surely was one of the Harbinger's own, his champion perhaps. Dagon whipped his massive tail with terrific speed. The red-thing sought to duck or dodge but the tail was too large, too swift; he had no chance. He put out his puny arms as if to catch the blow; the fool. The thunderous impact swept the red-thing away, as a man would swat a bug, to crash broken and bloody against the distant stones. He would move no more. So fell all Dagon's enemies.

The sounds of battle rose around him and the terrible screams continued; his poor children burned — fools that they were for not stopping these brutes at the sea — for not preventing the trap from being sprung.

Dagon dreaded the waves of energy he knew he would shortly sense. They would herald the Harbinger's entry into his temple and begin the battle that would cost at least one of them their life. Then he felt it. A stinging sensation across his hide and a buzzing in his ears. He knew then that those sensations had plagued him, had lingered at the edges of his consciousness long before the children took up their call, but he had been too groggy to heed them and take proper course. This meant the Harbinger had walked his island for some time, plotting and planning this cowardly attack. If only he had been more alert; more attuned to the signals. He had lain dormant too long; time had dulled his senses. But now he was ready — and none too soon for he felt a searing pain in his leg. He looked down to see a manling swing a great sword.

This manling wielded something of the arcane; some weapon of the outré realms, for no common blade could pierce his thick hide. Could this be the Harbinger at last? These manlings all looked so alike and he knew not the Harbinger's face, only his vile reputation. Dagon's heart ran cold, for waves of mystical power nigh erupted from the swordsman. Energy, invisible to mortal eyes swirled about him. This was a creature of power; great power. It could be no other but the Harbinger. Somehow, he had expected him to be taller.

Dagon pivoted his torso; his muscled foreleg with claws as long as manling swords, scales as big as shields, arced down and crashed through where the swordsman stood. He hit nothing but air. The swordsman was quick, or perhaps Dagon had slowed for his long slumber.

Dagon pivoted again and brought his other arm to bear. This time he took careful aim and moved much faster than before; faster than any mortal could move — but not fast enough, for again the swordsman skipped aside. Dagon felt a prick at his wrist, and black blood, thick as honey flowed down his hand, courtesy of some unseen strike from the manling's sword. A minor wound; no more than a momentary annoyance, though it shouldn't have been possible for such a puny thing to cut open the stony hide of the lord of the depths. Before Dagon could react, the swordsman lunged forward and thrust his sword deep into his calf.

Dagon howled, for this wound stung — the

sword was long for a manling weapon and it bit deep.

The swordsman danced back more quickly than he had ever seen a manling move, quick enough even to evade Dagon's tail once and then again when it whipped around to squash him.

Dagon's anger grew, his vision still blurred from the intense light; the wails of agony of his children still rang in his ears, and acrid smoke plagued his lungs. Dagon leaned forward, prepared to crush the swordsman between jaws stronger than any mortal beast's. He would devour him, body and soul. Dagon bent low, but the swordsman was already gone. He turned this way and that, searching, but through the haze and smoke of the battle, Dagon could find him not. At once, there was a prickling at Dagon's chest, then a sharp stabbing and tearing — a pain worse than he had felt in ages beyond count.

He looked down to see the swordsman rip from his chest his beloved heart stone — that ancient token that he had plucked from the bowels of Midgaard eons ago, retrieved by his own hand from the core of a smoldering volcano. The heart stone was flat, star-shaped, and held the aspect of obsidian, but was hard as steel and thrice again as heavy. All those long years Dagon had worn it about his neck on a silver chain that eventually corroded away and was lost, despite its thickness and rare quality, but the heart stone remained, adhered to his chest by means outside Dagon's ken. Time and anon, his thick hide grew about the heart stone's edges and it became a part of him, the oldest possession of his dismal exile. Dagon had ever sensed its powers and arcane nature, which is why he took the tiny thing at the first, but never learned its secrets, never probed its depths. He yearned to, but something always held him back.

Dagon leaned forward. He snapped massive jaws and clamped down with all his raw power on the swordsman, but his razored teeth crushed naught but air for the maddening thing dashed away at the last moment. A burning at Dagon's neck announced the swordsman's next slash. Then a deep thrust took him under his chin. Dagon roared with fury even as the swordsman's blade flashed before his eyes. Dagon's lightning-like reflexes saved his eye, but he took a long gash along his cheek.

Wizard's fire blasted Dagon from his left, then from his right. Not the petty magics of some dabbler or hedge wizard, these sorceries were thrown by archmages, learned masters of the mystic arts who commanded forbidden powers that could wound even a god of the gelid depths.

Dagon's hide was afire. Excruciating pain encompassed his body. He knew the manling magic, olden or not, could not consume him, for he had withstood the nuclear fires of the heavens in his travels, but that knowledge did little to lessen the pain.

Dagon roared his loudest and the stone amphitheater shook and shuddered. As he reeled from the scorching heat, he saw the manlings flee, one and all, the swordsman clutching the heart stone in his grasp. Only then did Dagon know for certain that the swordsman was not the

Harbinger, for the herald of doom was never wont to flee. That one would never stop, never give up — not until one of the two was dead. This swordsman was an imposter, some upstart; a brazen thief and red-handed slayer. It mattered not, whoever he was, Dagon would see him and his minions dead, one and all.

More wizards' fire blasted Dagon from one side and then another; this time, from a distance, as the cowardly wizards fled. He looked down and saw the robes of his high priest, but within them was not the young dweller he favored, but the broken body of an ancient creature, all wrinkled and gnarled, lying lifeless on the cold stone, stabbed and sliced by manling swords. His lifeblood pooled about him. Dagon leaned down, his face just feet from the corpse. He recognized his features, changed as they were by long years. His children lived long and aged slowly. They survived several spans of a manling's life before the void took them. How long had he slumbered for the priest to age so? Could it be so long since his last awakening? Dagon shuddered and his anger grew.

He had had enough. He would not suffer such humiliation or loss. He bounded from atop the altar and up the amphitheater's steps, taking many at a time, though his legs were weak in the unaccustomed atmosphere. The tattered and smoldering bodies of his poor children lay strewn about the stone tiers. If only he had arrived but a few minutes earlier or the manlings' attack come a few moments later, his sight and other senses would have been clear, the slumber would've been gone from his mind, the water fully purged from lung and gill, and his limbs would've been limber and strong again. Then he would have defended his children. The manlings would have met his full wrath and suffered it, wizards' fire or naught. But the timing of their assault had been too perfectly planned. Now his children were gone, wiped from the face of Midgaard. He could do nothing for them now, for not even one stirred; no spark of life remained in any. What was he without them? A god with no worshippers? How far he had fallen. He hoped that some few had escaped so in years to come, things could be again as they had been long ago. No matter, he would go on without them if need be. He could do naught else; he was Dagon.

Dagon reached the crest of the small valley that housed his temple, and gazed at the barren, uneven stone jungle beyond. He saw the pack of manlings scurrying away, cowardly vermin that they were. He charged after them with massive strides and explosive speed, the smell of manling blood urged him on, but the lingering effects of his long slumber yet hampered him. His lungs were still awash with water and sent him into coughing fits that slowed his pace. He was dizzy and his vision was still not fully clear. He careened now and again into rocky outcroppings and carved menhirs, his legs unsteady. The old stones of the isle slowed him but could not hope to stop him, his momentum relentless. With each impact, stone shards and massive boulders flew in all directions. Dagon ignored these annoyances and barreled forward, determined to exact vengeance.

He had not gone far before he caught a straggler — a fragile, sorry thing that hid within a suit of flimsy red metal. It hobbled along, trailing blood, part of its armor torn away. At least the children made some account of themselves before their end. Dagon's great foot rose up. The manling must have seen the shadow pass over him. He must have known his doom seconds before that massive foot slammed down and crushed him to pulp.

Dagon was on the rest at once. Before long, he had squashed another red-clad and took solace in its death scream. The smell of the thing renewed the hunger in Dagon's belly and displaced his anger ever so slightly. Then he caught a third. It looked tasty enough, so he wrapped his tail about it, lifted it to his maw, and bit it in two. The metal made the meal distasteful, but not inedible. Dagon spit most of it out, not wanting to waste the effort to chew the crunchy thing, though he savored the warm and delectable juices. Vengeance was sweet.

He sprang after the manlings once more, and came upon a sorry group that struggled along, carrying the red creature from the battle's start. For a fleeting moment, Dagon thought it strange that such primitive, heartless things carried away their dead. Then he realized that the red creature was their dinner. A savory prize to char over a fire, hung from a spit. Cold savages were they, cannibalism more proof of it. Only one amongst this group, the largest, wore metal armor — dull silver it was, not red and shiny like the others that still stuck in his teeth. This morsel would prove just as hard on his jaws, and not nearly as tender as his soft-shelled companions, but Dagon decided to sample him nonetheless. He swooped down and opened his jaws wide, but at the very last moment, without thought or intent, Dagon veered to the right, as if some unseen force nudged him, and his jaws instead found the head of a different manling. How this happened, Dagon did not know. No matter, for this one wore no annoying metal shell. Less tough, but just as sweet.

Dagon halted and lingered over this morsel far longer than he should. He forgot for a time his purpose, though he would have preferred to linger even longer and take a goodly rest. He grew tired of the chase. His pace slowed, but he remained determined to run the manlings from his isle, or catch and kill them all if he could. He trudged on until he reached the great lagoon. He stepped onto the black sand beach at the water's edge, marveled at the sights he saw. His roar so loud the heavens shook.

Dagon's hunger lingered, as did his anger, and his need for vengeance, but with his first step into the water, he sensed a presence he had not sensed in eons. An olden fear welled up from deep in his belly. An ancient entity of great power lurked on that ship of puny manlings. Dagon suspected what it was, but not why it was there. And then he realized that it was the heart stone the manlings were after from the first, no doubt at the behest of what abided on that ship. But for what purpose? To what end? Such questions vexed him, for he had no patience for intrigues. It was wiser to forego his hunger, put aside vengeance, and let the manlings slip away. But allowing them to escape came with its own consequences. They might spread word of his presence on the island. Eventually, the Harbinger would hear. Eventually, he would come.

Dagon watched the ship for some time before deciding what he would do.

***

The survivors of *The White Rose's* shore party fled for their lives across the desolate stonescape. Dagon of the Deep, a massive and monstrous being that had haunted the nether regions of Midgaard since the Dawn Age thundered at their heels. Dagon's every step shook the very stones beneath their feet and his bellowing near deafened them. The battered and exhausted men limped toward the beach as swiftly as they could, desperate to reach their longboats, trailing sweat and blood all the way.

Near the middle of the troop, Sergeant Putnam carried Little Storrl's limp form in his arms. By the lord's grace, the young lugron still lived and mercifully remained unconscious. Par Sevare staggered along beside them, supported by two of the Pointmen. His arms were at once numb but yet afire with pain from the magics he had lately thrown. His eyes were glazed over and he looked about to pass out.

Not far behind them, Frem and five burly lugron carried Mort Zag. Their every step was agony for the red giant weighed more than

249

several large men. One titanic blow from Dagon's tail had sent Mort Zag flying through the air. For him, that one blow ended the battle, and perhaps his life. For all Frem's great strength and skill, he would fare little better against such a monster. He couldn't hope to even fight it, little less defeat it. Might as well fight a mountain. And so he fled. Not often in his life had he run from anyone or anything. He was always the biggest and the strongest and the toughest. Not today.

Stranger still for Frem to see archmages and Azathoth's high priest with fear-filled faces. They fled with the rest, terror in their hearts. Strangest of all, to see the son of Azathoth, despite all his divine powers, running for his life. Disheartening in a way. Disappointing, though Korrgonn's face harbored no fear that Frem could discern.

A scream some distance behind Frem was quickly silenced, as was Dagon's pursuit. Frem thought to look back, but before he did, the booming footfalls began anew, signaling Dagon had renewed his chase.

Every step across the unforgiving stone jarred Frem's knees and the heavy burden he bore left his legs rubbery and weak. His arms ached as he struggled to maintain his grip on Mort Zag's arm and shoulder. Stinging blood dripped into his right eye, though he knew not if it was his or some other's. Every now and again one of the lugron with him would lose their hold or their footing and go down. The others kept moving; the falterer expected to catch up and resume his position. True to his duty, each man did.

More than once, the entire group stumbled

and crashed to the punishing stone. This brought Frem to the brink of panic, for each time they fell, more men passed them and put him closer to the rear of the group, closer to the roaring, bellowing, nightmarish death that hounded them. The overtakers could have relieved Frem's exhausted squad, but they didn't, they ran on and gave them barely a glance, if even that. Who could blame them, they weren't racing to outrun Dagon, for its great strides were too long, its powerful legs too swift. They ran to outpace their fellows so when Dagon caught and killed the group's stragglers, it would not be them. Every man amongst them knew this and every man fought to not be the straggler.

Frem could have carried Little Storrl instead of this red behemoth. With Storrl laid over one shoulder, he would have been halfway back to the beach by now and in no danger of becoming lizard food. But his honor wouldn't allow it. He couldn't let his men struggle with a burden that he feared to take on, so he had only himself to blame for his current predicament. Frem felt ashamed to do it, but each time they stumbled, he looked for the rise and fall of Mort Zag's chest. Contrary to all he valued, and only born of fear and desperation, he hoped to find Mort Zag's breathing halted, so he could be done with him and free of this burden without guilt or dishonor. He would gladly risk his life to save a comrade, even one that he never called a friend, but he would not die to carry a corpse.

Another scream assailed Frem's ears. He turned to see Dagon's tail wrapped about a sithian not ten yards back. It lifted the struggling man high in the air, and tore him in two with a single bite.

To Frem, this was madness. The whole ordeal surreal. He had fought more than a hundred campaigns and traveled farther and wider than most any man he knew. He had known death in its myriad forms. He had seen countless die at other men's hands. He had seen them fall to beasts, poison, disease, accident, and weather. But until Ezerhauten had hired the Sithian Company on with the League of Shadows, he had never seen a man die by myth or legend, monster or magic. How could he, for such things didn't exist — not in his sane, civilized world. But there was a secret world that lurked behind the shadows, well past reason, and just beyond sanity. He knew that now. Here resided the likes of Dagon, and the seaweed creature, the fish-men, the gargoyles of The Keeper's caverns, the skeletal messenger that Thorn had conjured, and who knows what many monsters more. Now, of a sudden, such creatures seemed everywhere, as common as dirt.

And magic — what he thought was the realm of card-tricksters, palm readers, herbalists, and assorted charlatans, was so much more. Real wizards lurked about — people like Par Sevare, Par Brackta, Father Ginalli, and Glus Thorn. At will, they launched blasts of fire and lightning and incinerated armies. They conjured creatures from other worlds to do their bidding. How could this be? Despite all his travels, he knew naught of such things. He had never seen their like before, save

252

for some small trickeries Sevare had displayed in past missions. He had only heard tell of them in children's tales and ghost stories whispered by the campfire. Frem no longer knew what was real. Was he lost in a nightmare? Did a fever grip his mind? Had death somewhere caught him and tossed him in some personal hell?

Frem and his group were the stragglers now. Dagon's pounding steps grew closer and closer. Its bellowing louder and louder, nearly on them.

They kept hold of Mort Zag and sprinted over the ancient stones. Adrenaline carried them forward at a superhuman pace. Frem urged the men on and pushed them to beyond their limits. Of a sudden, Frem felt a blast of air at his back and a sour, fishy scent washed over him. Something brushed his shoulder. *This is the end.* He looked over, and Dirnel, the tall lugron that ran beside him, was gone. He glanced back, and saw Dirnel enveloped in Dagon's giant, clawed hand. The beast effortlessly lifted him to its mouth, which stood agape and slavering, large enough to swallow him whole. Frem wanted to turn and fight, but the very thought was foolish and futile, for Dirnel was surely already dead, crushed in that unforgiving embrace. Another Pointman dead. Another of his men dead.

It could've been me. What whim of chance or twist of fate made the beast choose Dirnel, Frem could not fathom, but such thoughts plagued his nightmares forevermore.

The group staggered forward, their burden the heavier for the loss of Dirnel. Frem didn't even know whether they ran in the right direction. He trusted the men in front to steer their course. For the first time he noticed the strange echoes their boots made as they ran across the isle's old granite. Their steps induced a rhythmic pounding that reverberated off the surrounding stones. It amplified their footfalls and made them sound like a charging army. After a goodly time, the echoes were interrupted by Dagon's booming footfalls, now far in the distance. He'd finished his latest meal and hungered for more.

17
MALVEGIL

Lady Landolyn, consort of Lord Torbin Malvegil bolted upright in bed, her face pale, her hair askew, eyes wide with fear. Half-asleep, nightclothes disheveled and sans makeup, her beauty and youthful appearance were barely diminished. She was still blessed with the same unlined, glowing face, and melodic voice she had twenty-five years before when she married Malvegil, and in fact, now looked barely older than their son. "Torbin!" she said as she smacked her husband's back to rouse him. "Torbin, get up!"

"Don't hit me," said Lord Malvegil into his pillow, still half asleep. "What is it, another stinking dream? I need my sleep. Tell me in the morning."

Landolyn scowled. "Don't do that," she said sharply and smacked his shoulder. "You always act like I'm making it up. You know the women of my House have the sight. We've always had it. Now get up."

"More dire predictions of the future?" he said, his face still buried in the pillow.

"The present. You had best pay heed."

Malvegil sighed, turned onto his back, and rubbed the sleep from his eyes. "I'm sorry, alright. I know your visions of the present are almost always true."

"Not almost always. Always."

Malvegil sighed again. "I stand corrected.

What did you see?"

Landolyn's scowl remained. "Our son is in distress, if you even care," she said, her eyes glassy.

Malvegil sat up and turned toward her. He stared into her eyes, his full attention now focused. "Tell me. Does he live?"

"Of course he's alive. Do you think I would be sitting here arguing with you if—"

"—so what is it? What's happened?"

"It's hard to see. At first, I thought it was just the distance, but it's not. There's a veil of magic hanging over Glim's expedition. It clouds my sight, obscuring things."

"What can you see?"

"There's been fighting. Our boy's been in battle, Torbin. More than one. He's in pain and something has frightened him more than anything in all his life. But he's alive, and not badly hurt, thank the gods."

"Where is he?"

Landolyn's eyes narrowed and she looked past her husband, her eyes focused on vistas unseen by normal eyes. "Far away. Beyond this continent. Out at sea, the Azure Sea."

"The Azure? Dead gods, this I did not expect. Where in Odin's name are they going?"

She shook her head. "I cannot hope to tell."

"And Claradon? How fares my nephew? Can you tell?"

"I don't know," she said as she shook her head. "I tried to find him, to touch his mind, but at such a distance, with that mystic fog draped over them, I can't do it. I can't sense anyone there not of my blood."

"What is this fog you speak of?"

"It's as if a spell has been cast over them to mask their presence or their progress. It clouds their future. It's a sinister thing — dark magic. From whence it came, I cannot tell. It makes me feel helpless."

"Glim will be alright and he'll look after Claradon. After all, you've trained our boy well, haven't you?"

Landolyn looked surprised and searched her husband's eyes.

"Did you think I didn't know?" he said. "All those hours up in the south tower. You two disappeared over and again with little explanation. History lessons you claimed. Sometimes, mathematics. Then, for years it was lute practice. The boy can't pluck a single note to save his life. How daft do you think I am? You've many talents, Landolyn, but lying has never been one of them."

Landolyn's mouth was open in surprise.

"You keep your grimoires, your baubles, and bunk in that tower. Locked in some closet marked winter undergarments or some such foolishness. Do you think I don't know my own keep? I know its every crack and cobweb. You've kept nothing from me. It was magic you taught Glim up there, and little else. Trained him up right and proper in the olden magic of House Adonael."

"And if I did?" she said, wincing.

"Then you've given him a better chance to live through what he and Claradon are facing. The magic they taught those boys at the

Chapterhouse is no match for the olden stuff. I know that much. I taught him to use sword, dirk, and shield. You've armed him just as well, maybe better. You really didn't think I knew?"

"I was certain you didn't. I was sure you would never approve. You said you didn't want him to be a wizard. You said you would never allow it. You threw a fit over it more than once when we talked of it."

"I did. And so he's not a wizard. He's a knight, a warrior, born and bred. One of the best. And it just so happens he can also toss an old elvish spell or two when the need arises. How could I disapprove of that?"

She shook her head and smirked. "You've surprised me again, husband."

"Then after all these years you've still more to learn about me, my love." He leaned over and kissed her gently on the lips. She quivered at his touch, as she always did, her heart racing, then returned the kiss, passionately. Malvegil reached over and turned down the oil lamp beside the bed.

"Is there anything more you can tell me of the other dreams you've had the last few nights?" said Malvegil.

"I've gone over it a hundred times in my head and tried to remember more," said Landolyn. "There just aren't any details. All I know is that there's an evil rising in the east, another in the south, and a third in the north. The portents are there, but things aren't clear. Lomion is threatened on all sides, but perhaps the gravest threat is from within, as you well know."

A knock came at their door, despite the early hour. It was Gravemare. He presented Lord Malvegil an official missive from Lomion City. Malvegil unfolded the note and read it slowly, more than once, before he spoke. "Harringgold summons me to Lomion City. He wants me to speak before the Council of Lords. He says Barusa of Alder is moving to amend the Articles of the Republic."

"Can this be true?" said Landolyn, turning to Gravemare. "Can he do that?"

"The Articles have provisions for change, my Lady," said Gravemare. "Any such document must allow for the people to amend it, as times warrant, though the core and spirit of the original must remain sacrosanct."

"What changes do they intend?" said Landolyn. "And what does this mean for us?"

"Harringgold doesn't say," said Malvegil. "But anything Barusa is for can't be good for the republic."

"Could he get the votes?" said Landolyn. "Does he have that much support?"

"It must be close, or Harringgold wouldn't ask this of me. He knows what happened the last time I was in the city. He must think I can sway enough votes to put down this measure."

"If any man can, it's you, dear."

"There are others that can do this thing. He doesn't need me."

"I don't understand," said Landolyn. "You already decided to go to the city and to speak to the Lords. Why change your mind now?"

"That was when it was my idea. Now it's his.

Now if I do it, it's in response to a summons. Who does he think he is, summoning me to court?"

"He thinks he's the arch-duke of the realm, Torbin, and one of your oldest friends."

"I don't like it. Let him speak to the Lords himself. As you said, he's the Duke. Why should I do his job for him?"

"If I may, my Lord," said Gravemare. "Harringgold is Barusa's chief rival in all things. Their two factions will line up against one another. Most of those not so aligned will abstain, just to keep out of the fray. Things have been like that for all too long as you well know. The man to persuade the Lords must be an outsider to the Lomerian Court. Despite your long friendship with the Duke, you will still fill that role in the eyes of many. The independent Lords may well follow you."

"Aye, I know these things. I just don't like to be told what to do. It doesn't sit well in my stomach, not at all."

"Torbin — Jhensezil is no talker; Sluug is a soldier, not a statesman. Mortise doesn't have the charisma that you have. It must be you. There is no other."

"Aye, it must be me. So much for making a surprise entrance. No doubt, all of Lomion City is already waiting for me on their stoops, a great party in full swing at the city gates."

"The letter was sealed, my Lord, with the Duke's crest, unbroken," said Gravemare. "Its contents may yet remain secret."

"Doubtful," said Torbin. "This is not Harper's hand," he said, gesturing at the missive. "He must

260

have dictated to one of his aide's. Such men can be bought."

"Then you must go in force," said Landolyn. "A full brigade of our finest."

"Two brigades," said Gravemare. "It would take an army to waylay you with that many Malvegils at your side."

"I can't ride into Lomion City with a force like that."

"Have them escort you to within sight of the walls, then proceed with a picked squadron," said Gravemare.

Malvegil nodded. He paced the room for several minutes without a word. Landolyn and Gravemare stood waiting for some sign or statement. At last, he stopped before them. "I'll leave in three days. Hubert — see that the men are ready, but keep close our plans."

18
OLD ELVISH MAGIC

Ob jerked awake with a moan and bounced to his feet, scattering the collection of empty wine bottles beside his chair. Startled, Kayla nearly fell from her seat beside Claradon's sickbed. Ob winced and clutched his shoulder. Sweat formed on his brow.

"What happened?" said Kayla. "Are you alright?"

Artol, his face a bruised and swollen mess from his battle with DeBoors, reclined in a plush lounge chair beside a round table on the far side of the room. Glimador sat a similar chair nearby. They looked at Ob, his wine bottles, then each other, and shook their heads.

Ob ignored Kayla and paced the cabin floor, his breathing labored. All the while, he stared at his feet, rubbed his shoulder, and stretched his arm. "Something's coming," he said after a time, but whether to himself or the others, it wasn't clear. "Some stinking thing. Not good at all."

"What do you mean?" said Kayla. "What's coming?"

Ob halted before the bed. His eyes lingered on his unconscious liege for a moment and then bored into Kayla. "You have a weapon, lass?"

Kayla shrank back — a confused look on her face. "I wouldn't hurt him," she said, an edge to her voice. "Why would you even ask me that?"

"Have you got a weapon?" said Ob loudly, his

face pale and careworn.

"I've got a knife," she said as she pulled out a long, wood-handled blade from a bootstrap.

"Keep it close," said Ob. He walked to the cabin's door. "Something's coming. I need all of you to keep alert. Be ready for anything and keep him safe. Lock the door behind me," he said, exiting, his face filled with worry. "And bar it."

"Where are you going?" said Artol.

"To get Mister Fancy Pants," said Ob. "We'll be needing his sword."

"Is he drunk?" said Glimador as he bolted the door.

"No more than usual, I expect," said Artol. "But when his short hairs start rising, something bad is about to happen. Best we be on our guard."

***

Darg Tran walked the cargo deck's gloomy hallway, dressed again in his seaman's garb, and steered for the back stair. The Brigandir closely followed. Bire Cabinboy shadowed them, nervous and fidgeting.

Of a sudden, the door to the storage hold up ahead swung open and the distinctive voice of Bertha Smallbutt flooded the passage. "Did the crew nick it? Best you tell me now, for I'll have your hide if you hold out on me."

Darg froze — there was no time to slip out of sight. Several steps behind, Bire squeezed into a tiny, cleaning closet, though he turned immediately about and peeked out to see what went on.

Old Mock, a grizzled sea dog that had served with Slaayde for years stepped out of the hold, an annoyed expression on his face. "If the captain's stash got sampled, I would have heard, and I've heard nothing," he said. Mock glanced but a moment at Darg, his attention consumed by the banshee at his back. The Brigandir nudged Darg forward. The navigator continued down the hall and tried to act natural.

"Out of my way, you dolt," shouted Bertha as she pushed a second man into the hallway. That one, a young tough called Eolge, didn't have much smarts, and less to say, but was good in a scrape. Bertha stormed out of the hold, bristling, and scoured through the dog-eared ledger she held, her girth blocking most of the passage. Darg swore she grew an inch wider with each passing month. "The onliest other place it might be is the rear locker, unless some scalawags got into it, and if they did, they will rue the day that I catch them."

She looked up from her ledger and made eye contact with Darg, now just a few feet from her group. "By the luck of the Vanyar, just who I needed," she said from behind Eolge and Mock. "Darg — have you got my keg of Minoc Blue in the rear locker? I'm fixing to bring it to the captain to lift his spirits."

"Nope," said Darg. "No spirits at all back there. The last was that case of Kernian Brandy the captain called up months ago. Now it's as dry as a bone back there. Did you try the closets off the main hold?"

"Dagnabit! I had that one saved up for three

years at least. Some scum nicked it for certain. Fine thing to do when the captain's half-dead and has a need. I'll hang them from the yardarm by their privates — that'll fix them." She rolled up her ledger and stuffed it under her arm in disgust. "Who's that tall one with you? One of the Eotrus?"

"He's the young lordling's man — he got turned about and I'm setting him straight."

"No need for a hood in here, deary, it's dark enough," she said to the Brigandir with a smile, her voice softening. "Show us your face won't you — I like to see who I'm sailing with." She smiled from ear to ear, all white teeth and dimples.

"He's late for something, Bertha. No time for flirting with you, however fun that might be," he said with a wink.

Bertha rolled her eyes at Darg's remark and waited for the Brigandir to pull back his hood or respond in some way, but he stood rooted and silent.

"Fine, be all secret and rude," said Bertha, the edge returning to her voice. "I don't fancy tin-cans, anyways. Just stand aside. I'll scour the rear locker myself before I give up on that keg. Move it, I've no more time to waste with you."

"Wait," said Darg, holding his hand out. "My charts are laid out on the floor, arranged how I need them. I can't have them walked on or moved. We're on a tough course — we can't afford any mistakes. In any case, I'm quite sure the keg is not there."

"I'll be respectful of your charts," said Bertha. "I won't even let these dullards in, unless I find the keg. Now be a good man and stand aside."

Darg hesitated, his face reddening. "It was Tug."

Bertha's eyes narrowed. "What? Are you saying that Tug nicked my keg?"

"I'm no stoolie, but I can't have you walking on my charts. He had one too many one night and went looking for something better. Busted the Blue open, sloshed the floor with most of it, and chugged the rest until he passed out in his cups. Guj and a couple of others slopped up whatever was left. Don't tell him I told you — he'll toss me into the drink, or worse."

"Don't worry on that, Darg Tran. That big turd will be scrubbing the lower decks with a brush for the next month at least."

Relief washed over Darg's face. The arcane pattern on the rear locker's floor would remain secret for now — it needed to, at least until they found Theta, or else the alarm might be raised and the element of surprise lost. Unfortunately, Bertha noticed Darg's reaction. "Is there something you're not telling me?"

"Nothing. What do you mean?"

"Fine. I think I'll just have a quick look at the locker anyhow. Stand aside."

Nearly panicking and out of excuses, Darg pressed against the passageway's wall to give her room to squeeze by, but the Brigandir didn't budge. His broad shoulders squared across the hallway.

"Stand aside, tin-can," said Eolge sharply.

The Brigandir shook his head dismissively. "It is you that should stand aside," said the Brigandir, his voice deep and menacing. "You've delayed me too long already."

"What's this?" said Bertha.

"Come on, laddie," said Old Mock. "Don't be making any trouble. There's no call for that. You be a guest on this ship, and Bertha's our Quartermaster — an officer, so you best show some proper respect, or your Lord will hear of it."

"My lord is not on this vessel," said the Brigandir, "and respect is what you show your betters, not sea scum."

Eolge put his forearm to the Brigandir's throat and tried to shove him against the wall, but the Brigandir brushed his arm aside, and shoved him back. Despite Eolge's bulk, he careened into Old Mock and both men went down on their rumps. "Dare not touch me again," said the Brigandir.

"Oy," shouted Bertha. "There's been enough fighting on this ship. Stand down!"

Eolge bounced up and returned the Brigandir's shove with a double-handed one of his own. Surprise filled Eolge's face when the Brigandir didn't budge. Eolge's hand moved toward the hilt of his sword. In the next instant, the Brigandir's short blade penetrated clear through Eolge and lifted him into the air.

Blood splattered over Bertha and Old Mock as they gaped at the scene in shock.

"I forgave your first transgression," said the Brigandir, "but not again."

Eolge's mouth moved, but only gurgling sounds seeped out. His eyes bulged with shock; his hand gripped the Brigandir's as if to push it back and pull the blade out.

"Murder!" cried Old Mock. "No-good stinking

267

tin-can!"

Bertha screamed — a bellowing, high-pitched wail that would've been the envy of the banshee queen herself. Blood spatter dripped down her forehead and cheeks onto her nose and lips as she stumbled backward in a panic and fell on her rump. She scrambled to her feet, turned, and scurried down the hall with surprising speed — Old Mock just steps behind her.

With Eolge still held aloft, the Brigandir flicked his arm forward and Eolge slid off the end of his blade. He flew through the air for several feet before hitting the deck with a loud thump. His body twitched and spasmed as the last of his life left him.

Staring at Old Mock's back as he fled, the Brigandir spun his sword, and threw it underhanded. It struck the seaman just below his right shoulder blade.

Old Mock grunted in pain and stumbled against the corridor's wall, which dislodged the sword. He staggered on after Bertha, glancing over his shoulder in terror and disbelief as he ran.

At the end of the hallway, Bertha pulled the heavy rope that sounded the ship's alarm bells. That chord rang a chain of bells that could be heard all the way to the bridge deck. Its tone identified from which deck the alarm was pulled.

"Get up the ladder," said Old Mock as he pulled his cutlass and main gauche from his belt. He coughed and spit blood, bright-red and thick. He stared at the wad of blood in disbelief. He knew the wound had punctured his lung and that he was likely done for.

"Don't fight him," implored Bertha. "Follow me up," she said as she scampered up the ladder with speed and agility that belied her bulk. Her last backward glance marked the Brigandir's glowing, golden eyes, his hood now pushed back from his face.

Old Mock had no intention of fleeing any further. He'd only run to make sure that Bertha got clear. He felt the blood filling his lung and was having trouble breathing. The bastard had done him in, for certain. He would stand and fight now, and take whatever measure of vengeance he could before he breathed his last. If he had to die, he would die on his feet, fighting, not coughing up blood in some sickbed.

The Brigandir advanced, retrieved sword in hand. Deft as Old Mock was with his blades, two score deadly battles beneath his belt, not five heartbeats passed before he crumbled under a hail of blows, though he parried and riposted until his last breath.

The ship's ladder carried Bertha up to the captain's deck. "A demon," she bellowed as she ran down the long hallway and approached Claradon's stateroom. Artol and Glimador stood in the doorway conferring with Sergeant Vid and an Eotrus trooper regarding the twanging claxon. "It's right behind me with golden eyes," said Bertha. "It killed Old Mock and Eolge. It's got golden eyes! So help me, Odin! Golden eyes!"

Artol put his hand out to stop her, but she brushed it aside. "I gotta warn the captain." She dashed down the hall to Slaayde's stateroom, entered, and ushered the captain's door guards in with her.

At the end of the hallway, the Brigandir stepped off the ship's ladder onto the deck, a bloody sword in his right hand.

"I don't think he's one of the crew," whispered Glimador.

Artol turned to Sergeant Vid. "You men get inside and barricade the door. Don't open it for nothing." Artol moved to pull his sword from its scabbard, but found it empty. He grabbed his battle hammer instead. As he raised it to his shoulder, it scraped the ceiling.

"No room to swing that in here," said Glimador. Glimador drew his dagger, leaving his longsword in its sheath.

"Who are you?" shouted Artol.

"Justice, vengeance, and wrath," shouted the Brigandir as he stood beside the ladder and surveyed the passageway.

"Must be crowded in there for the three of you," said Glimador.

The Brigandir started towards them, his gait purposeful, but slow. No doubt, he was wary that men might emerge and assault him from the closed doors that lined both sides of the hallway.

"What's your business on this ship?" said Artol. "And how did you get aboard?"

"Point me to Thetan, stand aside, and you may yet live," he said.

"Pithy and well-spoken," said Glimador. "Refreshing."

"She was right about the eyes," whispered Artol. The Brigandir's eyes now appeared uniformly golden. They masked which way he gazed, and marred his face with an eerie, otherworldly appearance.

"Another of Nifleheim's finest," said Glimador. "Best not let him touch you, big guy."

"Unless you can conjure me a polearm, I've little chance of keeping him back."

"I'm fresh out of spears, but I've got something better — some old elvish magic." Glimador spoke a single word in ancient elvish and a ball of blue fire formed in his outstretched palm. It shot at the Brigandir, sparking and sputtering as it flew. He dodged to the side, but the fiery sphere followed him and exploded on impact with his chest. For a brief moment, the Brigandir took on his demonic appearance, all reddish-brown hide, horned, winged, and long-toothed, then returned to his human aspect. The explosion did him no visible harm.

"Crap," mumbled Artol.

Unperturbed, Glimador sent a second and then a third fiery ball of crackling energy fast on the heels of the first, and each blasted unerringly into the Brigandir's torso. With each impact, its demon form returned for but an instant, and with it came waves of heat and scents of sulphur that flooded the hall. The eldritch attacks left the Brigandir's shirt blackened and smoking, but seemingly did him no harm.

"Still coming," said Artol as he readied his hammer and braced against the Brigandir's charge. "Got anything else?"

Glimador spoke more mystical words as the Brigandir quickened its pace, now nearly on them. The ancient elvish words that dropped from his lips were soft and melodic, yet rich and tonal. In their wake, shimmering, translucent energy that resembled waves of heat on a hot day flared out from Glimador's hand, expanded across the breadth and height of the passageway, and coalesced just in front of Artol. The arcane forces formed a transparent and nearly invisible barrier of preternatural energy that stood solid as stone and as indestructible as steel.

The Brigandir's sword crashed into it with a loud thump and a shower of sparks that sent the blade spinning from his grasp. The Brigandir rammed his shoulder into the mystical barrier and sparks erupted around its perimeter and at the point of impact. The magic wall held, but it slid toward Artol and Glimador. Surprise on his face, the Brigandir bounced back from the barrier, wincing and momentarily stunned.

"Good work — he can't get through," said Artol. "How long will it stand?" he whispered.

"I can hold it one minute, maybe two," said Glimador through clenched teeth, his hand outstretched toward the barrier, his attention focused on fueling the mystical energy that comprised it.

The Brigandir recovered his sword and studied the mystical wall, focusing on its edges, which fit tightly to the contours of the corridor's floor, walls, and ceiling. He kicked it, once and then again — powerful strikes, far harder than a normal man could mount. The barrier sparked and shuddered and shifted ever so slightly with each impact. The Brigandir looked up and smiled. He sheathed his sword, leaned into the barrier, and strained with both arms and shoulder. At his touch, sparks and tendrils of crackling energy erupted from the magical wall and enveloped him — shocking and burning him, head to torso to toe, though he maintained his grip, growling in pain and anger all the while. The entirety of the invisible wall began to slowly slide, sparking along its edges as it went.

"Thor's Blood!" said Artol. "He's moving it."

"Hold it back," said Glimador.

"I'm not touching that — it'll fry me," said Artol.

"It's safe on this side. Trust me," said Glimador, his face now red from the strain of maintaining the wall against the Brigandir's assault.

"Can you anchor it down?" said Artol.

"No. You've got to hold it back."

Artol tentatively pressed hands and shoulder against the mystic barrier, though as promised no energy assailed him. Strangely, because the barrier had hardly any thickness, he and the Brigandir appeared to push against each other — at best, a wisp of clear glass between them. In his human form, the Brigandir was nearly as broad as Artol, more heavily muscled, but several inches shorter despite his significant height. Both strained and grunted. Sweat beaded on Artol's face. None formed on the Brigandir's, though his was a mask of pain.

Although Artol possessed such strength to best or match any man of Midgaard, the Brigandir slowly, inexorably, drove him back. Other men rushed down the ship's stair from the main deck in answer to the alarm.

"What the?" said one Lomerian soldier on seeing the strange struggle.

"Witchcraft!" said another.

"Help me, you fools," said Artol.

The first soldier lunged with his sword, aimed for the Brigandir's side. The sword's tip bounced off the barrier, sent sparks flying, and raked Artol's cuirass, though it did him no harm.

"Weapons won't work," spat Glimador. "There's a wall there, though you can see through it. Help Artol hold it back." The soldiers' suspicious stares bored into Glimador when they realized that he controlled the magic that powered the unseen barrier. Despite their aversion to all things arcane, the soldiers kept true to their duty, moved forward, and tentatively pressed their hands against the barrier wherever there was room. More soldiers appeared. Two pushed on Artol's back. All their exertions were for naught, for the barrier continued to slide, foot after foot. The Brigandir's growls assaulted their ears all the while.

"Get Claradon out," said Artol, not realizing that he and the barrier had already been pushed well past Claradon's stateroom door. Claradon, and those within his cabin, were trapped on the Brigandir's side of the barrier. Well enough that was, as long as he didn't turn his attention towards them.

"Bertha," yelled Glimador, "Get Slaayde out! Now!"

The captain's door sprang open and Bertha popped her head out, dagger in hand.

"Move him! Fast," she screeched at the guards inside the cabin, for the barrier now slid quicker down the corridor despite the soldiers' best efforts, and would soon reach the door.

Two guards, directed by Ravel, the ship's trader, rushed Captain Slaayde through the door. They carried him between them. One held his shoulders, the other his feet. Slaayde's eyes were open, but he looked more dead than alive. His hair was snow white; his face, drawn and pale; his skin, a sickly pallor; his leg, heavily wrapped in red-stained bandages.

"I can't hold it," said Glimador. Sweat poured down his face as he inched backward down the hall.

By the time Slaayde's crew heaved the captain up the stairs and through the door to the main deck, only ten feet of corridor remained at Glimador's back.

"Have we time to get clear?" said Artol.

"No," said Glimador. "When I turn, it'll fall," he said.

"Then don't turn!" said Artol. "Glim, stay where you are. The rest of you, break away now and get your butts upstairs." They did.

Artol spun from the barrier, ducked to avoid Glimador's outstretched hand or block his line of sight to the magical wall, scooped Glimador up about the waist with one meaty arm, and bounded for the stair. With Glimador draped over his shoulder, Artol dashed up the stair, skipping three steps at a time. Glimador groaned from the magic's strain, but he held it solid until the moment they crested the stair, then the barrier

275

collapsed with an odd, popping sound. Artol dived through the door and he and Glimador crashed to the main deck. The door slammed behind him.

19
LEVIATHAN

Frem's squad dropped Mort Zag's limp form and collapsed in exhaustion when they reached the edge of the black sand beach. Frem fell to one knee and struggled to catch his breath. "Keep watch for the muck monster," he sputtered to whoever was close enough to hear. He looked for the thing, but he could barely see — salty sweat marred his vision. Men yelled from all around. He raised his arm to wipe his eyes and found his limbs barely responsive. Both arms were half-numb, both legs were rubber. His muscles vibrated and shuddered — his strength utterly spent. His squad fared no better.

Meanwhile, the other squadrons strained to push the longboats back into the water while Ginalli shouted for everyone to pile in and shove off. The priest was in the lead boat, already away. He stood at the prow and waved everyone on. Korrgonn was beside him, shouting orders too, but Frem couldn't make his words out over the general din.

Then Sevare plopped down beside Frem, looking pale and queasy. He held his hands away from his body, fingers spread, as if the slightest touch caused him pain — aftereffects of his magic, no doubt. Putnam was there too, carrying Little Storrl, still unconscious. He gently passed the boy to Borrel and Ward who carried him to one of the boats. Lex and Sir Carroll supported Sergeant

Maldin who was badly wounded, a dweller's spear lodged in his chest. The rest of the Pointmen were there too, those still alive.

"Frem, get up," yelled Putnam. "We've got to get back to the ship." Panic dominated his voice and he looked every bit as exhausted as Frem felt. He grabbed Frem's arm and tried to pull him to his feet. As strong as he was, if Frem didn't want to get up, he couldn't lift him, and Frem wasn't moving just yet.

Frem looked over his shoulder and expected to see Dagon barreling down on them. He wondered if he would even bother to try to flee. "I don't see it. Is it still after us?"

"Maybe it gave up," said Putnam. "I can't hear it anymore, but we've still got to move, now. The ship is under attack. Get your behind up."

"What!?" Frem's head snapped toward the ship. *The White Rose* was anchored beyond the muck-filled harbor -- just where they'd left it, except now, smoke billowed from several points along its decks. Bright flashes that could be naught but sorcery pulsed here and there across the main deck, though the ship was too far away to make out what went on.

Frem's legs betrayed him, shuddering under his weight, but with Putnam's help, he made his feet. Around him, the lugron pulled themselves up. Frem grabbed Putnam, his eyes wide. "Bryton and Jorna! And the other wounded, we left them!"

"We ran back a different way," said Putnam. "We didn't pass them. But Frem, those boys are almost surely dead by now, the wounds they had. There's nothing we can do for them even if we

278

could go back and get them, and we can't. Not with that thing out there."

Frustration and anguish filled Frem's face as he grabbed Mort Zag's arm. "Heave him up, men, we're almost there."

"Leave him," said Sevare as he struggled to rise while avoiding putting pressure on his hands or arms. "He's done for. We've got to fly. Someone help me up for Odin's sake."

The lugron dropped their charge and poised to run for the longboats, but Frem's glare stopped them cold. "No," boomed Frem. "We just hauled him halfway across the stinking island. I'm not going to leave him on the beach now. Not him, or anyone else still breathing, darn it. Heave him up, men; let's move."

Frem and his Pointmen were amongst the last off the beach. They and several lugron stragglers from another squadron pushed the last two longboats clear of the sand and hopped in. Frem took his usual place near the stern, Sevare at the rudder, just behind him.

"If we lose the ship . . ." said Sevare.

"—We're done for," said Frem. "There's no other land the longboats can reach and we've no supplies to speak of. We've got to secure the ship."

The Pointmen pulled the oars for all they were worth, eager to get well clear of the beach, hoping that would put them beyond Dagon's reach, though all the while wary for any sign of the seaweed monster of their recent acquaintance. The strand was still clear, and of both monsters, there was no sign.

Frem looked down. His hands pulled the oars like mad, though he had no memory of taking hold of them. His arms ached. His legs were weak. His mind was clouded and dazed. It was difficult to concentrate and focus. It felt like a dream, a nightmare, but Frem knew it was real. As a soldier, he knew the symptoms of exhaustion, thirst, and shock. He had battled such things before, and he would endure them now.

He stared at the men's backs as they heaved at the oars, one man to each, though Frem pulled two with his meaty hands. When his rowing settled into a rhythm, his mind calmed, his heartbeat steadied. He smelled blood. Blood of the wounded, the dying, and the dead. With it came that foul odor you get when a man's insides kiss the air. That miasma hung over the wounded and drifted from the splattered blood and gore that afflicted every man in the boat. Frem realized that reek had been with them since the battle with the Dwellers, but only now did he notice it. Strange that.

Death loomed behind them on the island. It skulked about them, somewhere in the water, and lurked before them in whatever trouble plagued the ship. There would be more blood that day. What strength had they left?

Frem would've preferred to keep the remnants of his squadron together, but his boat was full, so Torak and Wikkle, along with a squad of lugron from Ezerhauten's command, pulled hard at the oars of the nearby longboat that held Mort Zag's limp form. Even supine, the giant's great bulk rose above the gunwales. His eyes were closed, but his head turned from side to side as if in a restless sleep. How he still lived after the blow he had suffered, Frem could not fathom. He had done all he could for the giant, though he wasn't sure why. Mort Zag had never respected him — tossing insults at Frem freely. Frem didn't abide that kind of treatment. He treated others with respect and expected the same in return, though many folks disappointed him, Mort Zag being no exception. Yet he had risked everything to save the giant. Aiding a comrade in dire need was the right thing to do, so he did it, no matter the consequences. He had too. Frem always did what he knew was right. Such notions had landed him in hot water more times than he could remember, but he couldn't change. He wouldn't, if he could. That was Frem.

In Frem's longboat, Putnam manned the bow. He looked sound enough — that man was a rock. Nothing ever seemed to harm him or even slow him down, though he was Frem's senior by a goodly number of years. Borrel, Royce, Ward, and Lex dragged at the oars, tired and battered but still with him and in one piece. Carrol's hand was clumsily bandaged, as was Moag's head, but they soldiered on and pulled with the rest. Given a bit of time to heal up, they would be fine. Little Storrl lay on the bench just in front of Frem, his face pale but peaceful, his arm's bleeding stopped, his form still. If his wound didn't fester, Frem thought the boy would live — he had to.

Sergeant Maldin sprawled between two benches and looked more than half dead; a Dweller's broken spear lodged in the right side of his chest. He was conscious and looking around. "How are you holding up, Sergeant?" said Frem.

"Fine, Captain, except for a splinter I picked up somewhere," said Maldin in a stronger voice than Frem expected. "Once we pry it out, I'll be right as rain."

A tough man, that one, but a bad wound it was. The kind that killed most men. Blood flowed freely from it. "Royce," shouted Frem. "Stay your oar and see to Maldin's splinter. Bind it tight and secure to get that bleeding stopped, but don't touch the spear — we'll get it out when we're back aboard." Royce complied without a word, and Maldin tolerated his ministerings just the same.

Frem didn't know Maldin as well as he did some of the others, but he seemed a goodly man and solid squad leader. It pained Frem to see him in such condition, but if luck were with him, he would recover quickly, or die quickly. It's the lingering death that soldiers fear. Frem wouldn't let a good soldier suffer through that; that's not how such men are meant to go. If Maldin didn't recover, Frem would need to promote another to take charge of his squad. He would worry about that if the time came.

All things considered, it was difficult to tell that they were the winners of the recent battle. When they set out from Lomion City, Frem had more than a full squadron under his command — two squads of twenty men each. His Pointmen were nearly all veterans and named men — an elite troop. Now only thirteen still lived. He had no interest in losing any more.

The longboat's progress was slow, uneven,

and challenging, for every few strokes an oar fouled in the thick seaweed and slid useless over the water's surface. The journey in was a joy in comparison. The putrid smell of the stuff was twice as bad now, the muck and weeds all the thicker and thrice as heavy as before, but whether that was truth or merely Frem's fatigue, he couldn't tell. Even the wet cloths they wrapped around their noses and mouths now did little to dull the fetid odor of the muck. Frem pulled the oars without thought, all muscle memory and instinct. His thoughts focused on reaching the ship as quickly as possible. He did his best to block out all else, with limited success.

Now and again Frem glanced at the beach, which slowly grew farther away. He expected to see Dagon stalk to the water's edge and make after them. It could surely swim, that thing, having come up from a well. It could wade out a ways, then slip under the weeds, glide through the water and be on them in no time. In a longboat, they would have little chance against that monster. A mere flick of its tail or swipe of its claws could capsize them with ease. Then it could pluck the men from the water at will and leisure. With his heavy armor, Frem would sink like a rock — not a way he wanted to go, if he had to go at all, but better than being eaten by a giant lizard, all things considered. Frem pictured his daughter's smiling face and rowed harder. He had to live to get back to her. Coriana needed him. She depended on him. It was bad enough that he was away so often and so long. He would not abandon her.

Behind him, Sevare struggled with the rudder as he wrapped wet cloths about his hands.

"You hurt?" said Frem. "Or is it just the burning from the magic?"

"It's just the magic," said Sevare. "But that was the most I've ever thrown . . . by a wide stretch. It feels like I've got a million ants crawling all crazy on my hands and halfway up my arms. I've never felt anything like it afore."

Frem looked over his shoulder at Sevare. "There are no bugs on you. Could be invisible, I guess." Frem shook his head. "That's just crazy talk. I'm losing it. I'm starting to think everything is magic. Can you see what's happening on the ship?"

"There's fighting on deck," said Sevare. "Magic is being thrown."

"I can hear it. How close are we?"

"We're still far. Korrgonn's boat is halfway there, but it looks like they're hung up on the muck."

"Can you tell who we're fighting or which way it's going?"

"Too far to see."

"I left my darned spotting scope on the ship," said Putnam. "You never have what you need, when you need it."

Yells erupted from Mort Zag's boat. The lugron were in a panic; they had dropped their oars, pulled weapons, and pointed toward the weed.

"The stinking muck monster must be back," said Frem as he looked warily into the water this way and that."

284

"One of the men is gone," said Sevare.

"What?"

"There were twelve men in that longboat," said Sevare. "Now there are eleven."

"Is he in the water?"

Even as they watched, thick vines, a mottled green and brown in color, all gnarled and sinewy, rose like a serpent from the muck and whipped around one of the men in Mort Zag's longboat. The tendril lifted him high into the air, the man's arms pinioned to his sides. Helpless, he screamed.

"Dead gods!" said Frem. "Turn the boat! Get us over there! We have to—"

Frem's words cut off when something slammed into him and sent him hurtling over the side.

The world spun with a deafening metallic clang. Frem sailed through the air; hit hard, his ears rang. On instinct, he tucked chin to chest and held his breath. He crashed through the surface muck and plunged into the depths; the impact, jarring. Most of his air, gone, though he remained conscious and kept the water from his lungs.

The thing that hit him, another tentacle or whatever it was, had no hold on him, thank the gods. His momentum shot him deeper — the bubbles and darkness blinding. His left arm, dead.

A glimmer of light that evaded the muck pointed the way up. Frem kicked and pulled, desperate one-armed strokes — his heavy steel armor fought him every inch. Air bubbled from his mouth; his lungs burned and threatened to burst, and still the surface eluded him. He fought against the darkness, against the terrible urge to give up, to rest, to sleep, to let oblivion take him. He wasn't ready for that. He had things left to do and Coriana to look after. He swam upward with all his strength, Coriana's little face etched in his mind's eye, and when he had held out longer than he thought he could, his outstretched fingers fell on a driftwood log. Frem's iron grip enveloped it, and pulled with renewed strength. The log, buoyed by the muck, offered resistance enough to aid his ascent. Frem breached the surface and took a breath. He couldn't move his left arm. He coughed, spewed water, and gasped for air, but he was alive.

Men yelled all around. The water was rough and waves slapped against his face. Before Frem got his bearings, an oar dangled in front of him. Sevare held it; his face grave and bleeding.

Still dazed, with the wizard's help, Frem scrambled into the longboat, his left arm hung limp at his side and putrid seaweed clung to his body. A chaotic din assailed him from all sides. Men yelled and screamed, water roiled, and thunderous impacts erupted everywhere. He looked up and saw several men held aloft and thrashed about by monstrous, sinewy tentacles, similar to but larger than those that attacked them earlier on the beach. One of those had hit him.

The putrid smell of the muck monster was overwhelming. Frem's stomach churned and twisted. More tentacles rocketed from the muck and showered water down on the boats. Others stealthily crept from the surface, trailing clinging, putrid algae. They swooped down on the men and plucked them from this longboat and that, wreaking havoc across the small fleet. They blasted men into the water, scooped others up, and slammed them to the surface of the muck, over and again, bludgeoning the life from them. Others, they squeezed within a pythonic embrace until ribs and spine shattered in their deadly grips. Some poor souls they pulled screaming beneath the surface, never to be seen again.

The gnarly, corded tentacles looked more like vines of some hellish, carnivorous sea plants than appendages of a giant squid or monstrous octopus of legend. But whether each was a separate creature, or a part of some vast monster of the deep still hidden beneath the waves, one could not say, save to note each tentacle didn't act in concert with its fellows. Like Dagon and the Dwellers, these beasts were beyond Frem's knowledge; beyond all reason and sanity; true monsters — heartless, soulless, living only to kill and to feed.

Men fought from each boat, sword, oar, arrow, and axe. None cowered or hid. These were fighting men all; not a one would go quietly to his end.

Par Brackta and Ginalli fired bolts of numinous energy at the thrashing tentacles, most as thick as a man's arm or leg — some as wide around as a large man's waist. Their magic left several burning and ruined. Ezerhauten and his men swung sword and axe, and cleaved and chopped any tentacle that ventured within reach, even as they kept their balance in longboats buffeted by the churning waters. Archers launched shafts at swooping tentacles. More than a few hit their marks, though most to little effect. Four tentacles lay severed in the water about the lead longboat, though they still writhed in their death throes.

The battle continued for some time, until at last, the water began to roil wildly not far from Korrgonn's boat, and a monstrous form slowly rose up from the muck. With it came a piercing, high-pitched roar and a rush of heady, putrid air. Higher and higher did it rise — its body globular and amorphous, colossal and vast, far larger even than Dagon. Its hide rough, mottled, and pitted; the very muck come alive. Its gaping, toothy maw was wide enough to swallow upright the tallest man, and housed myriad rows of wicked teeth born to both crush and tear its prey.

Three great eyes did it have. One lurked above the center of its maw, the others off to each side, where eyes are wont to be. Each, large, black, and yellow, though the central was near twice the size of its fellows. In its piercing gaze abided some spark of intelligence, some hint of purpose. These were not the dead eyes of a beast that marauded on instinct alone. They were alien eyes raised on truths unfathomed, unknown, and inconceivable to man. Every vast, destructive tentacle was but one of its innumerable digits, erupting from its sides and underbelly, vaguely as that of a squid, though this beast was far larger than the largest squid of truth, myth, or legend. It reeked of rot and decay, and offered only death, swift and painful, that day and every other.

For a moment, time stopped — each man

frozen in shock and horror, their heads craned back, their eyes affixed on the leviathan of the deep. The odor of the thing was rancid and burned the nose and tongue and set the men to coughing.

Korrgonn stood in the boat closest to it. To it, he was puny, an insect to be crushed, a tiny morsel to be devoured, barely even worthy of notice. He held his sword before him in both hands, seemingly immune to the stench that afflicted those around him. "Now would be the time," he said to Ginalli, urgency in his voice. "Throw all that you have at it. Swords will not avail us here."

Blood still dripped into Ginalli's eyes from some Dweller's blow. His face was smeared with it. His hair was all wild and disheveled, except at the front, where it was plastered to his head with blood and sweat. He was pale; his eyes unsteady, but he spoke his mystical words with strength and clarity. His incantation completed, red fire erupted from his hands. It coalesced out of nothingness, and grew into a blood-red sphere of churning, spinning fire. At Ginalli's command, it shot at the beast. The scent of ozone trailed in its wake.

Par Brackta rose at the far end of the boat. She held her arms outstretched, chin high, eyes closed. She stood statuesque, her face as beautiful and terrible as the goddesses of song and story. In a sultry voice, she emoted esoteric words from some nameless language unknown to the others, words that beckoned forth primal magics from beyond the pale. Her right hand began to glow, and quickly grew brighter and brighter until a bolt of sparkling white flame shot from it and rocketed at Leviathan.

The wizards' sorcery struck Leviathan squarely and the beast squealed, a sustained high-pitched, grating sound that stung the ears and left them ringing. Its flesh blackened and smoked where the flames smote it, but it did not burn, nor flee; in fact, it barely reacted. Its tentacles continued to thrash about and hunt for men as if each had eyes of its own, though none were visible. One boat snapped in half and sank when a huge tentacle crashed down on it, dumping its crew into the churning waters. Another boat was plucked clean when a gang of tentacles came up en masse and scooped up a half-dozen men and knocked the rest into the water.

Brackta spoke more mystical words and launched another ensorcelled blast — this one aimed for the beast's maw. Her latest sorcery was no instant stroke, but a sustained discharge of fiery, white energy that slammed into the beast and sought to burn it to cinders. The magic's crackling beam pummeled the monster as it thrashed from this side to that, though it would not turn. It would not flee. And it did not fall. Its maw opened wide, and from it gushed a roar that shook even the distant stones of the isle. The men clamped palms to ears in a futile attempt to hold off the skirling sound.

Brackta's spell still afire, Ginalli turned to Korrgonn with a look that bespoke futility. "We can't stop it, my lord," he said, fear taking hold. "We must flee."

"We can't kill it and we can't chase it away,"

said Ezerhauten. "It'll take us one by one, boat by boat. We need a diversion. Sacrifice a boat or two and make a run for it. It's our only chance."

"We've lost too many men already," said Korrgonn, his voice steady and calm. "I'll need the rest for what's to come. Priest — you must have a ward that can hold it back. Keep it off us for a few more moments and I'll deal with it myself."

"My Lord, you must not risk yourself," said Ginalli.

"We're all at risk. Just do as I commanded."

And he did.

Brackta's fire blast fizzled out. Her magic left little scar behind, the beast barely wounded, and still full of fight. Weakened from the strain, Brackta sank to her knees. Leviathan bellowed and its tentacles thrashed. Several rocketed toward Korrgonn's boat. Korrgonn swung his sword and cut the tip from a tentacle that dared venture too close. Ezerhauten sliced one in half as it came in and dodged another, but that one hit the man behind him. It scooped him up screaming, and carried his squirming form to its great maw where it swallowed him whole before his comrades' eyes.

As the battle raged on, Ginalli's hands waved before him and he mouthed rare words of power. A white light extended from his outstretched hands and morphed into the shape of a great translucent shield. It grew larger as the priest focused his concentration, all his formidable will bent on the task. The phantasmal shield expanded to nearly half the width of the beast. It was ghostly, insubstantial, and its edges sparked with arcane energies. Ginalli aligned it between Leviathan and their boat, offering whatever protection its mystical energies could afford. "I can't make it any larger," said Ginalli through gritted teeth, his face strained. "And it won't last long. Even now, the power drains me."

Par Brackta regained her feet, pale but determined. Before her, extending at first from her hands, then on its own, a rectangular wall of mystical energy coalesced, red and brown in hue, it grew mammoth in size; it brimmed with power, but looked as transparent and insubstantial as Ginalli's shield, which it stood beside, though it was the larger.

Leviathan lurched forward and crashed headlong into both sorceries. On impact, a great, hollow thump sounded and the mystical shields sparked and shuddered and bent, but held. Strangely, the blow's momentum was not transferred to the longboat, which moved not at all. Leviathan rebounded as if it had rammed a stone wall. It roared in defiance and anger, and lashed out with dozens of tentacles that flailed in all directions. They battered the magical shields. The echoes of the blows carried on the winds. Each one that struck Ginalli's shield, sounded as if it impacted metal; those hitting Brackta's, produced a dull thump, like stone. Other tentacles flailed the water and sent great plumes and scattered spray in all directions, which showered Korrgonn's boat with putrid water. Both wizards strained to maintain their magics. They poured all their strength into it; their faces masks of pain. They struggled to hold out until Korrgonn made his move. Brackta's legs buckled and she dropped to her knees, but her mystical wall held.

"We cannot hold," said Ginalli. His magic mantle sputtered and shrunk even as he spoke. Sweat and blood streamed down his brow and dripped from the end of his nose.

And then, the son of Azathoth whispered his own forbidden words in a voice too low for any to hear. What eldritch words from which forgotten tongue passed through his lips, what dark promises he made or unholy bargains he struck to call up the shocking magics he did, no one would ever know, thank the gods, for mortal man was never meant to know such things.

Korrgonn raised his black sword with his right hand and grasped the heart stone with his left. His sword began to glow with numinous energy, a scintillating, fiery red. He plunged it point first, not into the beast, but through the muck and into the water. At its touch, the muck sizzled and steamed as if the steel was lately plucked from Heimdall's forge.

The water and the surface muck took on a reddish glow and began to roil, smoke, and bubble. Leviathan rammed the wizards' shields again. Its tentacles thrashed — some arced over or around the mystical barriers and narrowly missed Korrgonn's boat.

Then did Korrgonn plunge his sword deeper into the water, now to the hilt, and he spoke terrible words of power that his comrades this time did hear — words that haunted them unto the end of their days. Words that dare not be repeated, even here, even now. Korrgonn's spell echoed and reverberated on the wind. His words boomed louder and louder, amplified by the strange topography of the cove, until the very heavens shook.

Leviathan cowered back. The great beast tried to break away, to flee. From Korrgonn's left hand or perhaps from the heart stone itself, emerged a ghostly hand that grew huge and menacing, as real, yet as insubstantial as the wizards' shields. The spectral hand reached out and clamped Leviathan in an iron grip that would not yield; a death grip that would not be sundered.

Leviathan howled. It was a piercing, high-pitched, pitiful cry that went on and on and varied in tone and pitch. Whether those horrid sounds were naught but the meaningless wails of a dying beast or baleful entreats to some demon of the nether realms was never known, save that whatever prayers it may have shouted went unanswered. Under Korrgonn's magic, its great form reddened, sizzled, and blistered. Its tentacles flopped and thrashed, and burst afire — combusting from within, not without. Its bulk surged this way and that, but the spectral hand held it back, denying any retreat. The few men still locked in Leviathan's grasp screamed and burned along with the tentacles that entrapped them. The men in the water shared the same grisly fate. Their flesh burned to cinders, but strangely, their armor, clothing, and equipment remained intact, and slowly disappeared beneath the waves, as did their whited bones. All the while, the water around the boats and for a distance beyond boiled and steamed.

At last, the beast's great form crashed to the water's surface in a smoking, ashen heap. It released a sound like a deep trumpet's rumble as it collapsed in on itself. Its cries gone silent, its form now still, save for some few tentacles that flopped about, owing to some residual, reflex energy. Leviathan, who had abided those waters for untold eons slowly slipped beneath the surface for the first time not of its own volition, but in answer to death's beckoning, relentless call.

With the beast's passing, so went the wizards' mystical shields and Korrgonn's spectral hand. Ginalli fell limp and would have pitched over the longboat's side save for Ezerhauten's retraining hand that steadied him and lowered him to the deck. How small he looked, thought Frem. How weak, the great man.

Brackta fell forward against the gunwale and puked over the side, her face gone green, her eyes sunken. Korrgonn sat on the longboat's bench and held his head in his hands, silent and still, and did not move for a goodly time. His right hand, whence the sorcery sprang, was blackened and charred, though Korrgonn paid it no heed.

The cove was silent save for the piteous screams of one soldier who had fallen from Leviathan's grasp and landed in Frem's longboat just as Korrgonn's spell had taken hold. Frem and his men looked on in horror as he screamed and writhed about. Much of his flesh had burned off and continued to sizzle and char. His entire head was blackened, his features unrecognizable. One eye was gone and bone showed through his face here and there, though his clothes and his gear were entirely untouched by the sorcery.

"Throw water on him," cried Moag, grabbing a bucket and dunking it over the side.

"It's boiling, you fool," shouted Putnam, but some water had already splashed over Moag's hands and sent him jerking back on his rump.

"I can't tell who it is," whispered Sevare to Frem.

"Me neither," said Frem. "I can't save you, my friend, but I can stop the pain." Frem pressed his boot to the man's torso to steady him and positioned his sword over the center of his chest. With all eyes in the fleet on him, and Frem's face full of anguish, he ran the man through, and ended his suffering.

All was calm and quiet for a full five heartbeats. Then came an earsplitting roar from behind, from the beach. Dagon of the Deep stood on the strand and bellowed.

"Oh, boy! All we need," said Frem.

"On your oars, men," shouted Putnam. The men scurried to their positions as fast as they could. Those in the other boats did the same. They rowed hard — their fatigue fallen away for fear of Dagon. After some minutes, they reached the edge of the muck-filled cove and continued rowing in the open sea toward their anchored ship, the going now much easier with no seaweed to hamper them.

"Why is that thing just standing there looking at us?" said Frem to Sevare, as he pulled an oar as best he could with his one working arm.

"Who cares," said Sevare. "As long as it's not

after us."

"Maybe he's afraid of Korrgonn's magic," said Frem.

"Or maybe he's just not hungry anymore," said Sevare. "Who knows. How's your arm?"

"Out of the socket," said Frem, "and throbbing like hell."

"You've got to get that arm back in place," said Putnam. "It will just be harder later as it swells up."

Frem dropped his oar and turned his shoulder toward Sevare. "Give it a tug for me, will you. Hard — hard as you can. And do it fast — I need to get back on this oar."

"I'm no physician," said Sevare.

"Just do it."

Three hard tugs, which Frem tolerated stoically, and the arm found its place, though Frem still had little use of it. Without missing a beat, Frem grasped his oar with his good hand and set right back to rowing. Then from the corner of his eye, Frem saw something in the water and turned toward it. Not far beyond the edge of the cove, he saw a fish's skeleton bobbing on the surface. Then he saw another and another, and turned about to get a better look behind them. The other longboats had all put up their oars and the men stared in amazement. For as far as the eye could see in all the directions, countless skeletons of fish of all varieties, great and small, floated and bobbed about the water's surface. "Dead gods," said Frem. "Korrgonn's magic did all this?"

"It looks as if anything alive in the water was

fried," said Severe. "Their flesh burned or dissolved clean off. Somehow, being in the longboats saved us."

Putnam stared at the bonefield. "Never seen or heard tell of anything like this. I wonder how far the dead zone goes."

"I hope it's not the whole darned ocean," said Frem. "We need to keep moving."

"On your oars, men," said Putnam.

"Do you still doubt him, Frem?" said Severe as he stared over at Korrgonn, beaming. "Only the son of the lord could do this. And since when do bones float, anyways?"

"Since we got hired by the League everything's gone upside down," said Frem. "The world don't make no sense anymore."

"It never made any sense. You just didn't have enough sense to realize it," said Severe with a smile.

"I can't argue with that."

In the distance, a large explosion rocked *The White Rose*.

"Oh, boy," said Frem. "Let's move men. Put your backs to it."

As they grew closer, yells and screams and sounds out of nightmare came from the ship.

"That's no minor skirmish or squabble," said Putnam. "It's a major battle across the whole main deck, and the bridge as well."

"We're not going to make it in time," said Severe.

"We need to get to *The Rose* now," shouted Frem. "Give it all you've got, men. Pull! Pull!"

"If *the Rose* goes down, we're all dead for

sure," said Sevare.

"She's listing to starboard," said Putnam.

Another explosion.

"Oh, no," said Sevare. "Dead gods, it's coming."

"What?" said Putnam, turning.

"Dagon," said Sevare. "It's coming after us."

Dagon waded out into the water, its great strides quickly carrying it far from the beach, its black eyes trained squarely on the fleet. It surely planned to kill them all. There would be no escape from that island. Not for any of them.

"Damn," said Putnam. "Why couldn't it have just been cannibals?"

"Shut up and row," said Frem. "Row for your lives." Frem pictured Coriana in his mind's eye and forced his left hand up to grip an oar and bit back the terrible pain in his shoulder. He saw her smile; he heard her laugh. That gave him the strength he needed to ignore the pain and to row like he never had before. "Row for all you hold dear," Frem shouted.

20
BRIGANDIR

The Black Falcon's main deck was crowded with men, weapons drawn and battle ready, waiting. Theta was there. So were Ob, Tanch, and nearly all of the expedition's soldiers and knights, along with most of Slaayde's crew. Most of them stood watching the main door that led below deck.

That door shattered to splinters, and a wave of brimstone-scented heat roared across the deck in the shrapnel's wake. In the gaping portal stood the Brigandir in his demonic form. The soldiers and seamen had never seen or heard of its like. The thing was a monster. Something out of a nightmare.

Gasps and expletives were spouted all around.

"By Asgard, what is that?" said Ob under his breath.

"Fire," shouted Theta.

A dozen shafts launched from point-blank range slammed into the Brigandir — neck, chest, belly, and thigh — but all dropped ineffectually to the deck, smoking and broken, the Brigandir's armor-like hide too hard to penetrate.

"Thetan," shouted the Brigandir. Smoke rose from where its feet touched the deck. It turned sideways as he came through the portal, for it was too broad to fit straight on. "Don't hide behind these puny pawns, coward. Come forward and face the lord's justice. Your reign of terror ends here; it ends now. Midgaard will be free of you at last!"

"Take it down," shouted Ob from somewhere in the throng.

Without hesitation, men charged from all sides, their eyes bright with bravery, war cries on their lips. Silver-armored, fresh-faced Lomerian soldiers of House Harringgold led the way with sword and shield, their intrepid captain, Seran Harringgold, at the van. Rugged veterans of House Eotrus charged beside them with sword, axe, or hammer. Scattered amongst the soldiers skulked the bravest of Slaayde's motley crew of cutthroats, wielding cutlass and dagger, knife and hatchet. The Brigandir met them all with a black sword now ablaze with the cold fires of Nifleheim. Its muscles bulged with strength beyond the ken of men. Its long, barbed tail whipped this way and that and stabbed with deadly purpose and precision.

> The epic battle engaged
> all wild and crazed,
> Men staggered wounded and dazed,
> a chaotic melee of blood, sweat, and rage.
>
> Stab and slash,
> thrust and crash,
> the strength of men ebbing fast,
> their courage and skill the beast would outlast.
>
> Scream and moan,
> slice and groan,
> a demon roared and men died
> in a bloody red and fiery tide.

Neither strength, courage, skill, nor force of numbers could bring the Brigandir down. Its very breath, when it so desired, was fire. It spewed flaming spittle into one man's face that burned him to the bone in an instant.

Its merest touch was death as two seamen discovered when its claws scraped over their arms' bare flesh. For reasons unknown, the creature's death grip was ineffective through armor, thank the gods. But naked flesh enjoyed no such reprieve. Flames erupted at the points of contact, but did not travel along the skin, burning into flesh as would any terrestrial fire. This hellfire instantly bored into the men's flesh and traveled inside their bodies in all directions, while leaving their skin, clothing, and gear untouched. They screamed in agony as the hellish flames spread, the flesh of their arms glowing, marking the flame's progress as it consumed them from within. In moments, they dropped to the deck, the flames utterly destroying them from the inside out. At last their skin blackened, charred, and collapsed in gruesome, ashen heaps.

The Brigandir's very body exuded a burning heat unbearable for more than moments to those within arm's reach. Even as it fenced with a dozen men, its barbed tail shot out, as it had several times before, and wrapped about a soldier's neck. It clamped down like a python, drew the man close, and squeezed the harder with each passing moment. Its sharpened ridges bit deep into the man's flesh and sent blood spurting. Desperate slashes of sword and axe along the tail's length did it no harm; the blows merely deflected off its scabrous hide. In moments, the tail sliced through the man's neck and his head popped off his body amidst a geyser of blood.

The men pulled back, out of range of the deadly sword and razored tail, breathing hard, some dripping blood, some broken and battered, some soon to be dead from their wounds. No one spoke a word, not even the dying. They stood a silent ring of steel about the Brigandir — shoulder to shoulder, winded and wounded, the hope of men.

And then Lord Angle Theta strode forward, his face stolid and chiseled. The ranks of men parted for him. His boot steps were loud and ominous amongst the silent throng. He gripped a massive falchion sword in his left hand; a polished round shield in his right. Both inscribed and etched with runic symbols at once beautiful and fearful to behold. A second sword was sheathed at his waist beside a massive war hammer that hung from a broad belt that brimmed with pockets and pouches. Here and there about his person was strapped a dagger, each ancient and ornate as his sword. Encased was he in blue-enameled plate armor, magnificently ornate, forged of exotic alloys in bygone days with skills long lost to the world. The golden coat-of-arms embossed on his breastplate shined proud and bold, a noble standard that bespoke depths of strength untold and a grand history that stretched back unto the

Age of Heroes. A midnight blue cape hung about his broad shoulders and fluttered in the breeze. Around his neck hung his misshapen ankh, that ancient relic of eldritch powers unfathomed by any but Theta. Theta's piercing blue eyes locked on the golden orbs of the Brigandir. They promised naught but pain and death.

The Brigandir broke the silence. "Comes now the coward at last. Send your dupes to fight and die in your stead whilst you cower behind and take my measure," it said, its breathing labored, some of the strength lost from its voice. "Oh, what a great hero you are, Thetan. How you find so many fools to follow you despite your black heart and cowardly ways has ever been your greatest skill. Know well that I have been prepared for ages beyond count for our meeting. My skills cannot be matched by you or any other. I lust to lay your black soul before the lord's feet. But first, I will devour your heart and—"

"—Cease your babbling, creature," boomed Theta, "and come now forth and meet your doom."

The Brigandir's eyes narrowed and flared with hatred. It strode toward Theta, the deck smoking beneath his feet. Fiery footprints and warped floorboards marked its trail.

The barbed tail arced up and sped down, aimed for Theta's head. His shield met it with a crash and sparks showered the deck. A black stain marred the shield's surface where the tail had touched it.

The tail flitted about and soared this way and that, feinting and bobbing. It searched for an opening in Theta's defenses. It struck again and again, but Theta's shieldwork was swift and sure and deftly deflected each strike — high or low, this side or that. Sparks showered the deck with each grating impact and the shield smoked and sizzled, dented and blackened across its once-polished face. For all his skill, Theta could not close with the Brigandir. He could not face him sword to sword without exposing his flank and back to the tail's relentless strikes.

The Brigandir snapped its tail at Theta's feet as it sought an opening beyond his shield's range. When the tail arced in, a curved blade extended from the shield's rim and Theta slammed its edge to the deck. The blade pinned the Brigandir's tail beneath it and part of the blade sunk deep in the deck boards. The Brigandir howled and strained to pull its appendage free, but it was held fast, its movement sorely hampered.

Theta wrenched his arm free of the shield and bounded forward. His falchion in his left hand, his scimitar now in his right, his expression stoic and determined. The Brigandir's great black blade hummed and crackled, alight with the fires of Nifleheim.

The great swords were a blur of movement. They sliced through the air faster than the eye could follow, humming all the while, each with its own tone — a signature sound that belonged to no other. The yellow and orange flames that danced and shimmered along the Brigandir's blade made it all the harder to track its lightning movements. Parry, riposte, slash and thrust, the blademasters battled, no quarter asked or offered while the soldiers and seamen watched in awe and fear. No human arm held the strength to strike those blows and no normal blade could withstand them without shattering. Artol, Seran, Kelbor, and others stood close by, waiting for an opening to jump back into the fray, but the blades of those titans permitted one another no respite.

When the Brigandir reeled from a blow barely parried, Theta spun about and slashed its pinned tail. Where other men's blades had bounced off ineffectually, Theta's cut severed clean through, the tail cut asunder. The Brigandir howled in agony and rage and staggered back. The severed portion of the tail writhed about and offered little sign that life was leaving it. It repeatedly crashed to the deck, and slammed into any man who drew too close, even as green ichor sprayed from its wound. That foul fluid smoked and sizzled when it hit the wooden deck boards. It ate through the wood like a powerful acid, leaving gaping holes to the underdeck behind.

Theta pressed his attack and pounded back the Brigandir's defenses with hammering blow after hammering blow, a punishing, brutal onslaught that would have cleaved through a brigade of Lomion's finest. Theta showed no mercy and offered not a moment's respite, but the Brigandir withstood it all. It parried, counterattacked, and sidestepped every cut, thrust, and chop. It never grew tired; its blows never weakened; its defenses and its resolve never faltered. Its courage never wavered. But Theta had the patience of the gods. He bided his time, waiting for an opening to appear in the beast's defenses, studying its every movement, its every breath. Until at last, he spied a fleeting gap in the demon's defenses. That was all he needed. Theta's falchion slipped under the Brigandir's guard, bit deep into its chest and slashed through its thick hide. Green ichor spurted through the air and spattered several nearby men, their clothing left singed and smoking where the merest droplets fell. The Brigandir fell straight back as a chopped tree and disappeared in a surge of dense black smoke when it struck the deck.

When the Brigandir fell, the men cheered and surged toward Theta, but halted when they realized he still stood at his guard.

"It's still alive," shouted Theta. "Stand ready." Theta stalked about, his swords held before him.

"Where is the bugger?" said Ob. "I saw it fall. It should be just there," he said, pointing to the deck.

"It didn't fall," said Theta. "It disappeared."

"Disappeared?" said Ob, his words slurred a bit from drink. "Are you kidding me? What do you mean, disappeared? Being a stinking, giant, winged, demon thing what breathes fire, bleeds acid, and that steel can't slice into ain't enough? Now it goes invisible too?"

"This is all too much," said Tanch, wringing his hands, his eyes half closed. "Dear Odin, just take me now."

"I've fought all kinds of men," sputtered Ob, his teeth clenched. "I've fought stinking lugron.

I've fought beasties in the woods and in the jungles — bears, lions, boars, and more. I've fought giants way up in the mountains. I fought a troll once down some cave. I've tackled worse than that over in the Dead Fens and deep in the White Wood. But you, Theta, you could find a stinking dragon in your drawers! Can't we go anywhere without some thing out of a fairy story coming at us, calling you out, and screaming for blood and souls? It's gotta be a stinking joke! Odin is looking down and laughing at us. Did you pee one of his temples or play naughty with some priestess? Why is the stinking universe out to get you, Theta? What the hell did you do!?"

"Shut up, gnome," said Theta.

"Every stinking unnatural thing there is has got the come hither for you, Theta. Is there some monster bait stuck up your behind or something? When is it going to end?" he shrieked.

"Stand back to back, men," Theta shouted. "Don't let it get behind you."

"How can we stop it, it's stinking invisible," screamed Ob.

A gut-wrenching scream marked the Brigandir's reappearance some yards away. Ob spun toward it. The Brigandir had stabbed a seaman from behind. The creature's black sword pierced clear through the man and protruded out from the center of his chest. The Brigandir slid the blade free and vanished from sight, disappearing before Ob's eyes.

The men scattered, some shouting in panic.

"Stay together, you fools," shouted Ob. "Shoulder to shoulder, and back to back like Theta said. It's our only chance."

Ob felt a blast of heat pour over him and the soldier beside him grunted and flopped to the deck, screaming, burning from the inside out. Ob turned in time to see the Brigandir remove its hand from where it touched the bare flesh of the man's neck. In a brief moment, too quick for Ob to react, the Brigandir vanished again. Ob's axe cleaved through the spot where it had stood, but parted only empty air. A shriveled, desiccated corpse that moments ago was a living man lay at Ob's feet. Ob couldn't even tell who it was.

"How did it get by us?" said Kelbor.

"It's got wings, you fool," said Ob.

"We would have heard it fly over us," said Dolan.

Another scream. This time from far across the deck. Another man died, skewered by the Brigandir's tail. Theta sheathed his scimitar and grasped his ankh in his right hand. He turned to the right and the Brigandir appeared in the distance, behind a soldier that crouched alone by the mast. Before any could react, the man was dead, the Brigandir's sword through his heart.

"Can you track him with that?" said Ob, referring to Theta's ankh.

"Aye, but it's too fast," said Theta. "It flits about the deck like a bird."

A minute passed and another man died in much the same manner as the last. Those who happened to be gazing in the right direction saw the Brigandir appear for a brief moment, slay the man with a single movement, and disappear just as quickly. The seamen began to panic. More than a few scurried up the rigging, hoping the monster could not follow. Others fled below deck. The fear on the soldiers' faces showed they too were close to breaking.

From somewhere, the Brigandir's voice called out, "Give me Thetan! Give me his head, or give me him bound and trussed or I'll slay you all, one by one."

"Show yourself," shouted Ob. "Cowardly scum."

Some time passed, and then a man fell from high in the rigging, screaming all the way down. He crashed to the deck with a sickening sound.

"There's nowhere for you to hide," boomed the Brigandir, still unseen.

Some moments later, another man fell screaming from on-high. This one hit the warped floorboards damaged by the Brigandir's passage, and the man crashed through to the deck below.

"Give me Thetan," boomed the Brigandir from somewhere. "Or slay you all, I will."

The sense of panic across the deck became palpable. "We have to give him to it," shouted one seaman, fear and anguish filled his face. "It's our only chance."

"It's him or us, lads," said another seaman.

A third sailor rushed toward Theta, cutlass in hand, shouting some war cry, mad with desperation and fear. The first two followed him.

Theta's falchion cut the first man completely in half in a single swing. His arm barely seemed to move, so quickly did he regain his former posture. Theta's face betrayed little emotion — neither shock, nor fear, nor regret. If anything, he looked sterner, harder, more stolid and resolute. Dolan's arrow took the second man in the throat, and dropped him to his knees. Blood poured from his mouth and neck. He didn't fall over, but he died there, on his knees. The third man sought to stop his charge and fell to his rump just in front of Theta. The blubbering sailor crumpled beneath Theta's withering, unforgiving gaze. Tears in his eyes, he dropped his cutlass, and mumbled something indecipherable, presumably begging for his life. Kelbor stepped forward, grabbed the man by the collar, and dragged him away from Theta.

"Slaayde," shouted Ob. "We need to work together, not turn on one another." Slaayde nodded from where he stood, supported and surrounded by his bodyguards, but he didn't have the energy to shout orders to his men. He leaned heavily on Guj, his face still deathly pale.

Several men ran to one of the longboats. As they tried to launch it, the Brigandir appeared in the boat and stabbed one, and then slashed another. It grabbed a third man — the one Kelbor had just pulled away from Theta. It lifted him into the air, and tossed him over the side — into the churning, cold waters of the Azure Sea.

Bowmen fired at it, but most missed their target. The Brigandir winced and roared when two arrows bounced off its hide, a light sea spray pelting it from some tall wave. A wayward arrow dented the Bull's armor as he dashed toward the Brigandir, battle hammer in hand. Then the Brigandir was gone again. Several arrows flew through where it had just stood, but hit nothing.

"Give me Thetan," shouted the Brigandir for the third time, now from a different part of the deck, its voice brimming with anger. "Or I will slay you all." A soldier wailed in agony on the bridge deck as he burned from the Brigandir's merciless touch.

One sailor ran to the gunwale and dived into the cold sea. Another followed, then other, and another, so desperate were they to escape the horrific death promised by the Brigandir. Slaayde's officers shouted for them to stop, but two more followed them over. Only one of the bunch carried anything that would float. Slaayde ordered the men to get below deck. Most dashed for the nearest door. The soldiers and knights remained and clustered tightly together in small groups. Theta stood in a tight circle, back to back with Ob, Artol, Glimador, Tanch, and Dolan.

"It's not just invisible," said Ob. "It's moving around too fast, too quiet. We should hear its steps or its flapping wings."

"It changes form somehow," said Artol.

"A flying bug," said Theta. "Not invisible — just too small to notice."

"That would explain it," said Ob. "Stinking magic. It's a shape changer."

"Wizard," said Theta to Tanch. "Can you reveal the beast or keep it from changing form?"

"No," said Tanch. "I don't know. I can't think of any magic that could do that. I'm not that kind of wizard."

"That bugger could punch holes in the hull and drop us to the bottom," whispered Ob. "Why don't he do it, I ask you?"

312

"Don't give him any ideas," said Artol. "I've no interest in swimming with the fishes. Besides, there's no land to swim to and the water's cold as death."

"Maybe he don't like the water either," said Dolan.

Theta and Ob turned to each other. "That's it," said Ob.

"It's the water," said Theta.

"What?" said Artol.

"The bugger is afraid of the water," whispered Ob. "When he was in the longboat and we hit him with arrows, he roared in pain at the same time as some spray from a wave doused him. Them arrows bounced off, same as all the rest. They didn't hurt him. So it must have been the water what done it. Maybe it burns him or something. Who knows, with demons?"

"If you're right, we've got him," said Artol.

"Get some buckets," said Theta.

The Brigandir appeared again, crashed into the knot of men surrounding Slaayde, and sent them sprawling. Tug kept his feet and sprang to attack. Old Fogey smashed into the Brigandir's sword and knocked it back against the beast's chest, forcing it to backpedal. It staggered and nearly fell, unbalanced from the loss of its tail. A second swing of Old Fogey caught the Brigandir full in the chest, sent it flying across the deck, and nearly smashed him through the wall of the captain's den. Men surged toward the Brigandir from all directions, but before they engaged it, it disappeared again.

"A count of sixty, no more," said Theta. "Then

it reappears. It can't hold its insect form."

"It stays in demon form for no less than a ten count," said Glimador.

"Then we've got to keep him on deck and douse him good and proper," said Ob. The men rushed to seal every door that led inside. Theta called out whenever the Brigandir was due to appear, and appear it did. The men bunched up close to one another, and it could no longer get behind them. Quickly as they could, the men filled and passed around buckets of seawater. The Brigandir caught on to the buckets quick enough and appeared before Theta in a rage, ready to make its stand.

Theta parried its strike and buckets of water flew wild at it from all directions. One bucket's contents grazed it and crackling steam erupted from its hide and evoked a deafening roar. Then it disappeared again. One minute later it reappeared and charged Theta. Theta sidestepped and it barreled into Artol as water doused them all from all sides. Artol careened backward and crashed to the deck. The Brigandir fell, but rolled to its feet in a but a moment, smoking and charred across much of its body. Theta's mighty slash cleaved almost fully through the Brigandir's sword arm and it staggered backward. Ob and Glimador doused its face and chest with full buckets of water and it collapsed, its flesh melting and dissolving.

"Aargh!" roared the Brigandir. "There will be no escape for you, traitor," it spat as the flesh of its face sagged and sloughed off, its gray skull exposed to the air. "Others will come for you—"

"No need," said Theta as he pulled the great war hammer from his belt. "I will come for them. I will destroy you all, unto the last, unto the end of time." Theta's hammer crashed down on the Brigandir's skull and smashed it to pulp, ending whatever life remained in it.

Where it died, the deck boards sagged and charred and near collapsed to the deck below. The men poured many more buckets of water on it, just to be sure, until Bertha appeared with a shovel and handed it to Tug who tossed what solid bits remained over the side into the cleansing sea. They washed down the deck and mopped it until no trace remained. They even tossed the mop and the shovel over the side. Until that work was done, the whole company stood there, watching.

"That was one tough bugger," said Ob. "Hope for our sakes there's no more of them lurking hereabouts."

Dolan looked around, bucket in hand. "Always hated lurkers."

"It promised there would be more," said Glimador.

"Not today, I think," said Theta.

Ob turned to Theta. "Why water?"

Theta wiped the ichor off his falchion with a cloth. "It's the essence of life," said Theta. "That one was the essence of death. The two cannot coexist."

"Dead gods," said Tanch, only now registering Ob's remark. "You don't really think there could be more than one of them, do you?"

"Relax, Magic Boy, or you'll soil yourself again. I think our fun's over for today."

"It's not," said Theta. "Not until we find out how that thing got on board. It didn't just happen by. Someone will answer for this."

"Could it have flown here from some island or even from *The White Rose*?" said Glimador. He was very pale and tired and winced as Kelbor bound cloth about his hands, both of which were bright red. "Maybe one of the Leaguers conjured it and sent it to stop us or at least slow us down."

"Maybe," said Theta, studying Glimador.

"If you're right," said Ob, "wouldn't it have flown away when we took up the buckets? It had to know it didn't have a chance."

"Maybe it feared going back to its master without killing Lord Theta more than it feared dying," said Glimador.

"More likely, its master is aboard," said Theta.

"Make no mistake, sonny," Ob said to Glimador, "It didn't fear us, not one bit. It feared old Mister Fancy Pants. Seems as if most folks do."

"What happened to your hands?" said Theta to Glimador.

"We just had a bit of battle in case you didn't notice," said Ob.

"I threw too much magic," said Glimador. "I've had them itch and sting before," he said, staring at his hands, which he held up before him. "But never anything like this. I held a spell far longer than I've ever done before. That's what did it."

Theta walked over and took a closer look at Glimador's hands. "What magic did you use?" said

Theta quietly.

"A shield spell. I held back the demon with it below deck. It gave us time to get clear."

"Your mother taught you that spell," said Theta.

Glimador didn't respond.

"Go carefully with the magic, young Malvegil, for there's far worse consequences to its use than burned hands, even for those who are masters of the art. Use your gifts sparingly, or better yet, not at all."

"Thank you, sir, for the advice," said Glimador standing tall and confident. "Though I claim no mastery of the mystic arts, I do know what I'm doing."

Theta turned to Dolan. "Let's go find the demon's master." They headed below deck, Theta with a hand on his ankh.

"Essence of death," said Dolan. "Good line."

"I thought so," said Theta, a grin on his face.

Sergeant Vid picked his way across the deck toward Ob. He stared aghast at the broken and mangled bodies, and the strewed wreckage. "Castellan," he said, standing to attention. "Lord Eotrus is awake and asking for you."

"Praise Odin," said Ob. "This calls for a drink."

END

GLOSSARY

PLACES

The Realms
Asgard: legendary home of the gods
Midgaard: the world of man
Lomion: a great kingdom of Midgaard
Nether Realms: realms of demons and devils
Nifleheim: the realm of the Chaos Lords / Lords of Nifleheim
Vaeden: paradise, lost
Valhalla: a realm of the gods where warriors go after death

Places Within The Kingdom Of Lomion
Dallassian Hills: large area of rocky hills; home to a large enclave of dwarves
Dor Caladrill:
Dor Eotrus: fortress and lands ruled by House Eotrus, north of Lomion City
Dor Linden: fortress and lands ruled by House Mirtise, in the Linden Forest, south of Lomion City
Dor Lomion: fortress within Lomion City ruled by House Harringgold
Dor Malvegil: fortress and lands ruled by House Malvegil, southeast of Lomion City on the west bank of the Grand Hudsar River
Dor Valadon: fortress outside Dover
Doriath Forest: woodland north of Lomion City
Dover, City of: large city situated at Lomion's

southeastern border

Dyvers, City of: Lomerian city known for its quality metalworking

Grommel: a town known for southern gnomes

Kern, City of: Lomerian city to the northeast of Lomion City.

Kronar Mountains: they mark the northern border of the Kingdom of Lomion

Lindenwood: a forest to the south of Lomion City, within which live the Lindonaire Elves

Lomion City (aka Lomion): capitol city of the Kingdom of Lomion

The Heights — seedy section of Lomion City

Southeast — dangerous section of Lomion City

Portland Vale: a town known for southern gnomes

Riker's Crossroads: village at the southern border of Eotrus lands

Tammanian Hall: high seat of government in Lomion; home of the High Council and the Council of Lords

Temple of Guymaog: where the gateway was opened in the Vermion Forest

Tower of the Arcane: high seat of wizardom; in Lomion City

Vermion Forest: foreboding wood, west of Dor Eotrus

Parts Foreign

Azure Sea: vast ocean to the south of the Lomerian continent

Dead Fens, The: mix of fen, bog, and swampland on the east bank of the Hudsar River, south of Dor Malvegil

Grand Hudsar River: south of Lomion City, it marks the eastern border of the kingdom
Emerald River: large river that branches off from the Hudsar at Dover
Ferd: Far-off city known for its fine goods
Jutenheim: island far to the south of the Lomerian continent.
Minoc-by-the-Sea: coastal city
R'lyeh: legendary island where a great battle was fought.
Shandelon: famed gnomish city
Tragoss Krell: city ruled by Thothian Monks
Tragoss Mor: large city far to the south of Lomion, at the mouth of the Hudsar River where it meets the Azure Sea. Ruled by Thothian Monks.

PEOPLE

<u>Peoples</u>
Emerald elves, Lindonaire elves, Doriath elves, Dallassian dwarves, gnomes, humans (aka volsungs), lugron, smallfolk, svarts

<u>High Council of Lomion</u>
Selrach Rothtonn Tenzivel III: His Royal Majesty: King of Lomion
Aldros, Lord: Councilor
Aramere, Lady: Councilor representing the City of Dyvers
Balfor, Field Marshal: Councilor representing the Lomerian armed forces; Commander of the Lomerian army
Barusa of Alder, Lord: Chancellor of Lomion
Cartagian Tenzivel, Prince: Selrach's son, insane; Councilor representing the Royal House.
Dahlia, Lady: Councilor representing the City of Kern
Glenfinnen, Lord: Councilor representing the City of Dover
Harper Harringgold, Lord: Councilor representing Lomion City; Arch-Duke of Lomion City
Jhensezil, Lord: Councilor representing the Churchmen; Preceptor of the Odion Knights
Morfin, Baron: Councilor (reportedly dead)
Slyman, Guildmaster: Councilor representing the guilds; Master of Guilds
Tobin Carthigast, Bishop: Councilor representing the Churchmen
Vizier, The (Grandmaster Rabrack

Philistine): The Royal Wizard; Grandmaster and Councilor representing the Tower of the Arcane

House Alder (Pronounced All-der)
A leading, noble family of Lomion City. Their principal manor house is within the city's borders
Batholomew Alder: youngest son of Mother Alder
Bartol Alder: younger brother of Barusa, Myrdonian Knight
Barusa Alder, Lord: Chancellor of Lomion, eldest son of Mother Alder.
Blain Alder: younger brother of Barusa
Edith Alder: daughter of Blain; a child
Edwin Alder: son of Blain
Mother Alder: matriarch of the House; an Archseer
Rom of Alder: brother of Mother Alder

House Eotrus (pronounced Eee-oh-tro`-sss)
The Eotrus rule the fortress of Dor Eotrus, the Outer Dor (a town outside the fortress walls) and the surrounding lands for many leagues.
Aradon Eotrus, Lord: Patriarch of the House (presumed dead)
Claradon Eotrus, Brother: (Clara-don) eldest son of Aradon, Caradonian Knight; Patriarch of the House; Lord of Dor Eotrus
Donnelin, Brother: House Cleric for the Eotrus (presumed dead)
Ector Eotrus, Sir: Third son of Aradon
Eleanor Malvegil Eotrus: (deceased) Wife of Aradon Eotrus; sister of Torbin Malvegil.
Gabriel Garn, Sir: House Weapons Master

(presumed dead, body possessed by Korrgonn)
Jude Eotrus, Sir: Second son of Aradon (missing)

Knights & Soldiers of the House: Artol 'The Destroyer', Sir Paldor Cragsmere, Sir Glimador Malvegil, Sir Indigo, Sir Kelbor, Sir Ganton 'the bull', Sir Trelman, Sir Marzdan (captain of the gate, deceased), Sir Sarbek (acting Castellan), Harsnip (deceased), Baret, Graham, Sergeant Balfin (deceased), Sergeant Vid, Sergeant Lant, Sir Miden (deceased), Sergeant Jerem (deceased), Sir Conrad (deceased), Sir Martin (deceased), Sir Bilson (deceased), Sir Glimron (deceased), Sir Talbot (deceased), Sir Dalken (deceased)

Malcolm Eotrus: Fourth son of Aradon

Ob A. Faz III: (Ahb A. Fahzz) Castellan and Master Scout of Dor Eotrus, a gnome

Stern: Master Ranger for the Eotrus (presumed dead)

Talbon of Montrose, Par: Former House Wizard for the Eotrus (presumed dead)

Tanch Trinagal, Par: (Trin-ah-ghaal) of the Blue Tower; Son of Sinch; House Wizard for the Eotrus. Alias: Par Sinch; Par Sinch Malaban.

House Harringgold
Harper Harringgold, Lord: Arch-Duke of Lomion City; Lord of Dor Lomion

Grim Fischer: agent of Harper, a gnome

Marissa Harringgold: daughter of Harper

Seran Harringgold, Sir: nephew of Harper

House Malvegil
Torbin Malvegil, Lord: Patriarch of the House; Lord of Dor Malvegil.
Landolyn, Lady: of House Adonael; Torbin's consort. Of part elven blood.
Eleanor Malvegil Eotrus: (deceased) Wife of Aradon Eotrus; sister of Torbin Malvegil.
Glimador Malvegil, Sir: son of Torbin, working in the service of House Eotrus.
Gravemare, Hubert: Castellan
Hogart: harbormaster

The Lords of Nifleheim
Azathoth: god worshipped by The Shadow League; his followers call him the "one true god".
Arioch; Bhaal; Hecate
Korrgonn, Lord Gallis: son of Azathoth
Mortach: (aka Mikel) — killed by Angle Theta

The Asgardian Gods (aka the Aesir)
Odin, Thor, Tyr, Frey, Freya, Heimdall, Loki, Balder

Other Gods
Dagon of the Deep
Thoth

Great Beasts, Monsters, Creatures
Duergar: mythical undead creatures
Dwellers of the Deep: worshippers of Dagon
Fire Wyrm: a dragon
Giants (aka Jotuns):

Leviathan: a sea creature
Trolls: mythical creatures of the high mountains

<u>The Crew Of *The Black Falcon*</u>
Slaayde, Dylan: Captain of *The Black Falcon*
Bertha Smallbutt: ship's quartermaster
Bire Cabinboy: ship's cabin boy
Chert: a young seaman
Darg Tran, son of Karn, of old House
Elowine: ship's navigator
Eolge: a crewman
Fizdar Firstbar 'the corsair': former first mate (presumed dead)
Guj: boatswain. A half-lugron.
N'Paag: First Mate
Old Mock: a crewman
Ravel: ship's trader and medic
Tug, Little: Near 7-foot tall part-lugron seaman; Old Fogey — Tug's battle hammer

<u>The Passengers of *The Black Falcon*</u>
Artol: former Sergeant to Gabriel Garn
Claradon Eotrus, Brother: (Clara-don) eldest son of Aradon, Caradonian Knight; Patriarch of the House; Lord of Dor Eotrus
Dolan Silk: Theta's manservant
Ganton, Sir (the Bull): a knight of House Eotrus
Kayla Kazeran: part Lindonaire elf, rescued from slavery in Tragoss Mor
Kelbor, Sir: a knight of House Eotrus
Lant, Sergeant: a soldier of House Eotrus
Lomerian Soldiers: a squadron of soldiers of House Harringgold, assigned to assist House

Eotrus.

Malvegil, Sir Glimador: first cousin to Claradon; son of Lord Malvegil

Malvegillian Archers: a squad of soldiers assigned to assist House Eotrus by Lord Malvegil

Ob A. Faz III: (Ahb A. Fahzz) Castellan and Master Scout of Dor Eotrus, a gnome

Paldor Cragsmere, Sir: a young knight of House Eotrus

Seran Harringgold, Sir: nephew of Arch-Duke Harper Harringgold — assigned to assist House Eotrus

Tanch Trinagal, Par: (Trin-ah-ghaal) of the Blue Tower; Son of Sinch; House Wizard for the Eotrus

Theta, Lord Angle (aka Thetan): a knight errant.

Trelman, Sir: a knight of House Eotrus

Vid, Sergeant: a soldier of House Eotrus

The Crew/Passengers of The Grey Talon

Alder Marines: squadrons of soldiers from House Alder

Bartol Alder: younger brother of Barusa; a Myrdonian Knight

Blain Alder: younger brother of Barusa

DeBoors, Milton: (The Duelist of Dyvers). A mercenary

Edwin Alder: son of Blain

Kaledon of the Gray Waste: a Pict mercenary

Kleig: Captain of *The Grey Talon*

Knights of Kalathen: elite mercenaries that work for DeBoors

Myrdonian Knights: squadron of knights

assigned to House Alder

The Crew/Passengers of The White Rose
Rastinfan Rascelon: Captain of *The White Rose*
Ginalli, Father: High Priest of Azathoth, Arkon of The Shadow League.
Ezerhauten, Lord: Commander of Sithian Mercenary Company
Brackta Finbal, Par: an archmage of The League of Shadows
Frem Sorlons: captain of the Sithian's Pointmen Squadron
Glus Thorn, Par: an archmage of the League of Shadows
Hablock, Par: an archmage of the League of Shadows (deceased)
Lugron: hulking, brutish humanoids
Mason: a stone golem created by The Keeper
Morsmun, Par: an archmage of the League of Shadows (deceased)
Mort Zag: a giant
Ot, Par: an archmage of the League of Shadows (deceased)
Pointmen, The: an elite squadron of the Sithian Mercenary Company
Sevare Zendrack, Par: Squadron wizard for the Pointmen
Sithians: mercenaries under the command of Ezerhauten; some are soldiers, some are knights
Stev Keevis Arkguardt: an elven archwizard from the Emerald Forest allied with The League of Shadows; former apprentice of The Keeper

<u>Sithian Mercenary Company</u>
Ezerhauten, Lord: Commander
Frem Sorlons: Captain, Pointmen Squadron
Landru, Par: a squadron wizard
Rewes of Ravenhollow, Sir: a knight

<u>The Pointmen (an elite squadron of the Sithian Mercenary Company)</u>
Frem Sorlons: captain, Pointmen Squadron
Sevare Zendrack, Par: squadron wizard for the Pointmen
Putnam, Sergeant: Pointmen,1st Squad
Boatman: Pointmen
Borrel: Pointmen; a lugron
Bryton: Pointmen
Carroll, Sir: Pointmen; a knight
Dirnel: Pointmen; a lugron
Held: Pointmen
Jorna: Pointmen
Lex: Pointmen
Little Storrl: Pointmen,1st Squad; a young lugron
Maldin, Sergeant: Pointmen,2nd Squad
Moag: Pointmen,1st squad; a lugron
Roard, Sir: Pointmen,1st Squad; a knight
Royce, Sir: Pointmen; a knight
Torak: Pointmen; a lugron
Ward: Pointmen
Wikkle: Pointmen; a lugron

<u>Militant Orders</u>
Caradonian Knights: priestly order; patron—Odin
Kalathen, Knights of: mercenary knights

Odions, The: patron—Odin; Preceptor—Lord Jhensezil; Chapterhouse: in Lomion City
Sithian Knights, The: Preceptor—Lord Ezerhauten
Sundarian Knights: patron: Thor; Preceptor: Sir **Hithron du Maris;** Chapterhouse: hidden in Tragoss Mor
Tyr, Knights of: patron—Tyr

Others Of Note
Angle Theta, Lord: (Thay`-tah) (aka Thetan) knight errant and nobleman from a far-off land across the sea.
Archmage / Archwizard: honorific title for a highly skilled wizard
Archseer: honorific title for a highly skilled seer
Arkon: a leader/general in service to certain gods and religious organizations
Azura du Marnian, the Seer: Seer based in Tragoss Mor
Gorb: Azura's bodyguard
Rimel Stark: Azura's bodyguard and famed Freesword
Dirkben: Azura's bodyguard
Black Hand, The: a brotherhood of deadly assassins
Brigandir: supernatural warrior(s) of Nifleheim
Churchmen: a generic term for the diverse group of priests and knights of various orders
Coriana Sorlons: daughter of Frem Sorlons
Dark Sendarth: famed assassin
Dolan Silk: (Doe`-lin) Theta's manservant
Dramadeens: royal bodyguards for House Tenzivel

Du Maris, Sir Hithron: Preceptor of the Sundarian Chapterhouse in Tragoss Mor; from Dor Caladrill

Einheriar: supernatural warriors of Nifleheim

Freedom Guardsmen: soldiery of Tragoss Mor

Freesword: a independent soldier or mercenary

Harbinger of Doom, The: legendary, perhaps mythical being that led a rebellion against Azathoth

Hedge Wizard: a wizard specializing in potions and herbalism, and/or minor magics

High Magister: a member of Lomion's Tribunal.

Korvalan of Courwood, Captain: Commander of the Dramadeens.

Keeper, The: elven "keeper" of the Orb of Wizard beneath Tragoss Mor

Kroth, Garon: newly appointed High Magister

Lindonaire Elves: from Lindenwood

Sluug, Sir Samwise: Preceptor of the Rangers Guild; Lord of Doriath Hall

Magling: a young or inexperienced wizard; also, a derogatory term for a wizard

Master Oracle: a highly skilled seer

Myrdonians: Royal Lomerian Knights

Picts: a barbarian people

Pipkorn, Grandmaster: (aka Rascatlan) former Grand Master of the Tower of the Arcane. A wizard.

Prior Finch: a prior of Thoth in Tragoss Mor

Sarq: a Thothian Monk. Known as the Champion of Tragoss Mor

Seer (sometimes, "Seeress"): women with supernatural powers to see past/present/future events.

Shadow League, The (aka The League of Shadows; aka The League of Light): alliance of individuals and groups collectively seeking to bring about the return of Azathoth to Midgaard

Snor Slipnet: Patriarch of Clan Rumbottle; a gnome

Talidousen: Former Grand Master of the Tower of the Arcane; created the fabled Rings of the Magi.

Thothian monks: monks that rule Tragoss Mor and worship Thoth

Vanyar Elves: legendary elven people

Volsungs: alternate word for men/humans

Wizard (aka Mage, Sorceror, etc.): practitioners of magic

THINGS

Miscellany

Alder Stone, The: a Seer Stone held by House Alder

Amulet of Escandell: a magical device that detects the presence of danger; gifted to Claradon by Pipkorn

Articles of the Republic: the Lomerian constitution

Asgardian Daggers: legendary weapons created in the first age of Midgaard. They can harm creatures of Nifleheim.

Chapterhouse: base/manor/fortress of a knightly order

Dargus Dal: Asgardian dagger, previously Gabriel's, now Theta's

Worfin Dal: "Lord's Dagger", Claradon's Asgardian dagger

Wotan Dal: "Odin's Dagger"; gifted to Theta by Pipkorn.

Axe of Bigby the Bold: made of Mithril; gifted to Ob by Pipkorn

Dor: generic term for a fortress

du Marnian Stone, The: a Seer Stone held by Azura du Marnian

Dyvers Blades: finely crafted steel swords

Ether, The: invisible medium that exists everywhere and within which the weave of magic travels/exists.

Ghost Ship Box: calls forth an illusory ship; created by Pipkorn and gifted to Claradon.

Mages and Monsters: a popular, tactical wargame that uses miniatures

Mithril: precious metal of great strength and relative lightness

Orb of Wisdom: mystical crystal spheres that can be used to open portals between worlds.

Ranal: a black metal, hard as steel and half as heavy, weapons made of it can affect creatures of chaos

Rings of the Magi: amplify a wizard's power; twenty created by Talidousen

Seer Stones: magical "crystal balls" that can see far-off events.

Shards of Darkness: the remnants of the destroyed Orb of Wisdom from the Temple of Guymaog.

Squad: a unit of soldiers typically composed of 15 men; can refer to any small group of soldiers

Squadron: a unit of soldiers typically composed of two squads of approximately 15 men each.

Tribunal: the highest-ranking judiciary body in the Kingdom of Lomion

Weave of Magic; aka the Magical Weave: the source of magic

ABOUT GLENN G. THATER

For more than twenty-five years, Glenn G. Thater has written works of fiction and historical fiction that focus on the genres of epic fantasy and sword and sorcery. His published works of fiction include the first ten volumes of the *Harbinger of Doom* saga: *Gateway to Nifleheim*; *The Fallen Angle*; *Knight Eternal*; *Dwellers of the Deep*; *Blood, Fire, and Thorn*; *Gods of the Sword*; *The Shambling Dead*; *Master of the Dead*; *Shadow of Doom*; *Wizard's Toll*; the novella, *The Gateway*; and the novelette, *The Hero and the Fiend*.

Mr. Thater holds a Bachelor of Science degree in Physics with concentrations in Astronomy and Religious Studies, and a Master of Science degree in Civil Engineering, specializing in Structural Engineering. He has undertaken advanced graduate study in Classical Physics, Quantum Mechanics, Statistical Mechanics, and Astrophysics, and is a practicing licensed professional engineer specializing in the multidisciplinary alteration and remediation of buildings, and the forensic investigation of building failures and other disasters.

Mr. Thater has investigated failures and collapses of numerous structures around the United States and internationally. Since 1998, he has been a member of the American Society of Civil Engineers' Forensic Engineering Division (FED), is a Past Chairman of that Division's Executive

Committee and FED's Committee on Practices to Reduce Failures. Mr. Thater is a LEED (Leadership in Energy and Environmental Design) Accredited Professional and has testified as an expert witness in the field of structural engineering before the Supreme Court of the State of New York.

Mr. Thater is an author of numerous scientific papers, magazine articles, engineering textbook chapters, and countless engineering reports. He has lectured across the United States and internationally on such topics as the World Trade Center collapses, bridge collapses, and on the construction and analysis of the dome of the United States Capitol in Washington D.C.

CONNECT WITH GLENN G. THATER ONLINE

Glenn G. Thater's Website:
http://www.glenngthater.com

To be notified about new book releases and any special offers or discounts regarding Glenn's books, please join his mailing list here: http://eepurl.com/vwubH

BOOKS BY GLENN G. THATER

THE HARBINGER OF DOOM SAGA
GATEWAY TO NIFLEHEIM
THE FALLEN ANGLE
KNIGHT ETERNAL
DWELLERS OF THE DEEP
BLOOD, FIRE, AND THORN

GODS OF THE SWORD
THE SHAMBLING DEAD
MASTER OF THE DEAD
SHADOW OF DOOM
WIZARD'S TOLL
VOLUME 11**+** *forthcoming*

THE HERO AND THE FIEND
(A novelette set in the Harbinger of Doom universe)

THE GATEWAY
(A novella length version of *Gateway to Nifleheim*)

HARBINGER OF DOOM
(Combines *Gateway to Nifleheim* and *The Fallen Angle* into a single volume)

THE DEMON KING OF BERGHER
(A short story set in the Harbinger of Doom universe)

Visit Glenn G. Thater's website at http://www.glenngthater.com for the most current list of my published books.

Printed in Great Britain
by Amazon